CRITICAL ACCLAIM F(

'A million readers can't be wror
day, sit back and enjoy a bloody g

'Taut and compelling' **Peter James**

'Leigh Russell is one to watch' **Lee Child**

'Leigh Russell has become one of the most impressively
dependable purveyors of the English police procedural' *Times*

'DI Geraldine Steel is one of the most authoritative
female coppers in a crowded field'
Financial Times

'A brilliant talent in the thriller field' **Jeffery Deaver**

'Brilliant and chilling, Leigh Russell delivers a cracker
of a read!' **Martina Cole**

'A great plot that keeps you guessing right until the very end,
some subtle subplots, brilliant characters both old and new and
as ever a completely gripping read' *Life of Crime*

'The latest police procedural from prolific novelist Leigh
Russell is as good and gripping as anything she has published'
Times & Sunday Times Crime Club

'A fascinating gripping read. The many twists kept me on my
toes and second-guessing myself'
Over The Rainbow Book Blog

ALSO BY LEIGH RUSSELL

Geraldine Steel Mysteries
Cut Short
Road Closed
Dead End
Death Bed
Stop Dead
Fatal Act
Killer Plan
Murder Ring
Deadly Alibi
Class Murder
Death Rope
Rogue Killer
Deathly Affair
Deadly Revenge
Evil Impulse
Deep Cover
Guilt Edged
Fake Alibi
Final Term
Without Trace
Revenge Killing

Ian Peterson Murder Investigations
Cold Sacrifice
Race to Death
Blood Axe

Poppy Mystery Tales
Barking Up the Right Tree
Barking Mad
Poppy Takes the Lead

Lucy Hall Mysteries
Journey to Death
Girl in Danger
The Wrong Suspect

Leigh
Russell

CAN YOU ESCAPE A
DEADLY
WILL

NO EXIT PRESS

First published in the UK in 2024 by No Exit Press,
an imprint of Bedford Square Publishers Ltd,
London, UK

noexit.co.uk
@noexitpress

ISBN
978-1-83501-026-6 (Paperback)
978-1-83501-027-3 (eBook)

2 4 6 8 10 9 7 5 3 1

Typeset in 11 on 13.75pt Times New Roman
by Avocet Typeset, Bideford, Devon, EX39 2BP
Printed and bound in Great Britain by
CPI Group (UK) Ltd, Croydon CR0 4YY

To Michael, Joanna, Phillipa, Phil, Rian and Kezia.
With my love.

Glossary of Acronyms

DCI   – Detective Chief Inspector (senior officer on case)
DI   – Detective Inspector
DS   – Detective Sergeant
SOCO – scene of crime officer (collects forensic evidence at scene)
PM   – Post Mortem or Autopsy (examination of dead body to establish cause of death)
CCTV – Closed Circuit Television (security cameras)
VIIDO – Visual Images, Identification and Detections Office
MIT   – Murder Investigation Team

1

TIME SEEMED TO CRAWL by as he stared at the intruder. He could only have stayed silent for a few seconds, but it felt like hours.

'No, no,' he croaked. His throat felt as though it was closing up. He tried again, forcing the words out in breathless bursts. 'Why are you doing this? Who are you?' His words rose in a shrill crescendo and he broke off, struggling to control his shaking.

'You don't need to know who I am.' The voice was hoarse, impossible to identify.

All he could see of the face were dark eyes glittering at him through holes in a balaclava. The stuff of nightmares. The intruder lifted one arm and a faint light from the window shone on the barrel of a gun.

'Get out of my house!' he yelled suddenly, terror finally loosening his tongue. 'Get out! Get out!'

Muffled by the disguise, the intruder's laughter sounded barely human. 'That's not how this works. You do what I say or—' There was a loud click and the gun jerked in a leather-clad hand.

'What do you want?' he gasped.

He took an involuntary step backwards, as though a few inches distance would shield him from a bullet threatening to rip through his flesh. Desperately he glanced around for his phone, but it wasn't beside the bed.

His initial burst of adrenaline gave way before a visceral fear that gripped him, making it difficult to move or utter a word. He struggled to control his thoughts. He knew he ought to be observing the intruder, memorising details to tell the police, but he couldn't focus. In any case, it was impossible to see anything under the shapeless jacket, balaclava and gloves, which concealed every inch of skin.

'What do you want?' he repeated. The words sounded unreal, but he ploughed on. 'I'm rich.' Sensing a way out of danger, he became garrulous in his relief. 'That's why you're here, isn't it? If it's money you're after, you've come to the right place. Come to my study and I'll open the safe. You can have everything. Only please don't hurt me,' he added, almost breaking down as the intruder stirred. 'You can have all my money, my wife's diamonds, passports. They can all be yours if you don't hurt me. Is it a deal?'

He was in no position to bargain, but he had to try. Dimly aware of the alarm wailing outside, he knew if he kept his nerve this harrowing situation could be over quite soon. Somewhere in the room his phone rang. The burglar alarm monitoring service was following up the alarm signal. When he didn't pick up, they would alert the police.

'Go to the garage.'

'What? There's nothing there. Only my car. The money's in my—'

'Stop talking and move!'

Unable to buy his way out of danger, he had no choice but to obey. With the barrel of a gun repeatedly prodding the back of his neck, he stumbled down the stairs and through the door that took them from the kitchen to the garage. Climbing into the driving seat, he picked up the remote control he kept in his car. Conscious of the masked figure sitting behind him, as if in a dream, he watched the electric door slide upwards.

'Drive or I shoot,' the voice rasped. 'Go! Now!'

As he reached the end of the road, he heard a siren in the distance. If the police were responding to his alarm call, they were too late. He didn't dare brake but continued driving down towards the river, the gun pointing at the back of his head. If only he hadn't insisted on tinted windows, someone might have noticed the masked face of his captor, directing him from the back seat. But the intruder and the gun were shielded from the outside world. Late-night carousers staggered along the pavements in a blur, oblivious to the drama speeding past them. On the crowded streets of the city, he was facing death alone. He wondered whether to crash the car deliberately, but was afraid any sudden impact might cause the gun to go off. His adversary might be injured or even killed in an accident, but he himself would almost certainly die. One tremor of a stranger's finger on a trigger was all it would take. So he drove on, doing exactly as he was told, while his senses seemed unnaturally alert, watching and waiting for an opportunity to escape.

They reached the river at just after two o'clock. There was no one else around as they pulled up in a secluded spot.

'Open your door and get out,' the passenger rasped. 'We don't want to make a mess in your expensive car.'

He held his breath, clinging to the steering wheel as though that could save him. 'What if I refuse?' he asked.

'It's your car.'

The barrel of the gun jabbed him suddenly in the back of his neck, and he let out an involuntary whimper. Trembling, he opened the door and stepped out of the car. Raw night air whipped at his face, and he realised he was sweating. He stared at moonlight rippling on the water, and wondered whether it was the last sight he would ever see. It struck him that he had never taken the time to appreciate just how beautiful the river was, flowing darkly under a night sky pierced by brilliant points of light. The moon hung ahead of him, a softly glowing crescent. For a fleeting instant he found it strangely comforting. He was alive in a beautiful world. As though celebrating his realisation, a shooting star shot across the sky in a wide arc, ephemeral as life itself.

'What do you want?' he asked. 'You can have anything. But don't hurt me, please.'

'Silence!' The voice was no longer disguised, and with a thrill of fear he understood.

2

AFTER HER INITIAL RUSH of excitement at the prospect of returning to work, Geraldine was seized by a spasm of guilt over leaving her six-month-old baby. Geraldine knew Tom so well, it was a wrench to hand him over to a childminder, and she almost changed her mind at the last minute. But Zoe, golden-haired and freckled, was relaxed and efficient and relentlessly patient. She seemed suitable, and had turned up at exactly the right time with impressive testimonials. Not only was Zoe happy to look after Tom, she was available at short notice just when Geraldine needed her. Ian questioned whether Tom might be better off in a situation where he learned to socialise with other infants, but Geraldine thought Tom would benefit from Zoe's undivided attention, and they both liked the fact that she had no car. So everything was arranged.

The day before Geraldine was due to return to work, she left Tom with Zoe for the afternoon, so he could get used to her. He seemed quite content with the arrangement, and when she picked him up, Zoe assured her he had been fine. But now that it was almost time to leave him for a whole day, Geraldine felt uneasy.

Ian dismissed her apprehension with a sympathetic smile.

'It's only natural to feel nervous about it,' he said kindly. 'But you're not doing anything wrong. Most mothers leave their children and go back to work.'

Geraldine nodded uncertainly. 'I know. It's nothing against Zoe personally. I'm just feeling anxious all of a sudden. And guilty,' she admitted.

'Well, there's absolutely nothing to feel guilty about. Do you want a hug?' he asked.

A hug was Ian's answer to most of her wobbles and, as usual, the reassuring warmth of his arms around her really helped. Rationally, she knew she was right to return to a job at which she excelled. As a detective, her skills had been honed over many years dedicated to investigating serious crimes. Tom would be better off with a woman experienced in child care. *Most mothers leave their children*, she repeated to herself as she drew up outside Zoe's neat little house. It was ridiculous to worry about him. And she would still be home to put him to bed. Holding him close, she peeled him away from his car seat, and hid her reluctance when she handed him over. Zoe put him down and handed him a soft toy that jingled when shaken. Dismissing her misgivings as natural, Geraldine turned to leave, but Tom seemed to sense what was happening and let out a wail of protest. Even though Geraldine had left him with the childminder before, there was a finality about her departure this time, an abandonment of their shared life.

'Don't worry. He's going to be fine,' Zoe assured her, ushering Geraldine out of the front door on to the chilly November street. 'As soon as he can't see you, he'll stop crying.' She was right. The crying had stopped and there was a faint sound of jingling coming from the house.

Uncertain whether she should feel relieved at Tom's easy acceptance of her departure, Geraldine forced herself to drive away, wondering whether she had done the right thing. Ian had encouraged her to stay at home for another six months, which she could easily have done. She had been desperate to return to work, but now that the moment had arrived, she couldn't remember why she had been so impatient to give up being a full-time mother. She almost turned the car around to go back and reclaim Tom. She would admit she had made a stupid mistake, and she wasn't ready to go back to work yet. Tom was her baby and he should be with her, not with some stranger who was only caring for him because she was being paid. This painful parting was unnecessary. She didn't have to do it. But she didn't turn around.

Her reservations vanished as soon as she entered the police station. She had done her best to adapt to living at home with a baby, but there was no denying the police station felt like home to her. The tension in her neck and shoulders seemed to ease as she crossed the entrance hall. Admittedly her job could be stressful, but she relished the familiar challenges of her work. The unpredictable demands of a baby were a different matter entirely, with Tom's needs a seemingly interminable reminder of her inexperience as a mother.

'If only you could tell me what you want,' she had murmured to him in the middle of the previous night, when he had woken up screaming for no apparent reason. After about fifteen minutes he had abruptly gone back to sleep, leaving her frustrated and exhausted. Her sister, Celia, who had two children, assured her Tom was just teething, or suffering from harmless colic, but Geraldine had no way of knowing if that was true. Skills acquired over years spent interrogating hardened criminals didn't help her when she was investigating why her six-month-old baby was crying.

The desk sergeant glanced up from a file he was studying and smiled at her. 'Hello again,' he greeted her, before looking back at the document he was reading.

And just like that, with no fuss, she was back. There was a similar absence of fanfare when she walked into the serious crime workspace where most of her colleagues were too preoccupied to give her more than a cursory nod and smile of welcome before returning to their tasks. What felt like a momentous change to Geraldine was unremarkable to everyone else. Only her friends, black-haired Ariadne and blonde Naomi, jumped up from their desks and hurried over to greet her.

'I'm so glad you're back,' Naomi said, her pretty face creased in a welcoming grin.

'We missed you,' Ariadne added, beaming.

Geraldine smiled back at her two colleagues. An experienced officer, Ariadne Moralis took after her Greek mother, with hair and eyes as dark as Geraldine's. Like Geraldine, she was in her early forties, while Naomi Arnold, not long ago promoted to detective sergeant, was barely out of her twenties. While they could not have been more different in appearance, both were intelligent and hardworking, and Geraldine considered herself fortunate to have such dedicated colleagues working alongside her in murder investigations. They made a good team.

'It's great to be back,' she said.

'We're not on a case right now,' Ariadne told her, 'but there's always the usual catching up to do.'

'Plenty of paperwork to keep us busy,' Naomi added.

Ariadne mimed a yawn and Naomi smiled.

Geraldine spent the morning getting to grips with the changes that had been introduced while she was away. There were the usual alterations to acronyms, and so-called improvements had been made to the systems she needed to use. It took time to update her passwords and note the changes, all of which was dull work, but she didn't mind. Hopefully they would be able to enjoy a relatively relaxed period in the run up to Christmas. She was having disturbed nights now Tom had started teething – or suffering from colic – and she didn't want any additional stress in her life, if she could avoid it. Ian was excited about Tom's first Christmas although, at little more than six months old, he wouldn't know anything about it. Geraldine was more concerned about what to give the childminder, and whether she ought to buy a present for Zoe's daughter who would be home from university soon. At lunchtime she phoned Zoe who reassured her that Tom was fine and reiterated a promise to call if there were any problems. Geraldine wasn't far away.

The nights were drawing in. While there were disadvantages to investigating murders in warmer weather, particularly when a body had been left exposed to the elements for more than a few days, nevertheless shorter days made investigations more challenging, especially in bad weather.

'Hopefully everyone is too focused on Christmas to be thinking of killing anyone just now,' Geraldine smiled.

'I don't know about that,' Naomi replied sourly. 'If you ask me, family gatherings are where vicious quarrels are most likely to break out. Throw in excessive drinking, and it's a tinder box waiting to ignite. Who wants to spend a whole day with their family? Surely that's exactly where most murders are plotted.'

Geraldine smiled uneasily, wondering what lay behind her colleague's remark. She and Naomi had worked closely together on several cases. Facing danger side by side on more than one occasion, they had formed a strong bond. Yet Geraldine knew almost nothing about Naomi's personal life. It was a salutary reminder not to make assumptions about other people.

3

THE BOYS WERE MESSING about on the dinghy. The boat belonged
to Dean's family, but no one ever used it apart from him and his
friends. He and Benjy had often gone out on the river together
when they were younger, but now they were away at different
universities and only occasionally had time to go rowing
together. They were both in York for a mutual friend's party,
and it was Benjy's suggestion that they take the boat out on the
water. At that time of year the river was deserted so early in
the day, and they had the stretch between the railway bridge
and Lendal Bridge to themselves. The morning mist had begun
to lift as the late autumn sun broke through the clouds, leaving
the air damp and fresh, but it was still freezing cold. Benjy was
already regretting having persuaded his friend to go out. His
gloves didn't seem to be doing much good. He let go of his oar,
one hand at a time, and wriggled his fingers. That didn't help
either.

'I'm freezing to death,' he called out as they reached Lendal
Bridge. 'It was a stupid idea to come out on the river.'

'It was your idea in the first place,' Dean pointed out.

'Well, I've changed my mind. It's no fun in this weather, and
it's going to start raining soon. I vote we go back and have a
coffee or something to thaw us out before we die of hypothermia.'

'All right,' his friend replied, laughing. 'If you're going to be
melodramatic about it. I'd hate to see you give up the ghost in
my– Hang on. What's that?' He raised his oar and pointed at
something floating at the edge of the water under the bridge.

'Let's just go back,' Benjy repeated. 'I'm freezing my bollocks off here.'

'Yes, all right, but first, I want to go over and see what it is.'

'Forget it. It's only a log or something, trapped under the bridge. It'll free itself in the current. And if it doesn't, who cares?'

'I think we should check it out. Someone could be in trouble.' He looked round at his friend with a worried expression. 'It looks like a body.'

'Don't be daft. Who the hell would want to go swimming? No one would last five minutes in the water at this time of year.'

'I'm not saying anyone's gone swimming, but they might have fallen in. Could be pissed. Come on, we're going over there to take a closer look.'

They rowed towards the floating bundle, Benjy grumbling all the way. At last Dean leaned over the side to inspect the floating object and yelled out in alarm.

'What?' Benjy asked, intrigued in spite of his freezing fingers which were beginning to really hurt. 'What is it?'

'I was right. It's a body. Bloody hell. Someone has fallen in. I can't see his face but he's not moving. Hello! Hello! Can you hear me?' He poked at it with his oar and it bobbed about without responding. 'Shit, I think he's dead.'

Benjy said that was hardly surprising. No one could survive in that freezing water.

'Are you sure it's human?' he added.

Dean nodded and said he could see it was a person, lying face down in the water.

'You'd better call the police,' Benjy said, snapping out of his fixation on his own discomfort.

They had left their phones in the locker at the boathouse, afraid of dropping them in the water. They now regretted what had seemed like a sensible precaution. After a hurried exchange they set off back to the boathouse. It wasn't far, but their hands were numb, and it seemed to take forever. At last they reached the boathouse, shipped their oars and moored up as quickly as they could. A moment later Dean was calling the police, while they hurried back along the path to watch what happened. A cordon was already in place by the time Benjy and Dean neared the bridge, and a police boat roared up as they arrived. One of the officers on the bank stopped them.

'I'm sorry, sir, I'm afraid you can't go any further. This section of the footpath is temporarily closed to the public.'

The policeman didn't look much older than Dean and Benjy, but he spoke with the authority of a man in uniform. Dean stepped forward officiously to explain that he wasn't just any passerby but was, in fact, the witness who had called the police to report finding a body underneath Lendal Bridge. The young policeman nodded equably and asked him and Benjy to wait until someone was available to talk to them.

'What happened to him?' Benjy asked.

'We don't have any details yet,' the policeman replied. 'We'll be bringing him out of the water shortly.'

'Can we watch?'

'You can't go past the cordon,' the policeman replied. 'I'm sorry, sir,' he added, 'but that's official. There's nothing I can do about it.'

'But we can't see anything from here,' Dean objected.

'Someone will be here to question you in a moment and then you're free to leave,' the policeman replied, ignoring Dean's protest.

'We don't want to go home,' Dean insisted. 'We want to see what's going on. We found him in the first place.'

The policeman nodded at that, but didn't reply. There appeared to be some activity on the far side of the bridge. They could hear shouts and someone calling out to 'Be careful there,' and 'Just a little more and we're clear,' but without being able to see what was going on it was difficult to work out what was happening.

'It sounds like they're pulling him out of the river,' Benjy said.

Just then, another policeman in uniform arrived. He was slightly older than the first one, and officiously echoed what his young colleague had told them. After making a note of their contact details and asking them what they had been doing before their discovery, he thanked them for their time and turned away.

'Wait,' Dean called out. 'We want to know who it is – was.'

The older of the two policemen didn't deign to reply.

The younger one gave an apologetic smile. 'I'm afraid we can't give out any details at this point.'

'They obviously don't know yet,' Dean said.

'Let's leave them to get on with their job. Rather them than me,' Benjy added, as they turned away.

'He probably jumped off the bridge,' Dean said.

Benjy shuddered. 'I suppose we'll read about it online.'

'If it's considered newsworthy,' Dean replied. 'It probably isn't that unusual for people to throw themselves off the bridge. Just before Christmas as well.' He sighed.

'It's a difficult time for a lot of people,' his friend said.

'Come on, let's go out for breakfast. I'm starving,' Dean added, cheering up.

Benjy nodded. 'Me too.' It had been an exhausting morning, even though they had spent most of the time standing around in the cold, waiting to be questioned.

It began to rain as they walked away, and they hurried along the path, debating where to go.

4

AT LUNCHTIME THE THREE friends met in the canteen. They were halfway through their lunch, enjoying each other's company and agreeing that it was 'like old times', when all of their phones buzzed simultaneously. They exchanged a glance.

'*Just* like old times,' Geraldine said, with a grimace

'At least it's not the middle of the night,' Ariadne added.

'Five minutes,' Naomi told them, reading the message.

They turned their attention to their lunch, eating as quickly as they could, before they hurried off to the major incident room together. Detective Chief Inspector Binita Hewitt was already in place, waiting, as the team assembled.

'A man's body has been discovered caught in weeds under Lendal Bridge,' she began straightaway, giving Geraldine a brief nod in acknowledgement of her return. This was no time for pleasantries.

'A jumper?' someone suggested.

'Possibly,' Binita replied solemnly. 'But the initial response team have reported suspicious circumstances. We need to see what they've got for us.'

Leaving the police station shortly after the meeting ended, Ariadne drove Geraldine down to the river, parking near Lendal Bridge. On the way, Ariadne enquired after Tom. Geraldine gave an appropriate response. She couldn't explain that she was trying to distance herself from her baby so she could concentrate on the crime scene. She trusted the childminder to do her job; she had to focus on her own. It was hard to believe how swiftly she had been able to switch from one mindset to another, as easily as flipping a switch. With luck they would solve this case quickly, leaving her free to think about her child once more. In the meantime, the investigation had to be her priority.

'Faster,' she said, switching on the siren, and grumbling about their speed as Ariadne accelerated for a moment only to hit the brakes again.

'We won't get there any quicker by trying to barge our way through the traffic,' Ariadne said.

'I know, it's just that we need to get there before they move the body.'

'Actually we don't,' Ariadne muttered.

As a rule, Ariadne was content to leave it to scene of crime officers and the medical officer on duty to determine what had happened at a crime scene, but whenever possible Geraldine insisted on viewing murder victims before they were moved. Observing the victim in situ could sometimes leave her with a sense of what might have happened, as though a kind of atmosphere hovered in the air around the scene. Many of her colleagues, including Ariadne, dismissed such speculation as irrational, but there was no doubt Geraldine's hunches often proved correct.

It was early afternoon when they set off. The sky was overcast and a cold wind was blowing through the trees that bordered the river, making their sparse leaves flutter as they clung to the branches. The forensic tent had already been erected by the time they arrived and a cordon was in place, blocking access to the path by the river. A uniformed officer had been posted at either end of that stretch of the bank to turn back cyclists and pedestrians. A lone car was parked nearby. Geraldine and Ariadne learned that the vehicle was registered to a local man named Martin Reed. The initial suspicion was that Martin had been pulled from the river, although the dead man's identity had not yet been confirmed. Several white-suited scene of crime officers were walking carefully over the muddy ground, examining footprints, taking photographs and marking potential evidence.

'It looks as though he drove himself here when it was dark, and slipped and fell in the river,' Ariadne said, adding that he might have thrown himself in.

It had been raining during the night, making the path slippery; it was reasonable to suppose the death had been accidental.

'So what are we doing here?' Geraldine asked, gazing around. 'It looks as though he fell in by accident, or jumped.'

'It's not that simple,' the officer leading the scene of crime team replied, coming forward and introducing himself. 'It's true the victim ended up in the river, but he didn't drown and he didn't freeze to death either, although both looked likely before we got him out.' He paused and screwed up his eyes against the wind before adding that the victim had been shot before he entered the water.

'Shot?' Geraldine repeated in surprise.

'Someone wanted to make sure he was dead,' Ariadne muttered.

'He was killed by a shot to the head at close range. Whoever did that wasn't taking any chances. The entry and exit wounds are both within his hairline, so it's possible his killer was hoping we would assume he fell in the water and drowned by accident.'

'Someone hasn't been watching enough *CSI*,' another scene of crime officer quipped. 'Anyone who watches crime on the telly knows there are obvious signs when someone's drowned.'

'And it's not difficult to tell when someone's shot,' Geraldine added drily.

'You're welcome to take a look,' the first scene of crime officer said solemnly, ignoring the flippant exchange. 'The doctor's gone, but his report won't be very illuminating. That's to say, he'll just confirm what I already told you, that the man was fatally wounded by a gunshot to the head, and his body was then thrown in the water. It looks like the killer brought a cushion along to muffle the sound of the shot. We found it further up the bank. It's been taken away for examination.'

'How long after he was shot did he end up in the river?' Geraldine asked.

The scene of crime officer shrugged. 'You'll have to wait for the report for a more detailed timeline. All we know is that he was dead before he hit the water, and he may have come here in his own car. There's a vehicle nearby registered to a local man, Martin Reed. Whether or not he was driving, or came here alone, is something for the forensic team to look into. They're checking the car now, but chances are they won't be able to tell you much until they take it away for a closer examination. There's not much more to say for now.' Swearing about the weather, he turned away to speak to a colleague.

After they both pulled on protective shoe covers, Ariadne went over to talk to the officers studying the car, while Geraldine put on full protective clothing and made her way along the common approach path to the tent. The seeming confusion outside gave way to an atmosphere of quiet and orderly activity inside. Like their colleagues outside on the path, the scene of crime officers in the forensic tent were scrutinising the ground, studying footprints that were faintly visible under the bright lights inside the tent, and collecting samples of earth and other detritus scattered on the muddy grass.

In the middle of the tent, the mound of a man's body was clearly visible. Geraldine approached as closely as she was allowed, and stared down at him. The dead man was lying on his back. Under the glare of brilliant electric lighting, she could see the thick dark grey hair on the top of his head was streaked with sludge. Through dirty crimson stains on his temples, tiny threads of white hair showed up like tapeworms. His open eyes bulged, blighting his otherwise handsome features. There were none of the usual visible signs of drowning, such as froth at the nostrils or around the mouth. The lips were stretched open in a semblance of a grin, and the tongue appeared swollen. The man's skin was pale and wrinkled, signs of maceration.

'Do we have a time of death?' Geraldine enquired.

The nearest scene of crime officer shrugged. 'Last night some time,' she replied. 'The doc thought any time from after midnight. She said it wasn't—'

'I know, I know,' Geraldine interrupted her. 'It's impossible to give an exact time, or even an approximation of it, because the body's been immersed in water for hours, not to mention exposed to all manner of muck and pollution.'

Her colleague's eyes creased in a smile above her mask.

'Well, he's dead anyway, so it makes no difference to him,' she said.

'But knowing when he died could help us find out who killed him,' Geraldine replied, more for herself than the scene of crime officer who had already turned back to her work.

5

THE FOLLOWING DAY, GERALDINE went to the morgue to find out as much as she could about the man who had been shot. She had often worked with the pathologist, Jonah Hetherington, and was pleased to learn that he was conducting the post mortem. His assistant, Avril, was happy to see her again. She was not the kind of girl Geraldine would naturally have befriended. For nearly a year before Geraldine's maternity leave, Avril's main topic of conversation had been her wedding plans, a topic which didn't interest Geraldine in the slightest. All the same, over the years they had become cordial acquaintances, if not exactly friends, in addition to being colleagues. Avril was keen to hear about Tom, and even more eager to talk about her own marriage which had taken place while Geraldine had been on maternity leave. Avril chatted happily about her party, and Geraldine duly admired the pictures of her dress and her venue and her exotic honeymoon. In return, Avril wanted to see a photo of Tom.

'He's just a baby,' Geraldine laughed, but Avril insisted.

'He's so cute!' she gushed, when Geraldine finally took a small photo out of her wallet. 'Are you planning on getting married?' Avril went on. 'You know I can give you lots of tips, and I can recommend the venue and the caterer we used. They get booked up so you'll need to plan way ahead, but by the time it happens, you'll be able to dress Tom as a page boy in a cute little outfit. Anyway, the point is, it all went really well for us in the end, so there's no need to reinvent the wheel. You can ask me anything and I don't mind if you do the same as us. Quite the opposite, in fact. It would be brilliant for us to see it all as guests. You know I would have invited you and Ian, if you hadn't just had Tom.'

'We've got no plans to get married just yet,' Geraldine interrupted her firmly. 'It's not long since Ian and his first wife divorced, and I don't think he's too keen on having another wedding.'

Avril stared earnestly at her. 'He can't let one bad experience scar him for life. That's hardly fair on you. What about what *you* want?'

Geraldine shook her head. 'Honestly, it's not something we've ever discussed. There just never seems to be time to think about it, and I can't say I'm that bothered.' She didn't add that with so many marriages failing, wedding celebrations had always struck her as a waste of money. 'But I appreciate your offer of advice,' she added kindly. 'I know you just want to help. If we ever decide to tie the knot, I'll be sure to take you up on your offer. And now, I'd better get on. Work to do.'

Jonah looked up as she entered, his squashed face lighting up in a smile. He held out his bloody gloved hands in a theatrical wave from the other side of the room.

'Well, well, well,' he greeted her. 'Hello, stranger. It must be getting on for a year since you were last here.'

'Nearly eight months,' Geraldine replied, returning his smile. 'But it feels like a lot longer.'

'So you missed me too,' he replied with a grin. 'That's a relief. I was beginning to think you'd forgotten all about me.'

'How have you been?' she asked.

'Other than pining for you?' he replied, with mock gravity. He placed a bloody hand on his chest and looked at her with a pained expression. 'The days have dragged so slowly while you've been away, it's been agony, sheer agony. And how's your little one?' he added, brightening up.

Geraldine smiled. For all his protestations of interest, Jonah evidently didn't know if she had a son or a daughter. 'He's fine,' she replied. 'He's called Tom.'

'Tom,' he repeated, nodding as though he was committing the name to memory. 'Congratulations on looking so well on it. Being a mother clearly agrees with you. Ah, I remember the sleepless nights.' He chuckled. 'Would you believe it? With my good looks, I actually looked worse than him for a while?' He gestured at the corpse.

Geraldine turned her attention to the body. 'What can you tell me about him?'

Jonah nodded. The time for banter was over. He told Geraldine that the victim had suffered a fatal gunshot wound.

'So he definitely didn't drown?'

'He was killed, instantly I would say, by a gunshot. The bullet passed through one of the ventricles through which cerebrospinal fluid flows. You have to appreciate that over ninety per cent of gunshot wounds to the head are instantly fatal, and this one was definitely one of the ninety per cent. So you're right, he didn't drown. There was no froth, and no cerebral anoxia.' He pointed at a repulsive heap of sludge which Geraldine barely recognised as what had once been a human brain.

She turned her attention back to the body with its mutilated head and pale hands and feet, wrinkled from immersion in the river. 'Do you think someone shot him and then carried or dragged the body to the river and threw him in?'

'There are no post mortem injuries, which suggests he wasn't dragged bodily from the car to the river, and no signs of resistance. My impression – and this is just speculation, so please don't quote me on it – my impression is that he walked right to the water's edge before he was shot and then fell straight into the water.'

'He might have been forced to walk to the edge at gun point,' Geraldine murmured.

Jonah shrugged. 'There's no way of knowing, but that would make sense, yes, given that he was shot.'

'He was shot from the side and then fell or was pushed into the water. We're examining the footprints along the river bank.'

Jonah grunted. 'Once your people have finished, I dare say you'll have a better idea of what happened. All I can tell you is that he was shot dead before he entered the water. I take it you know his name?'

She nodded. 'We suspect he was called Martin Reed. That's the registered owner of a car found abandoned near where the body entered the water, and as far as we can tell the body seems to match his appearance. It's not yet been confirmed, but we're confident that's who he was.'

'What else do we know about him?' Jonah asked.

'We're looking into the circumstances of his life. Now, what can you tell us about his death?'

'Oh, it's like that, is it? You'll show me yours if I show you mine.' Jonah teased her with a laugh. 'Very well then, I'll go first. We're looking at a man in his late sixties, I'd say, in very good physical shape for his age. He took good care of himself and exercised regularly. He had eaten well not long before he was killed: steak, green vegetables and potatoes. The medical examiner who attended the scene estimated the time of death at between midnight and four o'clock in the morning.'

She nodded, thinking. The scene of crime officers would already have studied the ground, but Jonah's report would be read alongside their findings and every different piece of information needed to be meshed together like a giant jigsaw. It was impossible to say exactly how long it would take to discover all the pieces, and then gather them into a coherent picture. They still hadn't confirmed the identity of the dead man. And, in the meantime, the murder weapon had not been found. An armed gunman was on the loose in the city, a gunman who had already committed one murder, and might be prepared to kill again.

6

THEY NEEDED TO MOVE quickly. However careful they were to avoid contaminating the crime scene, any traces left by the killer were inevitably deteriorating, exposed as they had been to the wind and intermittent drizzle overnight. The longer they spent closely examining the area, the less they were likely to find. While scene of crime officers carried out their painstaking scrutiny of the river bank, searching for recent footprints, Geraldine needed to establish the identity of the victim. The body was almost certainly that of Martin Reed, so she went to his house, a large red brick property in Friars Terrace, near the minster. The walls looked as though they had recently been repointed, and the tall windows were well maintained, with handsome bay windows on the ground floor.

A woman of around thirty opened the gleaming black front door. Her heavily made-up eyes widened on seeing Geraldine waiting on the threshold. She swept glossy honey-blonde curls back off her face, displaying long scarlet nails. Her elegant pink and silver dressing gown shimmered as it swirled around her.

'Have you come to see Martin?' the woman enquired in a low and gentle voice. 'Only he's not here and before you ask, I don't know where he is. He didn't leave any message and he's not answering his phone.' Beneath a show of insouciance, her eyes betrayed her anxiety. 'Who are you?'

Geraldine held up her identity card and the woman leaned forward to squint at it before she drew back with a scowl.

'May I come in?' Geraldine asked, taking a step forwards to prevent the woman from closing the door.

'I don't think so. What I mean to say is, it's not my house so it's not really my place to let you in. What do you want?'

'Can you tell me first who you are, and why you're here?' Geraldine responded with questions of her own.

The woman answered that her name was Serena, and she lived there with Martin. 'But it's his house. Like I said, it's not my place. I only moved in with him recently.'

'You just told me Martin's not here, and you said you don't know where he is.'

Serena nodded.

'We're trying to find him. I'm afraid we're going to have to come inside to look for any clues to his whereabouts.'

Serena frowned and she shifted her weight, poised to retreat and close the door. 'I don't understand. Has something happened to Martin?'

'What makes you say that?'

'Why else would you be here? What's happened to him?' Suddenly alert to the situation, Serena responded with a series of questions. 'Tell me what you're doing here. Something's happened to him, hasn't it? What? Tell me!' She was becoming slightly hysterical.

'I suggest we go inside and you can sit down and answer a few questions.'

'I don't understand what you're doing here,' Serena insisted. 'I haven't reported him missing.'

'Let's go inside where we can talk more comfortably.'

Her outburst over, Serena nodded and led Geraldine past a grandfather clock and a tall vase of flowers, across a narrow hall with several closed doors leading off it, and past a broad staircase with a wooden balustrade that swept upstairs. Geraldine waited until they were both seated in a lavishly furnished living room before she started questioning Serena.

'When did you last see Martin?'

Serena stared at her, no longer defensive. 'Where is he? Is he all right?'

'We're not sure. When did you last see him?'

'I was away for the weekend. When I got home on Monday morning, he wasn't here. I thought he'd be back in the evening, but he never appeared. I tried his phone but couldn't get hold of him. I kept trying all day yesterday, but he still wasn't answering. When he hadn't called me by the evening, I called every hospital in the area, but no one had any record of him being admitted. They all said the same thing – to wait, he would probably turn up. I guessed his car had broken down, or something had come up and he had gone out without telling me, but by last night, I was really worried. He had been gone for more than twenty-four hours, and possibly longer because I didn't speak to him over the weekend. I was planning to go to the police station in person this morning to report him missing. It's better than phoning, I think.' She shrugged. 'But anyway, now you're here I'd like to report him missing. Can we do that? I mean, officially? It would save me having to go to the police station, although I'll probably do that anyway.'

'Tell me about your relationship with Martin Reed,' Geraldine replied, ignoring the question.

'We worked together. That is, I worked for him as his personal assistant. But then, after his wife died, we fell in love. The truth is, I'd always had feelings for him, but he was married, so nothing ever happened between us and I thought nothing ever would. But after she died, I discovered he felt the same way. I know there's a bit of an age difference between us.'

'Forty years,' Geraldine murmured.

'Forty-five. I know what you're thinking, but we love each other. There's no point in pretending we don't. Martin asked me to come and live with him, and I agreed. Why wouldn't I? I love him. We love each other. So here I am.' She gazed at Geraldine, her attractive features creased in a worried frown. 'Only I don't know where he is. Why would he go off without telling me? Do you know where he is?'

Geraldine listened as Martin's girlfriend justified moving in with a man so much older than herself. Serena didn't mention Martin's wealth, although Geraldine supposed that might have been part of his attraction. She took down details relating to Martin's disappearance and concluded by asking for his toothbrush or comb. Serena gasped and covered her mouth with both hands.

'You think he's dead, don't you?' Serena whispered, her eyes glistening with tears. 'You've found his body. That's why you want his DNA, isn't it? Isn't it?'

Watching her closely, Geraldine wondered whether Serena's concern for Martin was as fake as her nails and eyelashes.

7

RETURNING TO THE POLICE station, Geraldine discussed the case with her colleagues.

'According to the pathologist's report, there was nothing to indicate he had been dragged along the ground, no contusions or scratches inflicted before or after death, which suggests his killer must have carried the body quite carefully right to the water's edge. So that means we're probably looking for a man,' Naomi suggested.

'A man or a strong woman,' Ariadne added.

'Not necessarily,' Geraldine said. 'Let's not jump to conclusions when there are other possibilities. The victim could have been forced at gun point to walk to the water's edge and then been shot right there so he would have fallen into the water without needing to be pushed. Even carrying him carefully might have left some bruising, but there was nothing, and no defence wounds.'

'He could have been shot actually *on* the water, forced to stand up in a boat,' Naomi speculated.

'Or even once he was *in* the water,' Ariadne added. 'You're right, there are all sorts of possibilities.'

'We need more evidence, and in the meantime we have to keep open minds. It's a pity other people walked along the muddy footpath before SOCOs got there to examine it, but there's still a chance they'll come up with something.'

'There might have been two sets of footprints, but we'll never know,' Ariadne said.

'The body could have been carried there really carefully, but it does look like no one dragged it to the water's edge,' Naomi added.

Geraldine sighed. 'I know it's difficult when you have a theory that seems to make sense, but just because something could be true doesn't mean it is. And so far, the evidence isn't helping much.'

They finished their coffee and were about to go back to work, when they received confirmation that the DNA on Martin Reed's toothbrush was a match for the body pulled from the river. No one was surprised. While it was never a cheerful discovery, it made their job simpler knowing the identity of the victim. Confident Martin Reed was the dead man in the river, Geraldine had already instructed Naomi to start looking into his background.

'Our upright citizen Martin Reed had an interesting past,' Naomi told them. 'He was married to his second wife Ann for nearly forty years, since he was thirty, and they had two children, a son and a daughter.'

'What happened to his first wife?' Geraldine asked.

'His first marriage didn't last long, and his ex-wife went abroad after the divorce. She lived in America for around forty years and only returned to the UK two years ago when her partner there died.'

'She came back around the time his second wife died,' Geraldine said.

'Yes, although there was no suspicion of foul play at the time. It was a brain tumour, all very sudden.'

'So it was a coincidence, his first wife returning just then?'

Naomi nodded. 'It seems so. She lives in Surrey and doesn't appear to have had any contact with Martin for many years. As far as we know, she didn't attend Ann's funeral. So she seems to be out of the picture, although we'll check, just to make sure.

What may be more interesting is that six months after Ann died, his young PA moved in with him.'

'How did his children feel about that, I wonder?' Geraldine murmured.

Naomi nodded. 'We need to find out whether he made any changes to his will,' she added thoughtfully.

There seemed to be a handful of potential suspects, all of whom might turn out to have alibis. Until they knew for certain who could be ruled out as guilty, there was a lot of work to be done. DNA suggested the pillow found at the scene had come from Martin's own bed, but it wasn't yet clear who had brought it to the river bank. Possibly Martin had kept it in his car.

Ian had collected Tom and by the time Geraldine walked through the front door and kicked off her shoes, the baby was already asleep. She felt a flicker of disappointment that she hadn't been there to put him to bed.

'You could have waited for me to get home,' she muttered.

'He was tired,' Ian replied. 'And I thought you would be too, after your first day back. I hope it wasn't too much of a shock?' He smiled kindly. 'Why don't you go and put your feet up and I'll get something out of the freezer?'

Geraldine was pleased that Ian seemed supportive, now he had accepted that she was back at work. All the same, she hesitated to tell him about the case she was working on. She was afraid he would remonstrate with her, arguing that she ought to ease herself back into work slowly. She could imagine him questioning whether she was in the right mental state to deal with the demands of a murder investigation. She knew she ought to reassure him before he could mention his concerns to the detective chief inspector, who could easily take her off the case. Puzzled by the shooting, she was determined not to abandon the case without a fight. She certainly wasn't prepared to step back because Ian took it upon himself to worry about her needlessly. Tom was fine with the childminder, and she was enjoying the challenge of being back at work. Objectively, Ian had no reason to be concerned.

They were living happily together in the flat Geraldine had bought with the proceeds from the sale of her London flat which she had purchased with the help of a sum inherited from her family. Following an acrimonious divorce, Ian had lost his marital home to his ex-wife. He steadfastly maintained he was too pleased to be rid of his ex-wife to care about his material losses. He claimed to have realised fairly early on that his marriage had been a mistake. He had done his best to make it work, until his ex-wife had run off with another man. Ian insisted he had been happy to see the back of her, but it had been a difficult period in his life, and he had been grateful to Geraldine for standing by him. She had done more than that, admitting that she had been in love with him for a long time.

After dinner, when they were sitting at the table with a glass of wine, Geraldine broached the subject of her work obliquely, asking Ian how his day had gone. He grunted before launching into a detailed account of his current caseload. Preoccupied by what she wanted to tell him, she wasn't really listening. She needed to preempt his inevitable disapproval of her leading a murder investigation by telling him how well she was coping, but she didn't know what to say. She couldn't admit that she was relieved to be handing the responsibility for child care to a stranger. At last Ian drained his glass and asked her how her day had gone. She was about to reply, when Tom let out a howl and she jumped up, secretly relieved at the reprieve. Telling herself she would tackle the issue of her workload as soon as Tom had gone back to sleep, she went into the small bedroom that had once been her study and was now the nursery. They were going to have to move before Tom was very much older, so he could have some space of his own, but for now the flat was fine and by all accounts it wasn't a good time to be moving anyway.

'If we wait until it's a good time to move, we'll never go anywhere,' Ian had complained when he had first moved in with her. 'We might as well put the flat on the market and start looking around, and see what happens.' But then Tom had come along and they had been too tired to organise moving, so had agreed to shelve the idea for a while.

Now Tom was possibly teething, which was making him tetchy, and he refused to settle. Geraldine resorted to rubbing Calpol on his gums and eventually he fell asleep in her arms. Gently she laid him in his cot, hardly daring to breathe for fear she would wake him and he would start yelling again.

'I hope he sleeps tonight,' she said, joining Ian in the living room.

'You never told me about your day,' Ian said.

This was her opportunity to talk about the murder case she was working on, but she was too tired to face a row, so she just smiled and assured him everything was fine.

'You're confident you can find him?' he asked.

'Find who?'

'Your shooter. When were you planning to tell me about it?'

Geraldine hesitated. If she confessed how tired she was, Ian was bound to object to her taking on the case.

'I was going to tell you,' she replied, annoyed with herself for sounding apologetic even though she had done nothing wrong.

'It's not like we have many shootings in York,' he said. 'The media's going to go crazy. You do realise it could be quite a lot of pressure. I think you should have discussed it with me first, before jumping in with both feet.'

'I only found out about it today,' she protested, hating that she had to defend herself to him. But he was right, she probably ought to have mentioned it to him earlier. 'I was going to tell you only then Tom starting crying and it went out of my head.'

'Really?' He sounded understandably sceptical. 'It went out

of your head? I know you, and once you're on a case, you won't forget about it for a moment.'

'I meant, it went out of my head to talk about it just then. Tom was crying. And now, let's get some sleep while we can. I've got a feeling he's going to be awake again during the night.'

Relieved that they had talked about it, she wondered whether to tell him she regretted having held back from discussing it with him before this, but decided it was best to say nothing. Any attempt to justify her reluctance would sound clumsy or, worse, insincere, and she was too tired to think about what she might say that wouldn't sound awkward.

'Don't worry about Tom tonight,' Ian said as he climbed into bed.

'What?'

'We're both working. We should take alternate nights.'

'What if one of us is on night duty and he doesn't wake up? Does that count or will it roll over?'

Ian gave a sleepy smile. 'Why don't you write out a rota?' he teased her. 'Now get some sleep.'

'Thank you.'

'What are you thanking me for? He's my son too.'

He smiled and Geraldine felt an overwhelming rush of love for him. She lay beside him for a while, watching him as he lay beside her with his eyes shut, looking like a larger version of Tom.

'I'm so lucky to have met you,' she said, but Ian was already snoring and she realised, with a guilty pang, that she wasn't the only one who was worn out.

8

HAVING ESTABLISHED THE DEAD man's identity as Martin Reed, other DNA detected in his car was being processed and samples had been taken from anyone who might have travelled in it, so they could be questioned and eliminated from the enquiry. Members of his family and anyone who had worked closely with him were being contacted. Leaving the police station, Geraldine drove to see his daughter who lived not far away, off the Holgate Road. There were cars parked along the street but she managed to find a space not far from the house. A light rain was falling, and she zipped up her jacket and pulled up her hood as she hurried to the front door to shelter under the porch. Daisy Reed lived in an apartment in a converted detached house. It must have once been a handsome red brick property but the exterior was now neglected. Grass and scrubby weeds poked up between the paving slabs in a narrow front yard where garbage spilled out from a bin. Wooden window frames were so ingrained with grime that scrubbing them would probably remove flaking paint as well as dirt; the brickwork was in need of repointing and the paintwork on the front door was chipped and filthy. It formed a stark contrast to the house where Daisy's father had lived.

A short, squat woman came to the door. Like the house, she looked as though she had seen better days. Her lank brown hair was threaded with grey, and she wore no make-up on her pockmarked face. Clutching a threadbare grey cardigan around her chest, she peered warily through the narrow gap between door and jamb. Seeing a stranger outside, she began to close the door. Geraldine promptly stepped forward and introduced herself.

'Am I speaking to Daisy Reed?'

'Yes, I'm Daisy Reed,' the woman replied, pulling the door further open. 'What do you want? A constable's already been here to tell me my father's car's been found, abandoned down by the river. That's what your colleague said. Abandoned,' she scoffed, as though an abandoned car was something shameful. 'It's his car all right, but they refused to return it, and said no one was allowed to go and pick it up. No explanation, just a flat no. So when are you going to let him have it back? Only he's going to want it, isn't he? And he's going to need to get it checked because it was stolen by joy riders and goodness knows what damage they might have caused, speeding around. And what the hell do you need my DNA for? Do you think I stole his car? You think I'm a closet car thief? I can't even drive!'

'May I come in?' Geraldine interrupted Daisy's tirade.

'No, you bloody well can't come in. You listen to me. That car is my father's property. You've got no right to keep hold of it. Your colleague said they had it towed away. I just hope for your sake you haven't damaged it, towing it away. You need to return it to him, and it had better be—'

Geraldine interrupted Daisy's rant, insisting she accompany her inside. Finally falling silent, Daisy gave a reluctant nod and led the way upstairs to a small living room off a narrow corridor. Three worn brown leather armchairs were arranged around a scratched wooden coffee table, facing a small television that was fixed to the wall. There was a musty smell, as of a place long empty; paint on the skirting boards was chipped and the ceiling was stained with water marks. Despite all the evidence of neglect, the room looked lived-in and comfortable, with a half-drunk cup of tea on the table beside a small pile of well-thumbed copies of *Reader's Digest* magazines. Geraldine wondered whether Daisy's apparent financial deprivation had caused any friction between her and her wealthy father.

'I'm sorry to tell you your father is dead,' Geraldine told Daisy gently, when she was seated.

She watched the other woman covertly as Daisy took a tissue from a box on the table and blew her nose noisily. She tucked the tissue in the sleeve of her cardigan and frowned. 'Yes, well, I expected you to say that. It's the easiest conclusion, isn't it?'

'I'm not sure what you mean.'

'What I mean is, you're taking the obvious way out. You found a body somewhere near the car, so of course you jumped to the conclusion that the dead man must be my father. But you don't even know if he's dead. We're very close. No one knows him like I do.' She gave a twisted smile and leaned back in her chair. 'You might not want to believe this, but I would know if my father was dead, and he isn't.'

Geraldine waited a moment to hear if she would say anything else, but Daisy closed her eyes as though signalling that the conversation was over.

'Do you know why his car was left near the river?'

'I told you, it must have been stolen. Unless it was her doing,' Daisy muttered. 'But don't ask me why she would leave it there. She's such an airhead, it's impossible to say what goes through her mind, if anything. Have you seen her? All make-up and hair and fancy clothes, and nothing between her ears.'

Geraldine leaned forward. 'Who are you talking about?'

'She got round him when he was vulnerable. My father was never quite the same after my mother died. We both thought that.'

'We both?'

'Me and my brother, Nigel. We weren't convinced by my dad's claim he was happy with that bitch.'

'Who are you referring to?'

Daisy heaved a sigh. 'Listen, my parents were married

for nearly forty years. Mum died just over a year ago. Nigel suggested our father have bereavement counselling when Mum died, he was that lost without her. I mean, he just went to pieces. But you can't force someone to get help if they don't want it. My father's a very proud man, very independent. But then a few months after our mother died, this gold-digger, Serena, moved in with him. He told us she'd been working for him as his personal assistant, but before we knew anything about her, she'd become more than that. A lot more. And Mum had only just died.' Her voice rose indignantly. 'Serena made her move while he was still grieving for our mother. Anyway, my brother and me, we don't think Dad was ever happy once Mum died. It's tragic, the way he lets her manipulate him. It's not as if he's a fool. He's a highly intelligent man and he knows I'm always here for him. When Mum died, I went to his house every day to clean for him, and do his laundry, and I cooked for him every evening. He doesn't need anyone else. I still can't believe he was stupid enough to let her move in with him. He didn't have to be lonely. He had me.' She broke off, her features crumpled in grief, and a solitary tear made its way down the pitted surface of her cheek.

Geraldine spoke very gently. 'I'm afraid your father is dead. There's no room for doubt. I'm sorry to tell you he was murdered.'

Without warning, Daisy pitched forward. Her head on her knees, she burst into noisy weeping.

'Is there someone who can sit with you?' Geraldine asked. 'Would you like me to call your brother?'

Daisy shook her head. 'No way. No, just go away, leave me alone,' she mumbled. After a few seconds, she raised her head and spoke clearly. 'Go and arrest her.'

'Arrest who?'

'Serena, of course.' Daisy let out a curious snort, her shoulders shuddering. Her eyes glittered with fury. 'Isn't it obvious it was her?' she hissed through clenched teeth. 'Serena. She killed him.'

'That is a very serious allegation. What makes you believe she was involved in what happened to your father?'

'It's not a question of what I *believe*. I *know* it was her. I had a bad feeling about her right from the start. Ask my brother. He'll tell you it was her. Who else could have done it?'

'Please accept my condolences. I assure you we are investigating the circumstances of your father's death and we will find whoever is responsible for what happened.'

'I'm telling you, it was Serena. You need to arrest her now, before she gets away,' Daisy insisted tearfully. 'She killed our father. She has to be punished.'

Repeating her assurances that the police were doing everything in their power to apprehend Martin's killer, Geraldine took her leave of his daughter. Back at the police station she learned that scene of crime officers had found a bullet in the grassy verge on the river bank, not far from the bridge where the body had been discovered. DNA on the bullet matched Martin's. Now they knew he had been shot right by the water, but they hadn't found the gun, and they didn't know who had fired the fatal shot.

9

IT WAS THE FIRST time either of them had been in their father's bedroom since their mother's death. Walking in there without his permission, Daisy felt awkward, as though they were intruding on his privacy which, in a way, they were. Gazing around uneasily, she half expected her father to burst in and demand to know why she and her brother were snooping around in his room. She tensed, waiting to be startled by his booming voice, but the room remained shrouded in dusty silence. She took a tentative step forward; her feet made no sound on the thick carpet.

Until their mother's death, their father had always been strong, mentally as well as physically. When his wife died, suddenly and unexpectedly, he had fallen apart. Perhaps it would have required superhuman strength to cope with her dying so unexpectedly only days after her condition had been diagnosed. Or perhaps he had always been a weak man, cowering behind a domineering exterior, propped up by a submissive wife. Whatever the truth about their father, there had been no time to discuss their mother's treatment, no time to process the terrible news.

Their father had staggered around in a daze for weeks. 'If only we'd had some notice,' he kept repeating. 'If only we'd had time to prepare.'

'If only your doctor would stop dosing you up on sedatives, or whatever it is he's giving you,' Nigel had muttered, loudly enough for Daisy to hear.

It had never occurred to Daisy that their father might go to pieces like that. He was too solid a figure to crumble. Daisy and Nigel had both been confident he would soon be back on his feet, running his business with his characteristic authority. They had discussed the situation without a hint of apprehension. With hindsight it should have been easy to spot the warning signs that they had overlooked at the time. They had even quietly congratulated one another on how seamlessly he had managed to pass the responsibility of his day to day work on to his personal assistant, while they had both been too preoccupied to involve themselves in their father's business affairs.

Neither of them had met Serena before their mother died but she seemed very efficient and they were grateful to her, at first. In any case, they too needed time to come to terms with the sudden loss of their mother. Their father had been largely preoccupied with his work throughout their childhood, while their mother had always been there for them, encouraging and supporting them into adulthood. She had died suddenly without giving them a chance to say goodbye. It had been a terrible shock for them both. And now their father was gone too.

'We're orphans,' Daisy said, looking sadly around the bedroom. She was determined not to cry. 'Do you think *she* killed him?'

Nigel shrugged. He understood immediately to whom she was referring. 'Who knows?'

'Of course we don't *know*. I'm asking what you think.'

'I wouldn't put it past her,' Nigel replied, gazing around his parents' bedroom, his brow lowered in a frown. 'Who else could it have been?'

The room held few reminders of their mother after a marriage of nearly forty years. There were no pictures of her on display anywhere in the house, and when Daisy looked in the wardrobe, she didn't see any of her mother's clothes hanging inside. There were only signs of Serena's occupation, from the framed photograph of her and their father on the mantelpiece in the living room to the flamboyant dresses hanging in the wardrobe that had, until recently, been filled with their mother's grey and beige.

By the time his children realised the nature of Martin's relationship with his so-called personal assistant, Serena was already living with him.

'There's no fool like an old fool,' Nigel said bitterly. 'He should have waited. It's indecent to move on so soon.'

'I know. And she's so young,' Daisy agreed. 'She must be ten years younger than me.'

'How old is she, exactly?'

'I don't know, but she can't be thirty yet. It's disgusting.'

'A lot of men like younger women,' Nigel said, turning on her, suddenly testy. 'It's not exactly unusual.'

Daisy regretted her tactless comment as soon as it left her lips. She never said as much, but she thought Nigel had been lucky to find a wife at all. Despite her lumbering hips and flat chest, Carol wasn't unattractive and, at thirty, she was sixteen years younger than her husband. Nigel, by contrast, was possibly the ugliest man Daisy had ever met, and that wasn't just because he was her brother. Prematurely bald and chinless, he looked like an egg squashed on to a lanky body. Daisy found it hard to understand what Carol saw in him. But what had happened to their father was different. Martin had been seduced by a younger woman at a time when he was grieving and vulnerable.

'I wasn't talking about the age difference,' Daisy said quickly. 'It's just that she's blatantly a gold-digger. It's hard to believe he didn't see through her.'

'What I find so offensive about the whole thing is that our mother was barely cold in her grave when Serena made her move,' Nigel said.

'I know. I will never forgive her. Never. That grifter spotted how vulnerable he was, and couldn't wait to leap in and exploit him.'

'And he was stupid enough to go along with it,' Nigel said angrily.

'Yes, the conniving bitch fooled him into believing she actually cared about him and not just his money.'

'As for how he died and who did what to whom, we don't know what she was capable of, but I'm sure she wasn't acting unselfishly when she moved in with him,' Nigel said grimly.

'It's perfectly obvious what she was after all along,' Daisy said, opening a drawer in the dressing table. 'Take a look at this.'

She held up a large pear-shaped diamond. It swung gently on its gold chain, sparkling in the light from the crystal chandelier overhead.

'He never bought Mum anything like that,' she added sourly.

'Is it real?'

'It looks real.'

'What do you suppose something like that is worth?'

It was Daisy's turn to shrug. 'We'd need to take it to a jeweller's to get it valued. It could be anything from two bob to tens of thousands of pounds.'

'Two bob?' Nigel laughed.

Daisy giggled. 'You know what I mean.'

'When did you ever say two bob before?'

'There's a lot about me you don't know,' she teased him.

'I very much doubt that,' he replied, serious again.

'What I want to know is what Serena was doing when Dad died. The police need to question her. I wouldn't be at all surprised if they find any alibi she gives them is an out-and-out lie. We ought to let them know what she's done before she manages to pull the wool over their eyes as well.'

'I don't think she's clever enough to fool the police.'

'You're probably right,' Daisy agreed. 'The inspector who came to see me was sharp as needles. But we can't take any chances. We have to make sure the police know she was only ever targeting him for what she could get out of him.'

'She was certainly quick enough to move in here,' Nigel said, gazing around the room. 'And that does seem to confirm that she only cared about his money.'

'It's our money now,' Daisy pointed out softly.

'As long as she didn't have time to talk him into changing his will,' he muttered.

'Changing his will?' Daisy looked startled. 'What are you talking about?'

'It's just something Serena said. I came to visit Dad one day and he wasn't here. She was.' Nigel frowned. 'She wouldn't let me in and she said something about making us sorry for how we treated him, living so near and hardly ever visiting him.'

'What?'

'And she said something about how things are going to be different one day. She said she had no intention of indulging us like our father did. I told her she was talking nonsense, and she shut the door in my face.' His face grew taut with anger. 'I'll do the same to her, now Dad has left everything to us. You and me. Do you understand? It should all be coming to us, every single penny of it.'

'I don't believe he would leave everything to her,' Daisy replied, but she looked anxious.

'We'll find out soon enough. But the question is, if he didn't change his will, why would she kill him? What would she gain from his death?'

It occurred to Daisy that their father might have promised to alter his will in Serena's favour, but not yet got around to doing so.

'We have to find his will,' she muttered. 'And if he was besotted enough with her to change it, well, we'll just have to change it back again to what it should be. We're his children. No one else can take what's rightfully ours.'

At last they found what they were hunting for, carefully folded in a brown envelope and hidden away at the back of a drawer in the desk in his study.

Nigel studied it. 'This certainly looks genuine,' he said. 'Signed and witnessed and everything.'

'And leaving everything to her,' Daisy snarled. 'We have to destroy it before anyone else finds it. It's our future at stake, yours and mine. We won't let anyone steal our inheritance. We'll do whatever it takes. Whatever it takes,' she repeated fiercely. 'And now, all we have to do is destroy this.' She snatched the document from him with an exultant cry.

'Don't be stupid,' Nigel snapped. 'This is obviously a copy. Look. The signature isn't the real one. It won't make any difference if we destroy it. A solicitor probably has the original. It won't have been left here in the house, where we might find it.'

'Then we'll have to make another one, a later one. We'll do whatever it takes,' Daisy said.

'We'd have to forge the witnesses' signatures.'

'We'll use the same names,' she replied. 'They're not going to remember the details of what the will said, are they? And if we date it the following week, they'll never know. What other choice do we have?'

He shook his head, insisting it couldn't be done. For an instant their eyes locked. But before she looked away, Daisy saw her own cupidity reflected in her brother's eyes.

'There is another way,' she murmured under her breath, almost too softly for him to hear her.

10

'WHAT ON EARTH HAVE you done?' Serena demanded shrilly, turning to examine herself again in the mirror. Her hair hung down to her shoulders in glossy chestnut brown curls. 'I said I wanted highlights, like last time. I always have highlights. Blonde highlights. That's what I come here for. I could have done this myself. What do you think I'm paying you for?'

The young stylist shrugged. 'You never told me you wanted highlights. I thought you said you wanted something different.'

'You thought?' Serena's voice rose in irritation. 'What do you mean, you thought? Your job is to do what I want. No one asked you to think.'

'You said you wanted something different,' the stylist repeated, sounding less sure of herself.

'I said *you* were a different stylist. I never said anything about wanting anything different for my hair. Are you deaf, or did you just not bother to listen to what I said? Just look at me! I can't see any blonde streaks when I look in the mirror. This is a complete disaster. I'm going to have to walk out of here looking like this.'

Serena stared at her reflection in the mirror and decided it didn't actually look too bad. In fact, the colour quite suited her. But it wasn't what she had requested. The manageress of the salon bustled over to enquire what was wrong. Coldly Serena explained that the stylist had made a complete hash of her hair and should be sacked on the spot.

'And I expect a full refund,' she added. 'It was a complete waste of time coming here. Who would pay your exorbitant prices to look like this? It's dreadful, just a dull mousy brown.' She turned to the stylist who was glaring defiantly at her. 'Really, what on earth were you thinking?'

The manageress smiled brightly, told Serena her hair looked lovely, and offered a fifty per cent reduction on her next visit. Serena retorted that she wouldn't be returning, and demanded a full refund. Tougher than she looked, the manageress refused to budge.

'We foster a tranquil atmosphere here and don't welcome vexatious clients,' the manageress said, raising her voice slightly so that other clients could hear her. 'I suggest you take your custom elsewhere. Lucy, give this lady her coat.'

'I just told you I'm never coming back. You're not the only hairdresser in York.'

Serena grabbed her jacket and flounced out without paying. Thoroughly disgruntled, she drove home. Since Martin's death, she had struggled to deal with even the most trivial of setbacks. But worse was to come. As she was turning her key in the lock, the front door swung open. Startled, she let the key slip from her hand and watched, shocked, as Daisy snatched the key. Her eyes were red and puffy but if she had been crying over her father's death, she had regained control of her emotions sufficiently to stare impassively at Serena.

'I'll take that,' Daisy said, glaring at her.

'Give me back my keys,' Serena cried out furiously. 'Give them back at once.'

Daisy shook her head. 'In your dreams,' she said. 'Now get lost. You're not wanted here.'

Her dark hair was greying at the temples, just like her father's. With sharp features and a spiteful sneer, she seemed to exude malevolence. Serena had always thought her name was inappropriate, because Daisy suggested someone dainty and pretty, like Serena herself. The woman confronting her was ugly and, far from delicate, her figure was dumpy and she had no waist.

'You can't take my keys,' Serena protested. 'What do you think you're doing? What are you even doing here? Get out of my house.'

'Your house? This was my father's house.'

'I live here,' Serena protested.

'Not any more you don't. There's no need for you to come here again. We'll pack all your belongings up and you can come and collect them tomorrow,' Daisy said, adding spitefully, 'we don't want your trashy clothes.'

'Don't you dare touch my things!'

'If you don't want your jewellery back, we can dispose of it for you. We'd be happy to bundle everything up and give it away to charity,' Daisy gloated.

'You can't do this. This is my home. You can't shut me out.'

'This is my home now,' Daisy said. 'Mine and Nigel's. You are no longer welcome here.'

Serena drew in a deep breath. There was no point in losing her temper, but this was a disaster and, in the meantime, Daisy seemed to have taken possession of the property. Somehow Serena would have to outwit Martin's children. With sudden determination, she lunged forward and tried to snatch her keys from Daisy's grasp, but she was too slow. The door hit Serena's outstretched fingers as it slammed shut.

'You can't do this to me!' she called out, nursing her bruised fingers and adding forlornly, 'I loved him. I was the only one who loved him. And he loved me.'

Realising that Daisy had taken her set of keys, including the one to her car, along with her house keys, she blew her nose and wiped her eyes, before ringing the bell. This time Daisy opened the door on the chain.

'What?' she snapped, glaring at Serena through the gap between the door and the frame.

Nigel was standing behind her, head and shoulders above his sister.

'You've taken my car key,' Serena said.

'It's not your car any more, is it?' Daisy replied smugly.

'It belonged to our father and now it belongs to us,' Nigel added firmly, as though his decision was final.

'It's my car,' Serena said. 'Martin gave it to me. You can't steal it from me. Martin would be horrified at what you're doing. I'll make sure you don't get away with it.'

'That's rich, coming from you. You're the one who's trying to get your hands on what's not yours,' Daisy said. 'We're keeping what belongs to us, and there's no way you're getting your hands on any of it. Everything our father owned is ours now, so you might as well get used to it. Go and find some other vulnerable old man to sponge off. You've had all you're going to get here and that's more than you deserve.'

The door slammed shut again. Serena rang the bell repeatedly, but the door remained closed. She half expected to see her belongings hurled out of an upstairs window, all her new clothes and expensive jewellery scattered over the immaculate lawn and flowerbeds. She would be forced to scramble around on her hands and knees to gather everything up. She waited, but nothing happened and the house remained closed to her.

'How am I supposed to get home?' she called through the letterbox, and then paused, because the house they had locked her out of *was* her home.

She had been living with Martin for months, and she actually had nowhere else to go. The house and everything in it belonged to her. She would have to come back with a locksmith. But before she returned, she needed to work out how she was going to handle the situation. Her grief at Martin's death was momentarily overwhelmed by her anger at what Daisy and Nigel were doing. They were his children, but Martin had loved her, and he had left his whole estate to her. They were effectively squatting in her house and she would have them removed at the first opportunity. She would begin by changing the locks and getting inside, and then she would call the police and complain that they were persecuting her.

As she walked away, she wondered angrily whether the police would actually be her best bet. Perhaps she needed someone more forceful to help her out, someone who would act more swiftly than the so-called justice system. If Nigel and Daisy contested Martin's will, it could take months for the case to be concluded, and even then there was no guarantee the decision would go in her favour. Nigel seemed like a clever man, and he could afford to pay a lawyer. Without her inheritance from Martin, she had nothing.

11

TOM WAS DEFINITELY TEETHING and the pain was making him grizzly. It was an ongoing struggle to soothe him. Since Geraldine was working on a murder case, Ian had taken over seeing to the baby when he cried for attention during the night. While she was grateful, at the same time she felt guilty because Ian was also working full-time. She felt ashamed of being so selfish, but she was too tired to refuse his offer of help.

On Friday morning, she dropped Tom off at the childminder's on her way to work.

Tom grumbled all the way there, but he stopped crying as soon as Zoe picked him up. Geraldine felt a flicker of envy watching her baby snuggle into the childminder's shoulder, but she had to get to work. Zoe gave her a curious look and Geraldine had a fleeting impression she was gloating at her discomfiture. Dismissing the notion, Geraldine promised she wouldn't be back late and turned to leave. She had to force herself to drive away, but as soon as she entered the police station her attention switched to the investigation. While they were certain of the identity of the dead man, they had made no progress in finding out who had shot him. A team was compiling a list of the legal movement of firearms, and other colleagues were looking into illegal sales of weapons in the area.

The detective chief inspector was becoming impatient. 'We need to discover who shot Martin Reed,' she said. 'This is urgent.'

'We're doing what we can to trace who bought the gun, but it's going to take time to question everyone,' Geraldine replied.

'There's a murderer who is armed and at liberty, and we know they're prepared to shoot to kill,' Binita said. 'Time is something we don't have. We need to find that gun and we need to arrest whoever used it on Martin Reed.'

An enquiry had been ongoing for twelve months into illegal possession of firearms in the county, and Geraldine went to chat to one of her colleagues on the team involved in tracking down weapons. Neil was a broad-shouldered Northerner with a shaven head and a whiskery face. He carried himself with an air of belligerence but Geraldine knew him as a gentle giant of a man. He smiled on seeing her, realising straightaway what she had come to ask.

'We haven't tracked down your murder weapon yet,' he told her as she approached him.

'What about the bullet?' she asked. 'Does that help at all?'

He shrugged. 'It narrows it down. It would be more helpful if we could examine the gun, and that's probably lost somewhere on the river bed where the chances of finding it are currently virtually nil. The powers that be have decided it's not worth dredging the river for it, and I dare say they're right, for once. It would take a real stroke of luck to come across it any time soon. It's likely to be a long, drawn-out process. Think looking for a needle in a haystack. Anyway, they're refusing to spend limited resources on something that's such a long shot, if you'll pardon the expression.' He chuckled.

Geraldine nodded. 'I can see it would be time-consuming and expensive,' she agreed reluctantly. 'But we need to get some answers quickly. I suppose there's not a lot you can tell me?'

Neil shook his head and held out his palms in a gesture of helplessness. 'Like I said, finding the bullet narrows it down.' He mentioned a common kind of pistol. 'But that doesn't help us find this individual weapon. There's nothing definite yet. Nothing confirmed.'

'How about what's unconfirmed? What about your gut feeling? Does anything spring to mind?'

'You want me to tell you who might flog an illegal firearm for cash? How long have you got?' Neil gave a deep throaty laugh. 'Trust me, we're talking to all the usual suspects, but nothing's come out of it so far. Don't worry. If we pick up any information we'll pass it on straightaway. No one relishes the idea that there's an armed killer roaming the streets. Believe me, we're working round the clock to discover who was behind the shooting, and we're all keen to get a result as quickly as possible. We've got a good team and if there's anything to find out, we'll get to it. It's just a matter of time. I don't know about honour among thieves, but most of the scum we deal with are willing to squeal at the sight of a few bank notes. Sad but true. Most of them can't see further than their next fix.' He shook his head. 'You don't want to know.'

After talking to Neil, Geraldine met Ariadne in the canteen for a coffee. Ariadne had been overseeing a team of forensic auditors who were looking into Martin's company records.

'So,' Geraldine said as they sat down with their coffees. 'Have we uncovered any dodgy dealings that might have led someone to want to silence him?'

Ariadne shook her head. 'So far everything seems to be above board. No unaccounted for money transfers. He might have exaggerated a few expenses to reduce his tax bill, but the Inland Revenue challenged his accounts more than once over the years and nothing came of it. There's no reason why anyone would have wanted to kill him on account of his company's financial affairs. It looks like we're going to draw a blank on this line of enquiry. If anyone wanted to commit murder,' she added ruefully, 'it would have been him wanting to kill his tax inspector.'

Geraldine laughed. 'If a murder was committed every time someone failed to get away with a tax fiddle, there'd be no one left working for HMRC.'

Leaving the canteen, she went to speak to Naomi who was in charge of a search team that had gone to Martin's house. Martin's alarm had been activated at one forty on the night of his murder. The police had arrived shortly after one fifty. Entering the property through an open window, they had found the house deserted. There had been no sign of any disturbance and the security alert had been shut down as a false alarm. By now it was clear the conclusion at the time had been incorrect.

'Binita wasn't pleased when the search team reported that an intruder might have entered the property,' Naomi added.

'She does have a point. Either the window was forced open or it wasn't.'

'I know. Forensics are re-examining it and Binita has said she wants a definite result this time, not some vague speculation about what might or might not have happened.'

The intruder had left no obvious trace. Serena assured them that nothing in the house had been disturbed, although Martin had left his phone behind. She had discovered it on the floor near the bed.

'So we know he left home between one forty and one fifty, and drove down to the river,' Naomi said.

What they still didn't know for certain was whether he had gone out alone or with someone else.

'The alarm going off suggests it wasn't Nigel or Daisy who was with Martin on the night he died,' Naomi said. 'So that's one positive to come out of this whole debacle.'

'Unless it *was* one of them, and they were hoping to misdirect us,' Geraldine replied.

It would have been a very risky strategy, gambling on the police not arriving immediately, but it was possible.

'I haven't met Nigel, but I suspect Daisy could be that sneaky, and we haven't been able to confirm Serena's alibi for that night yet,' Geraldine said.

'It could have been any one of the three of them,' Naomi agreed.

'Or someone we haven't even considered yet.'

'Or someone else entirely,' Naomi echoed.

12

LATER THAT AFTERNOON, GERALDINE was called to speak to a park keeper who had found a gun in one of the bins in Museum Gardens and had come to the police station to hand it in. He was about forty, with black hair turning grey at his temples and a thick black moustache. He was pale and seemed quite shaken as he repeated that he had found a gun in a bin in the park.

'What if a child had found it?' he asked several times, his voice husky with anxiety.

While Geraldine was questioning the park keeper, the gun was being dusted for fingerprints. Disappointingly there were no prints matching those of Daisy, Nigel or Serena, but it didn't take long to discover some that matched those of a small-time criminal registered on the database. He was one of Neil's informers, known to the police as John. Later that afternoon Neil called Geraldine to say John had been picked up and was waiting for her in an interview room. She joined Neil to face a scraggy young man with an emaciated face. He was wearing a khaki anorak that was too big for him and he looked sick, with sunken cheeks and greasy hair. Nevertheless, he seemed sober. It was difficult to judge his age; Geraldine guessed he probably wasn't even out of his twenties.

'Tell the inspector here exactly what you told me,' Neil said.

The man who had been introduced as John glanced nervously from Geraldine to Neil and back again. 'It wasn't me,' he mumbled after a brief hesitation. 'I never deal with weapons. Guns aren't my thing. You know I don't break the law—'

'Leave it out,' Neil interrupted roughly. 'You'd sell your grandmother for a hit. I know you've been involved with passing on illegal firearms more than once, so don't give us any of your flannel. We're looking into a murder, so you'd better start talking because this isn't going away.'

John swore. 'What you're talking about, that was before,' he replied, fidgeting nervously with the buttons on his jacket. 'I don't do that any more.' He gazed at Geraldine earnestly for an instant before dropping his eyes. 'I'm on the level now,' he muttered. 'You got nothing on me.'

'We have evidence you've been handling an illegal firearm,' Geraldine said.

'Not me,' he replied, with a flicker of animation. 'You can't prove it was me.'

'We have a gun and it's got your prints all over it.'

John squirmed in his seat. 'Yeah, well, someone handed it to me,' he said. 'I told him I wasn't interested. I told him no way.'

'Told who?'

John shrugged. 'Dunno who he was. I'm not saying another word.'

'Do you want to be charged as an accessory to murder?' Neil demanded with fake ferocity.

John's face paled. 'Murder?' he repeated, suddenly looking frightened. 'Are you sure?'

'Neil said you have some information for us,' Geraldine prompted him.

He nodded anxiously. 'It wasn't me,' he repeated plaintively.

'What wasn't you?' Geraldine asked.

John scowled until his eyebrows met over the bridge of his nose.

'Did you sell a gun recently?' Geraldine asked him.

John screwed up his eyes but said nothing.

'Listen to me, John,' Neil spoke more gently. 'Your name

doesn't need to come up, not officially. You're too valuable,' he added with a grim smile. 'If you cooperate, we can protect your anonymity.' He looked at Geraldine who nodded. 'But you're not going to walk away from this without answering our questions. So, start talking or you'll be charged with obstructing a murder enquiry and end up facing a long stretch inside. Is that really what you want? Or would you prefer to tell us what you know and walk out of here a free man? Those are your options. Tell us the truth or risk being banged up for a long time. Do yourself a favour and choose wisely. We'll make it worth your while,' he added, and John licked his lips nervously.

He dipped his head, mumbling.

'I didn't catch that,' Geraldine said. She leaned forward. 'Were you involved in passing on a firearm recently?'

'You can speak freely,' Neil reassured him. 'But let's get this over with quickly, shall we, before my patience runs out.'

'All right, all right, yes.'

'What does "yes" mean?' Neil pressed him.

'I sold a gun, yes,' John admitted grudgingly.

'Where did you get it?'

John shrugged and muttered that he couldn't remember. 'It's not difficult to get hold of one,' he added sullenly.

Clearly he wasn't willing to reveal his source, but Geraldine had no time to waste. Leaving any enquiry about the supplier to Neil, she turned her attention to the buyer.

'I sold it to a woman,' John said. He insisted he had no idea who she was.

'Can you describe her?'

John shook his head, muttering that he hadn't seen much.

'What about her hair? Was she fair or dark? What about her eyes? Anything you can recall would be helpful.'

John shook his head again. 'She was wearing a hood. I didn't see her face or her hair. I didn't see nothing. I didn't look at her. People get twitchy if they see you clocking them.'

'Did you notice her height, or her figure, or anything at all about her?'

'She was wearing a loose coat, dark, and I didn't see anything more than that.'

'What about her hands? You must have seen her hands when she took the gun from you?'

'She was wearing gloves.' He paused. 'They looked like a man's gloves, too big for her.'

'You must have some idea who she was, or how she came to find you?'

'It doesn't work like that,' he replied, glancing around nervously, and shifting on his seat, eager to get away. 'We didn't exchange names and phone numbers. What would be the point? It would only put us at risk. You don't know who to trust. If someone wants something, they just ask around, see who's hanging out. No names.'

'So how do I find out who sent her to find you?'

John shook his head. 'We don't keep records,' he replied, with a slight sneer. 'People just turn up, hand over the dosh, no questions asked. I've told you everything I know.'

'Wait. Where did you meet this woman to hand over the gun? And when?'

John looked at her suspiciously for an instant and shook his head, unable or unwilling to respond.

'I need to know where you met her,' she insisted.

'Union Terrace car park,' he said at last, adding that he had no idea when they had met. 'We arranged it, of course we arranged it, but I can't give you no details. I don't keep a record of all my comings and goings. Things just happen, innit? Go with the flow.'

'You must have agreed a time to meet?'

Geraldine waited impatiently for John's response. If they could nail the transaction down to a specific time, there was a chance they would be able to find the woman on a security film as she hurried to and from the car park.

John shrugged. 'It was eleven fifteen one night,' he said, surprising Geraldine with his precision. She wondered if he was saying the first thing that came into his head. 'Don't ask me what night it was.'

'How long ago was it? Days? Weeks?'

Please give me something so we know at least where to look, she thought. If it was more than a week since John had sold the gun, any CCTV footage would probably have been wiped and might take months to recover. Even if it was still relatively accessible, it could still take weeks to trawl through all the footage from around the car park.

'About a week ago.' He didn't sound very sure.

Geraldine wondered if what he was saying bore any relation to what had happened.

'What else can you tell me about how the meeting was set up?'

But John refused to say any more. All Geraldine had learned was that the gun had been sold to an anonymous woman in a deserted car park, possibly at eleven fifteen one night. She threatened to charge the informer with supplying a murder weapon, but he clammed up and refused to give her any more information, insisting that he wasn't a grass.

'More than my life's worth to get a reputation as a snitch,' he explained so earnestly that he was probably being honest about that, at least.

He hadn't told them much, but it was a start. At least she knew where the exchange had taken place. There was a chance the buyer might be seen on CCTV arriving at the scene, or departing. At a prompt from Neil, she thanked John for his cooperation and left her colleague to decide whether to pay him for the information he had shared, or send him off with a warning.

The gun found in a bin and the bullet from the crime scene had been sent off for forensic examination to determine whether the weapon had been used to shoot Martin. The results were disappointing.

'Inconclusive!' Naomi grumbled. 'If this was a TV show, forensics would have found a flaw in the barrel of the gun that matched a scratch on the bullet and bingo. Why can't real life be that helpful?'

'The gun might yet help to nail the killer, if we find one of our suspect's prints on it,' Geraldine replied.

'If they were stupid enough to hold it without wearing gloves,' Ariadne muttered.

13

IT WAS LUCKY THAT Serena had not yet come to the end of her rental agreement on her flat in York or she would have found herself homeless. It was a simple bus ride away from Martin's property. Her flat was part of a converted house and fortunately her neighbour on the ground floor was home and let her into the building. On hearing that Serena had left her keys at the house of a friend who had gone away, her neighbour lent her a set of keys, including Serena's own spare key. Although she was able to get back into her flat without any difficulty, she knew her problems were only just beginning.

Before she moved in with Martin, she had found her own lodgings comfortable enough, but the rented flat now seemed dingy and cramped, with space only for a bed with a lumpy mattress, and one single wardrobe. It had not taken her long to become accustomed to a spacious room and a more comfortable bed. Her old wooden wardrobe wouldn't have space to hold all the new clothes she had bought since she had gone to live with Martin, but there would be no point in moving them, even if she could get hold of them. She was going to return to the house Martin had gifted her in his will, the house that belonged to her. But first she had to outmanoeuvre Nigel and Daisy.

Exhausted by grief at her loss, and anger at Martin's horrible children, she flung herself down on her narrow bed and wept. She wouldn't put it past Nigel and Daisy to have thrown out all her possessions by the time she moved back in, but they were only things. Once she came into her inheritance, the house and everything in it would be hers. Anything missing could soon be replaced. It was only a matter of time and she could be patient. Even so, it was a pity. She gazed sadly at the few possessions she had brought with her from her recent home: the jewellery and clothes she had been wearing when Daisy had refused her entry to Martin's house. Whatever clothes she had left behind in the flat when she moved in with Martin looked shabby and old, but they still fitted her. They would have to do until the will was read and she came into her legal inheritance. Imagining Daisy's fury on hearing the terms of the will cheered her up, and she stopped crying.

In the meantime, she faced an immediate problem. She was broke. There was nothing else for it. She would have to find a job to tide her over. She thought it might help if she could dress fairly smartly for job interviews, so she decided to return to the house – her house – and insist they at least allow her to collect some of her clothes. This time she would be firm if Daisy tried to slam the door in her face again.

She told herself it was anger, not fear that made her hand shake as she reached for the bell.

'What do you want?' Daisy demanded, once again opening the door on the chain. 'Haven't you had enough? Just go away and stop pestering us. You're never going to get your hands on anything of my father's, you vulture. We knew all along you were only after him for his money. Now get lost before I call the police.'

'The police?' Serena replied, making it clear she was surprised by Daisy's words. 'Is that supposed to be a threat?' She laughed, and was afraid her laughter sounded fake.

'Yes, the police,' Daisy snapped. 'You think you can get away with pestering us but I'm warning you, don't ever come back here again, or you'll be sorry, I promise you. We'll have you arrested for harassment.'

Daisy shut the door without another word, her face red with anger. Daisy and Nigel had claimed the property for themselves and had changed the locks on all the doors to ensure no one could break in. Serena understood it had been done to keep her out. She suspected the valuable jewellery Martin had given her would very soon be sold or otherwise disposed of. She had no hope of retrieving any of it. But after the will was read, she had every expectation that things would be very different, starting with the removal of Daisy and Nigel from Martin's house, by force if necessary. If possible, she would sue them for the cost of the belongings they had stolen from her.

In the meantime, it was hard not to give way to despair. She had lost her job as well as her home, and without Martin her life was empty. But her immediate and most pressing concern remained money. Back at her old flat, she phoned the estate agents where she had worked before she met Martin, and her call was answered by a woman she had never met.

'I'm Serena Baxter,' she began and paused, because the girl gave no sign she had recognised the name.

'Are you looking to buy or rent?' the woman replied, confirming Serena's impression that she had been completely forgotten in her recent work place.

'Oh no, I'm not looking for somewhere to live,' she said quickly. 'It's not that. I – It's just that I used to work at Magenta Properties.'

'That must have been before my time,' the woman on the phone replied. 'I can't say I remember your name. Who did you say you were again?'

'My name's Serena Baxter. I left Magenta Properties about a year ago to work somewhere else, but that didn't work out so I'm looking for a job, and wondered if there might be a vacancy there?'

'I'm sorry. We're not looking to recruit anyone at present,' the woman replied, a trifle frostily. 'If you'd like to send us your name and contact details, I can send you an application form.' With that, she hung up.

The woman's dismissal stung, making Serena feel as though she had been presumptuous in her request. Refusing to give in to grief and despair, she resolved to go out and do something, anything. She washed her face and carefully applied her make-up before rummaging through the contents of her small wooden wardrobe. It didn't take very long. Most of her clothes were in the house in Friars Terrace. Having selected the smartest of her old trouser suits, she set out. The rebuff on the phone was not going to deter her. Making an appearance in person would hopefully produce a different result. She arrived at the estate agents in Foss Lane and was greeted by a young woman whose hair was tinged with bright pink. She was wearing a pink and purple T-shirt next to which Serena's self-consciously professional outfit seemed frumpy and middle-aged. Ignoring her qualms, Serena introduced herself and explained the purpose of her visit. Before she had finished speaking, the girl with pink hair broke into a grin and told Serena that she was the second person to turn up asking for a job that day. Someone else had called only an hour or so earlier, making the exact same request.

Noting with satisfaction that the girl's front teeth were crooked, Serena explained she had made the call.

The girl laughed, but she seemed uneasy. 'That was you as well, was it? Goodness, you're keen, phoning and coming here like this.'

'That's because I used to work here and I thought there might be a vacancy for me, seeing as I know how things work here. I need something to do,' she added, embarrassed at sounding so pathetic in front of a stranger. 'The point is, I really need a job.'

'Yes, I remember that's what you said on the phone. But I did tell you there are no vacancies here. I look after the lettings, and Ronny deals with sales. The boss isn't looking for anyone else. I can keep your name on file in case anything crops up, if you like, but I don't think anything's likely to come up in the near future. You'd be better off looking elsewhere. Why don't you try an employment agency? There must be tons of places recruiting at the moment. I mean, there always are.'

She spoke with the indifference of someone who didn't really care what she was saying before turning her attention to her screen with the obvious intention of closing the conversation. There was nothing Serena could do but thank her and leave. She called in on several other estate agents she knew of in the city to ask whether they had any openings, but was disappointed. Eventually, worn out, she went back to her cheerless apartment where she flung herself down on the bed and wept all over again for the loss of the life she had so recently enjoyed, a life that had taken her away from the need to find a job so she could pay her bills. At least this disaster was only temporary. She just had to keep going until she came into her inheritance. She would never stop missing Martin but, in time, her life would become easy again, thanks to him. Thinking of Martin made her cry all over again.

14

BACK AT THE POLICE station the following morning, Geraldine checked her report and scanned everything that had been logged overnight, before joining Ariadne in the canteen for a quick bite of lunch. Friends as well as colleagues, they liked to take their breaks together when they were working on a case.

'My money's on Serena,' Ariadne said as soon as Geraldine sat down. 'She's the obvious suspect. She clearly had means and opportunity and my guess is she expects to clean up now her lover's dead. He was so much older than her, you'd think she could have just waited, but I guess she was impatient. She probably only moved in with him in the expectation that he wouldn't last long.'

'That's a lot of guessing,' Geraldine replied, smiling. 'First of all, Martin was only seventy and he was fit and healthy, according to Jonah Hetherington. So he was hardly at death's door. In fact, he could easily have lived for another twenty years or more. Second, we don't know Serena stands to inherit anything. Whatever Martin might have told her, she couldn't have known for certain what he was planning to do. Wills are funny things. Let's wait and see who inherits his estate.'

'It seems obvious enough,' Ariadne persisted. 'Serena turns up, talks the old man into changing his will in her favour, and then shoots him before he has time to change his mind. And even if it turns out he never changed his will, how do we know she wasn't convinced he had? He could have promised he'd leave everything to her, without ever intending to do so. Or perhaps he did mean to do it, but thought better of disinheriting his children. It comes to the same thing in the end, I suppose.'

'More guesswork?' Geraldine teased her friend.

'Surely she's the obvious suspect? I mean, if she didn't kill him, then who did?'

Geraldine shrugged. 'Without any evidence one way or the other, I'm not going to jump to any conclusions. Although you'd think if Serena was living with him, she could have come up with something more subtle than a bullet in his head.' She picked up her sandwich and stared at it as she continued. 'It could just as easily have been his daughter, determined to stop him disinheriting her, or maybe taking revenge because she was too late to stop him changing his will in Serena's favour.'

She began to eat, and they finished their lunch in thoughtful silence.

'Right, let's not waste any more time on idle speculation,' Geraldine said briskly, standing up. 'Let's get going checking any CCTV we can find, and see if we can discover where the woman who bought the gun came from, or where she went afterwards. If we can find her, we may have our killer.'

A team had been tasked with checking CCTV cameras anywhere in the vicinity of the car park where John had recently sold a gun. They studied any film they could access that had been recording at the approximate time of the transaction. The sergeant in charge of the video images identification and detections team was a stout, forthright woman who greeted Geraldine with a warm smile, and assured her that her team had already set to work.

'It's likely to take us a while,' the video images identification officer added. 'If you could find out exactly when they met, that would help to narrow down our search. As it is, we're going to have our work cut out. But don't worry, we'll keep at it. I've already asked for the team to be expanded so we can speed things up.'

The sergeant looked faintly worried as she spoke, and Geraldine tried to feel confident that the search would produce a result very soon. There was nothing else she could do but wait and hope they would discover some useful information. Neither she nor the sergeant admitted that, even if they were able to find an identifiable image of whoever purchased the gun from John, there was no proof they had actually killed Martin. The weapon could have changed hands again, possibly more than once, before it reached the killer. But it was at least the start of a possible lead.

While they were waiting to see what the CCTV might disclose, Geraldine and Ariadne were sent to question anyone who might possibly have witnessed Serena's movements on the night Martin was killed. They started with the people who lived closest to Martin's house. The couple who lived next door were quite elderly. Only the wife was home when Geraldine called. It was a few moments before she came to the door and gazed anxiously out at Geraldine.

'Yes?' she asked in a quavering voice. 'Who are you? What do you want?' Her white hair fluttered as she shook her head. 'My husband's not here, and I don't...' She drew in a breath. 'We don't want anything, thank you. I'm sure what you're selling is very nice, but I'm afraid we're not interested.'

As the woman began to close the door, Geraldine introduced herself and explained that she was enquiring about the woman who had moved in next door.

'I won't disturb you for long,' she added. 'But there are a few questions I'd like to ask you. Perhaps I can come in? You don't want to keep the front door open in this weather.'

'Oh, a young police officer has already been here asking us about them,' the woman said anxiously. 'Is it true he was murdered?'

Geraldine held up her identity card again and invited the woman to call the police station if she wanted to confirm her caller was a genuine police officer, but the woman shook her head.

'That's all right,' she said. 'You come in out of the cold, love.'

Geraldine stepped inside and the woman nodded at her.

'I know you're only doing your job, but I don't know what you expect me to say that I haven't already told your colleague.'

The neighbour evidently wanted to be helpful, once she knew who Geraldine was, but she didn't seem to know very much about Serena.

'We keep to ourselves,' she added almost apologetically. 'Serena seems like a nice young girl, I suppose, but we really hardly speak to her. We are very private people. What was it you wanted to know?'

Aware that her question was futile, Geraldine enquired whether the neighbour could tell her anything about Serena's movements on the previous Sunday night. As Geraldine expected, the neighbour shook her head.

'We haven't actually seen anything of her for a while, until yesterday,' she replied.

'What happened yesterday?'

The neighbour described how Serena had rung their bell, having locked herself out.

'We couldn't help her, and she went away. Apart from that, we've not seen her recently. We used to catch sight of her occasionally, coming and going, off to work in the mornings, and back in the evenings, but we've not seen her lately. We thought maybe she'd gone away.'

Geraldine and Ariadne spoke to people in the neighbouring houses, one of which was divided into flats. They were successful in that they succeeded in questioning at least one person living in each residence, but their efforts revealed nothing new. No one had seen Serena for a long time, if ever, and most of her neighbours didn't even know her name. She was just 'that young woman who moved in with Martin'. They learned nothing about Serena's movements on the night of the murder.

15

GERALDINE AND IAN BOTH had the day off on Saturday and they had agreed they would spend the day sorting out the flat which was beginning to look a bit dusty and neglected. There was plenty to do, and they were soon busy emptying bins, hoovering and doing laundry. While she had been on maternity leave, Geraldine had insisted on doing all the chores at home, and Ian had been perfectly happy to hand over his domestic duties to her: taking out the rubbish, putting the hoover around, and clearing up after dinner. Since Geraldine had returned to work, everything but the bare essentials had been neglected.

They spent three hours tidying and cleaning, while Tom sat in his bouncing chair and watched them, jigging about and gurgling with pleasure as they moved around the room. As far as he was aware, they were capering around solely to keep him entertained, and they kept up a stream of conversation, mostly directly at him.

'I'm just going to wipe the shelves in here,' Geraldine sang. Tom chuckled, making her laugh, which made him squeal with delight.

'At least one of us seems to be enjoying all this cleaning,' Ian said, smiling and nodding at his son who was waving his fat little hands in the air.

'Yes, I don't mind it. Oh, you mean Tom. I thought you were talking about me.' She laughed.

'You really do seem to like doing this,' Ian said.

'I do. Cleaning's so satisfying,' she replied. 'All you have to do is wipe the surfaces in the kitchen or bathroom, or hoover the living room, and you can actually *see* the result of your efforts.'

She sighed. She didn't need to add that the immediate satisfaction from cleaning was very different to the results she achieved at work, where every fragment of evidence had to be scrupulously weighed up and considered in the light of every other angle of each step in a labyrinthine investigation. Anything that seemed obvious at first soon became obscure again, and as soon as they felt they were making progress, something invariably turned up to send them spiralling backwards. One of the advantages of living with a colleague was that Ian understood without her having to explain herself.

It couldn't last. After a while Tom grew fractious and began to wail.

'I'm getting bored of this as well,' Ian said, lifting Tom out of his chair and swinging him up in the air. 'Phew, he needs changing. Look, it's nearly one o'clock. Why don't we call it a day and go out for lunch?'

It took a while to pack Tom and his bag in the car, and then they drove to an out-of-town pub they liked, which served decent food. Tom nodded off in the car and didn't stir when Ian carried him very carefully into the pub. Even the ambient noise didn't wake him up. For a while, Geraldine relaxed and forgot about the murder case she was working on. They took their time studying the menu, even though they were both hungry. She was surprised how quickly she slipped into feeling like any other family, having lunch together on their day off, and looking after their baby who was sleeping peacefully and causing no trouble at all.

They chatted happily as they ate, until Ian decided to resurrect a conversation that that been interrupted by the discovery that Geraldine was pregnant. Until then, they had been sporadically discussing the possibility of moving from their flat. From the moment Ian had moved in with her, he had been trying to persuade her they should sell up and buy a house together. With two salaries they could afford something bigger, especially since there was no mortgage on the flat, thanks to money Geraldine had inherited from her family. Ian was keen for them to buy a place together instead of continuing to live in a flat that had belonged to Geraldine before he had moved in. Geraldine understood his feelings, but she batted away his attempt to discuss moving.

'Let's not talk about that right now,' she said. 'It's going to be time-consuming and tiring and, to be honest, I'd prefer to wait until Tom's a bit older and less disruptive at night. Can't we just relax and enjoy ourselves for now?'

He didn't press her, and the conversation moved on.

'Are you okay?' Ian asked when they finished and Geraldine glanced at her watch. 'You are having a good time, aren't you?'

Geraldine nodded and smiled affectionately at him. 'Never better.'

She was trying not to think about Martin Reed, but was finding it difficult. Ian prolonged their lunch by ordering coffee, but they couldn't stay in the pub forever. At last they stood up and Geraldine lifted Tom out of his seat and wiped the tray which was splattered with baby spit and goo, while Ian began gathering up their bags. They stopped at the supermarket on the way back and, once they were home, Ian put the frozen food away while Geraldine settled Tom down for his nap. As Ian was unpacking the rest of the shopping, she glanced at her phone and said she needed to pop into work.

Ian frowned. 'I thought we might spend the rest of the day together... ' he began.

'I won't be long,' she interrupted him. 'I'll be back before Tom wakes up.'

If Ian had remonstrated, she would have capitulated, aware that she was being unfair to him in choosing to work on her day off. But a man had been shot, and tracking down the killer had to be her priority. So she gave Ian a peck on the cheek and was gone, hurrying out of the door before he could stop her. By the time she reached her car, she was already regretting abandoning Ian on their planned day off together, but whatever she did these days felt like the wrong decision. Ever since Tom was born, she seemed to spend her entire life feeling guilty.

16

MARTIN'S SOLICITOR, JAMES BENSON, had his office in St Saviourgate, round the corner from Daisy's maisonette. On Monday morning Nigel arranged to pick up his sister on the way, so they could go together to hear their father's will read.

'Do you really think he could have cut us out of his will?' Daisy asked, as she returned from the kitchen with a tray of tea and plain biscuits which she set down on a rickety side table. 'We're his children.'

'I can't believe he would have left everything to her if he was in his right mind,' Nigel agreed, frowning at her as she poured the tea. 'He wouldn't have done it willingly,' he repeated, attempting to hide his disgust at having touched the sticky surface of the side table.

Daisy looked up. 'Are you saying you think she coerced him into changing his will?'

Nigel grunted. 'If he *did* change it. We don't know what the will says yet, do we, so let's not run ahead of ourselves.'

Daisy finished pouring the tea, taking care not to jog the table and talking all the while. 'Well, it doesn't matter what he did, as long as no one else believes it was his choice if he made any changes. We have to be ready to persuade Mr Benson that our father was being unduly influenced if it turns out to be necessary.' Nigel drank his tea in silence. 'We can say she was always getting him drunk,' Daisy went on. 'No one can disprove that, can they? Not if we both say it. We're his children, aren't we? They'll have to believe us.' She slurped her tea.

Nigel sighed and shook his head. 'You carry on with your plotting if you like. I've heard enough. Listen, you know we're going to hear the official reading of our father's will in less than an hour. Just be prepared for the worst, because I don't see how anyone's going to accept he wasn't in full possession of his faculties, right up to the end. We'd need to have got power of attorney, or at least have evidence from a doctor that he'd lost his marbles. We can't just helicopter in and take control and expect everyone else to go along with what we want. You're being ridiculous. You can't take people for fools. Even an idiot would see through your lies, and this man's a lawyer, for Christ's sake.'

Daisy frowned as she set down her cup. 'If she persuaded him to change his will, we'll either have to convince everyone he wasn't in his right mind, or we'll have to come up with a later version, and say we found it somewhere in the house. We can say he told us where it was. I really think that might be the best idea, and no one would be able to argue with us. Not if we can produce a more recent will.'

Daisy's face flushed as she explained what she wanted to do. Nigel listened in silence until she finished and then shook his head.

'We've discussed that harebrained scheme before, and I told you it can't possibly work,' he said, glaring at her and speaking very forcefully. 'We'd never pull it off. Not in a million years. You're crazy if you think we could get away with it. We could end up in prison.'

'We could do it, we can, and we have to,' she replied, her voice rising in frustration. 'How hard can it be?' she went on, controlling her irritation with a visible effort. 'All we have to do is copy the usual template and make sure we date it before he died but after any other will. That's all we have to do. We can date it the day before he died, just to be sure. What other choice do we have? We can't just take this lying down. It's not fair and we both know it's not what Father would have wanted, not really. He hardly knew that woman.'

'Don't be absurd. You're not thinking straight. We can't possibly forge a legal document. What about the witnesses? A will has to be witnessed or it's not legal. I'm telling you, it's not that simple. If it was, everyone would be doing it, and wills wouldn't be worth the paper they're written on because no one would ever be able to trust they were genuine.'

She shrugged. 'We can forge a few signatures. How hard can it be? I'll do it. No one will ever know. Why would anyone suspect it wasn't genuine?'

'Because there's a lot of money involved.'

They fell silent, both brooding on their inheritance.

'It's time to go,' Nigel said at last. 'We might as well walk. It'll be quicker than trying to find somewhere to park. Come on, let's get going.'

He waited while Daisy insisted on clearing away the dirty cups and stale biscuits, and 'doing her face' as she called it although, as far as he could see, all she had done was put on a smear of lipstick. After that, he had to wait while she laced up her sensible shoes. When they were about to leave, she halted on the doorstep and went back to fetch her coat, muttering that it might rain. In her worn grey coat and stout brown shoes, she looked like a retired impoverished low-grade civil servant, or something equally boring. Finally they set off, with Nigel complaining that it was 'about bloody time'.

'I should have brought the car,' he grumbled as a fine light drizzle began to fall. 'Whatever happens in there, don't react,' he added. 'Are you listening to me? Whatever happens, don't say anything until we're alone together. Just don't. The situation is fraught enough as it is. Let's not give Serena the satisfaction of knowing how we feel. And let's not do anything that might end up with us both behind bars. Forging a legal document is a serious crime. We'd never get away with it.'

Daisy glared at him. She shivered inside her raincoat and pulled up her collar. 'Do you really think the will can go in her favour? I mean, why would it? We're his children. She was nothing to him. Nothing. She moved herself into his house but he would soon have got tired of her.'

Nigel grunted. 'You're probably right. He was only using her to distract himself from Mum's death. That was all it was. Serena couldn't control him.'

'Stop mentioning her name to me!' Daisy hissed.

'That's exactly what I'm talking about. You can't speak like that in front of anyone else. You have to control yourself at the solicitor's or it will be obvious you've got it in for her. We have to appear calm and resigned, as though we have nothing against her. Let the lawyer think we're grateful to her for supporting Dad. That way, it won't look suspicious if we find ourselves forced to question the will.'

'Don't worry, I'm not an idiot. This is just between us. You know perfectly well he can't have been in his right mind if he really left everything to her.'

Nigel didn't answer at first.

'Well,' he said at last. 'Let's hope he didn't, eh?'

They walked on.

'If he *has* changed his will, and if we can't produce a later one, there's only one other way to deal with her,' Daisy said as they reached the solicitor's building.

Nigel frowned. 'I don't know what you mean. What are you talking about?'

She lowered her voice. 'If we can't fake a will, we'll just have to get rid of Serena. How hard can it be?'

17

THE LAWYER'S OFFICE WAS located in an unprepossessing
building sandwiched between a newsagent's and a hairdresser's.
It would have been easy to miss, a brass plate beside the door
the only indication that Benson Melrose and Partners could be
found there. Nigel rang the bell and a buzzer sounded. Once
they stepped inside, a young woman materialised and invited
them to wait. She gestured at a row of wooden chairs in the
reception area, before resuming her seat behind a small desk at
the end of the hallway. The carpet appeared to be new and the
corridor looked well maintained. Clearly money had been spent
on the décor, but the chairs were hard and uncomfortable.

'I do hope he isn't going to keep us waiting long,' Daisy said
loudly after a couple of minutes, tapping her foot and gazing
around with obvious irritation.

Nigel seemed to be engrossed in examining convoluted
whorls on the red and gold carpet. The receptionist raised her
eyes and gave them a professional smile before returning her
attention to her screen.

'I said I hope he isn't going to keep us waiting long,' Daisy
repeated, raising her voice impatiently. After all, this was an
important meeting, and the receptionist ought to be treating
them with more respect. 'There's a lot of money involved,' she
added. 'A lot of money.'

'Mr Benson will be with you soon,' the woman replied,
without lifting her eyes from her screen, seemingly unimpressed
by Daisy's words.

They waited, while Daisy grew increasingly exasperated. Her annoyance intensified when the door buzzer sounded and Serena walked in. Typically, she was inappropriately overdressed, in black from the collar of her raincoat to the stiletto heels on her elegant patent shoes. Even her earrings were jet. She sat down and crossed her black stockinged legs, the tight black skirt beneath her coat barely reaching her knees. Daisy sniffed. Remembering what Nigel had said, she did her best to keep quiet, but she couldn't conceal her feelings for long.

'What the hell is *she* doing here?' she growled. 'My brother and I are waiting to hear our father's will. It has nothing to do with anyone else, anyone who isn't *family*.' She stressed the last word.

'Be quiet,' Nigel warned her. 'I told you,' he went on under his breath, 'don't say anything. We can't show our hand, not yet. We don't know what's going to happen and we don't know what we're going to have to say if things don't go the way we want.'

'Why does *she* have to be here?' Daisy hissed angrily.

Serena turned to face them. Her large blue eyes fixed on Nigel with a faintly puzzled expression; Daisy she ignored completely.

'Nigel,' she murmured. 'You remember me?' Her question didn't require an answer. 'I'm Serena Baxter, Martin's girlfriend. His partner.' She held out one slender hand, while she pressed a tissue to her nose with the other and stifled a sob. 'We are all shocked and grieving,' she went on, leaning towards Nigel and gazing earnestly at him.

Serena must have heard Daisy sneer, 'Lousy actress.' She raised her voice. 'You do know my brother's married? Is it impossible for you to see a man without making a pass at him?'

Serena continued to ignore Daisy.

'Of course we remember you,' Nigel replied stiffly, before turning away.

Daisy sniffed and glared at Serena. After that, the three of them sat in awkward silence until the receptionist ushered them into a small rectangular office, dominated by a large wooden desk. A row of metal filing cabinets along one wall made the space seem even more cramped, while a high window did little to make the room feel less claustrophobic. A man seated behind the desk half rose to his feet when they trooped in. Tall and stocky, James Benson seemed to fill the room. He was middle-aged, with sleek grey hair and a square head. He looked at them gravely, a stolid presence gesturing to them to sit down.

'I'm sorry to say I didn't know Martin well,' he said in a clipped but sympathetic tone, as he resumed his seat. 'We met several times, but only in a professional capacity. He always struck me as a fine man. I understand his wife's death hit him very hard.' He glanced at the three beneficiaries and let out a grunt of satisfaction. 'And now, thank you for being so prompt. You all know why you are here.' He put on a pair of horn-rimmed glasses. Opening a file on his desk, he slowly drew out a buff folder. Daisy felt as though they were waiting interminably as he leafed through the papers. 'Here we are.' He smiled solemnly at each of them in turn.

'Oh, do get on with it,' Daisy muttered under her breath. 'We don't want to have to wait all day.'

Nigel's head flicked round as though he had been stung, and he frowned at her.

'I realise you've been waiting to hear the contents of the will. So yes, let's get on with this.' Mr Benson cleared his throat. 'Without further ado,' he said, and proceeded to read the will aloud in a level voice.

If she hadn't been so interested in the detailed contents of the will, Daisy thought the lawyer's steady boring voice would probably have sent her to sleep. As it was, she was perched on the edge of her hard wooden chair, listening attentively as he announced that her father had left his house and all his savings to Serena. Daisy was to receive nothing apart from her mother's jewellery. The assets left to Nigel were listed, including a ten per cent share of the business.

'Ten per cent?' Nigel blurted out, his composure shattered for once.

There was no question that Daisy and Nigel's legacies were trivial compared to Serena's. Once he had finished, the lawyer replaced the document in the folder. Daisy and Nigel sat in shocked silence for a moment, while Serena covered her face with her hands and began to sob noisily. The lawyer pushed his chair back and rose to his feet.

'Wait!' Daisy cried out. 'We're not done yet.'

'I warned you to keep quiet,' Nigel muttered.

'Stop telling me to be quiet,' she snapped at him.

'Do you have any questions?' Mr Benson enquired impassively. 'Is anything unclear?'

'No, thank you,' Nigel replied quickly. 'Everything's clear. It appears that our father left his entire fortune to a stranger.'

'Yes, on condition she writes a will of her own, leaving her estate to be divided between you and your sister on her death. He didn't wish any children she might have to benefit from his estate in the future.' He turned to Serena who was still sobbing quietly. 'The will is very clear on that point. The money is tied up. Unless you spend it all, of course,' he added with a faint smile.

'It's pointless anyway, seeing as she's younger than either of us,' Nigel interjected. 'And in any case, as you say, there's nothing to stop her spending it all,' he added crossly.

'He can't have left everything to *her*,' Daisy protested, unable to restrain her indignation. 'I don't believe it. We're being conned. How do we know you're not part of the fiddle?' She stared straight at the lawyer, who looked faintly affronted.

'I understand this must be difficult for you,' he said frostily. 'It's not uncommon for people's expectations to be disappointed on the death of a loved one. It's generally best to expect nothing.

That way, you cannot be disappointed. Naturally, you are free to contest your father's will, should you wish to do so, but I advise you against pursuing such a course. There is no chance the will could be overturned, and you will incur legal fees to no end. I assure you, your father's will is unequivocal.'

'No, no, that's not what happened,' Daisy countered angrily. 'It can't be. Our father would never have done that to us. Disinherited us, I mean. We're his children. He promised us everything would be ours one day. He promised. He wouldn't go back on his word.'

The lawyer sighed and straightened the file that he had put down on his desk. 'The terms of the will are here in black and white.'

Daisy bit her lip and managed to hold back from saying anything else, but she knew perfectly well that Serena had manipulated their father into changing his will. One way or another, she and her brother were going to find a way to stop Serena cheating them out of their inheritance.

18

GERALDINE LOGGED OFF AND made her way along the corridor
to the interview room where Daisy was waiting. She wondered
what new information Martin's daughter had for her. Geraldine
suspected Daisy was just going to come up with more bile
against her father's girlfriend, and as soon as she entered the
room, her suspicions appeared to be confirmed when Daisy
leaped to her feet.

'At last!' she burst out, her voice shrill with rage. She took
a step towards Geraldine, pointing at her with a hand that
trembled with pent up emotion. 'I know who did it. You need to
arrest her, now! Go on. What are you waiting for?'

Daisy's face was unhealthily flushed, with bright spots of colour
on each cheek. She was wearing brown trousers that looked as
though they might be homemade, and a shapeless beige jumper.
As before, she wore no make-up and her greying hair looked
greasy. Geraldine wondered whether she ever stopped to look in
a mirror before leaving her home. Seeing Geraldine frown, she
lowered the hand that was pointing in a somewhat aggressive
gesture and clenched both her fists at her sides. She could have
been preparing to launch a physical attack. Her features looked
sharper than usual, and her eyes blazed with anger.

'Please, sit down,' Geraldine said quietly, gesturing at a chair.
'Now, why have you come here today?'

'I'm here about my father, of course. About his murder.'

Geraldine drew in a deep breath. 'Yes, of course. Once again,
my condolences. Now, you asked to see me. What is it you

want to tell me? You know we're very busy looking into what happened. Please, sit down,' she repeated quietly but firmly.

Daisy snorted and resumed her seat. Folding her arms, she glared at Geraldine.

'I just told you what happened,' she said crossly. 'It was her. Isn't it obvious? When are you going to arrest her? Are you even listening to me?'

'By "her" I take it you are referring to Serena Baxter?'

'Yes, yes. Serena, of course. Who do you think I'm talking about?'

Geraldine spoke very slowly and softly. 'To be absolutely clear, am I right in understanding that you're accusing Serena Baxter of murdering your father?'

Daisy nodded and repeated that Serena was guilty. According to her, it was the only possible conclusion. She became frustrated when Geraldine pointed out that they were unable to arrest Serena without any evidence against her, even though Daisy was convinced she was guilty.

'However sure you may be,' Geraldine explained patiently, 'this is only your opinion, and we need proof before we can charge anyone with murder. If someone levelled such an accusation against you, would you expect us to arrest you just on the strength of one person's accusation?'

'It's not just me,' Daisy protested. 'Ask my brother. He'll tell you. He agrees with me.'

'Let's go through this accusation again. What makes you so sure Serena killed your father?'

'Isn't it obvious?' Daisy asked.

Geraldine waited.

'I mean, it stands to reason, doesn't it? She wormed her way into his life. It's disgusting. She's younger than me, and I'm his daughter, for Christ's sake. Is everyone blind or stupid?'

Geraldine waited once more, but Daisy didn't say anything else.

'Being younger than him isn't a crime,' Geraldine pointed out at last.

'Killing him is.'

'Tell me what you think happened.'

Daisy's face darkened and she squinted at her interlocutor from beneath lowered brows. In a voice that shook with barely suppressed emotion, she described how Serena had inveigled herself into Martin's company where she had manoeuvred her way into working closely with him.

'She wanted to make him dependent on her,' she explained. 'He had a perfectly decent secretary for years but once Serena turned up, Dorothy was fired for no reason. According to my father, she retired voluntarily, but I don't believe that for a moment. I didn't believe it at the time, and I don't believe it now. And nor should you. Serena had Dorothy pushed out to make room for her. She's like a cuckoo. She deliberately got rid of Dorothy so she could get her claws into Dad, and then she persuaded him to change his will, leaving everything to her. That was her plan all along. That's what people like her do. I've seen documentaries about them. They're all young and attractive and they target lonely old rich people and seduce them with sex and lies. Once she'd got him to change his will, she got rid of him.' She paused for a response, but Geraldine waited to hear what she would say next. 'Isn't it obvious what happened?' Daisy repeated impatiently. 'How stupid can you be? She was only interested in him for his money. Why else would she want to have anything to do with a man so much older than her? She'd only known him for six months when he was killed, and then all his money is suddenly hers. She was after his money all along. That's what this is all about, isn't it? It must have been her.'

Geraldine stirred in her seat. 'You didn't like your father very much, did you?'

Daisy glared at her. 'I loved my father. She's the one I didn't like, but that's not the point. She killed him and you need to arrest her before she gets her hands on the money that belongs to me and my brother. The longer you hang about, the more likely it is she'll take all the money and run off with it. Just get on with it! If you don't do something to stop her, we will. We're not going to sit back and watch her get her hands on our money.'

Geraldine said she would question Serena again, and stood up.

'Is that it?' Daisy asked.

Geraldine nodded. 'You'll have to leave this with us. Go home and we'll let you know as soon as we have anything further to report.'

Daisy scrambled to her feet, scowling. 'You'd better arrest her soon, before she runs off with our money.'

Geraldine ushered Daisy from the room, reiterating that the police would be in touch with her and her brother once they had any further information to impart. They walked along the corridor together, Daisy muttering loudly enough for Geraldine to hear.

'And she actually threatened to kill Serena?' Ariadne asked, when she had read Geraldine's report.

Geraldine nodded. 'Not in so many words, but she was furious about the inheritance,' she replied. 'It was probably just bluster. All the same,' she broke off, uncertain what to think about Martin's daughter. 'She seemed quite fixated on her father's money, and she struck me as quite unhinged.'

'She's grieving,' Ariadne said. 'It's understandable. She was very close to her father. He was the man in her life. I don't think she's close to her brother, and she didn't have anyone else.'

'Yes, but is she upset about the loss of her father, or about losing what she saw as her inheritance?' Geraldine asked. 'Granted, people act irrationally when they're emotionally vulnerable, especially where money is at stake, but would Serena have wanted to kill Martin when he had given her a home and showered her with gifts? Why would she want to lose all that, and risk losing her freedom into the bargain?'

'And he was so much older than her, all she had to do was wait and it would all have come to her in time anyway,' Ariadne added.

'Do you think Daisy could have been angry enough about Martin's will to have wanted revenge? She and Nigel were expecting to inherit a small fortune each. It must have been a big disappointment to them.'

'Perhaps Daisy killed her father because she was angry with him for seeing a young woman so soon after her mother died,' Ariadne said. 'Was she jealous of Serena for taking her father away?'

'Or was she angry with him because she had found out he had changed his will in Serena's favour?' Geraldine added.

They gazed at each other for a moment, nonplussed.

'If she didn't know about the new terms of the will, she might have killed him to prevent him changing his will,' Ariadne added.

'We're going round in circles. We'll have to question Serena again,' Geraldine said at last. 'And I think we should look into Daisy's alibi very carefully. She seemed very keen to accuse Serena, didn't she?'

'You suspect Daisy killed him,' Ariadne replied, almost triumphantly.

Geraldine shrugged. 'Honestly, I don't know what to think. It could have been Daisy or Serena, but it could equally well have been someone else, someone we haven't even considered yet.'

'What about Nigel?' Ariadne asked.

'And there's an ex-wife, isn't there?' Geraldine added.

She had worked on murder investigations with no obvious suspects and others where there was a confusing number of suspects. She wasn't sure which was more difficult to resolve.

'We certainly have a lot of plausible suspects,' Ariadne said, sharing Geraldine's thoughts.

19

SHE HAD GONE THROUGH a worrying few days, but at last everything was getting sorted out as it should be. She didn't have to wait long for the locksmith who turned up within minutes of the agreed time. Tall and lean, he displayed brilliant white teeth in his tanned face when he smiled. He worked quickly, and she was soon inside the familiar house, slightly surprised at how easy it had been to gain access. She had prepared a story about losing her bag and wanting to change the lock in case anyone found her missing keys and tried to use them, but the locksmith had nodded and set to work before she had said more than a few words. She had even come armed with a copy of the will proving her ownership of the property, but the locksmith hadn't once questioned her right to enter.

'Easily done,' he had commented when she told him she had lost her keys. He hadn't questioned her wanting to have all the locks changed, front and back, in case someone found her keys and broke in. Within a matter of minutes he had the front door open and it wasn't long before he had fitted shiny new locks, front and back, and handed her the keys, together with a spare set. She paid him and closed the door behind him, grinning with relief. Daisy had locked her out and she had responded in kind. If Daisy tried to enter the house again, she was in for a shock. Serena's next task was to have the burglar alarm serviced, so that no one could get away with changing the lock again. Martin had left the house to her, and she had no intention of letting anyone take it away from her.

After popping out for some milk, she made herself a leisurely cup of tea before turning on her phone and researching burglar alarms. Having booked an urgent appointment, she went upstairs to see what Daisy and Nigel had stolen or thrown out. Expecting to find some of her belongings were missing, she wasn't surprised to discover her jewellery had vanished. It was annoying, but there was not much she could do about it, and no point in making a fuss. What was gone was gone. None of it had been particularly expensive, although some had sentimental value: an attractive glass bead necklace Martin had bought her in Venice; a cameo brooch she had taken a fancy to in Covent Garden in London; and a silver replica Viking bracelet bought right there in York, all of which brought back memories of happy times spent with Martin. With a sigh, she remembered how he had liked to indulge her.

The only really expensive items of jewellery he had given her were a diamond and pearl ring which she never took off, and a matching pendant which she had fortunately been wearing when Daisy and Nigel had made their crass attempt to lock her out of her own house. She would have been sorry to lose those diamonds and pearls, not only because of their monetary worth, but because she genuinely liked them, and she knew that reclaiming them from Martin's children would have taken more than a simple change of locks. She was sorry about the rest of her jewellery, but she would never give Nigel and Daisy the satisfaction of knowing they had got their hands on anything she wanted.

Apart from her jewellery, on a first look around she couldn't see anything else missing. All her clothes still seemed to be there. She went downstairs. Feeling slightly guilty, she went into Martin's study. Even though they had lived together, she had never been in there without him. Somehow the opportunity had never arisen. He had been generous to her and the last thing she had wanted was for him to suspect her of poking into his affairs. Despite knowing she was alone in the house, she stole quietly into the room and closed the door softly behind her before going over to the desk, glancing around as she rattled the drawers. There was nothing of interest in the lower drawers, just random items of stationery and a tin of mints, but the top one was locked. After a moment's hesitation, she went to the kitchen for a knife so she could try to force it open. Thinking better of her initial response, she went up to the bedroom and searched his bedside cabinet where she knew he hid his spare set of keys. At the back of the bottom drawer she found them, concealed beneath a few folded handkerchiefs.

The smallest key on the ring fitted the drawer of Martin's desk. Gingerly she turned it and the drawer slid open. It was empty. Either he had emptied it himself, or someone else had been there before her. She locked the drawer again and sat down on the large swivel chair behind the desk. It swung very slightly under her weight. She planted her feet on the floor to steady it. The chair was comfortable, if too big for her. When she leaned back, her feet didn't reach the floor. Seated, she gazed around the room with a tentatively proprietorial air. Everything she could see belonged to her: the solid wooden desk and strong swivel chair, the cabinets and bookshelves, and the soft thick rug. She wondered what use she could make of this room. Martin's belongings would have to go. Without the desk and Martin's old books, the study could be turned into a cosy sitting room. She would feel more at ease there once all signs of Martin had been removed. It was gradually sinking in that he had gone and everything in the house now belonged to her. The house was hers. She was startled out of her reverie by a ring at the door.

Serena recognised the woman gazing steadily at her.

'Good afternoon,' the dark-haired inspector said, with a solemn smile, 'I'd like to ask you a few questions. May I come in?'

Talking to the police was the last thing Serena wanted to do right then, but she could hardly refuse.

20

SERENA LED GERALDINE PAST the grandfather clock in the hall. Today the tall vase was empty of flowers. Only a scummy green ring indicated where the water had reached. Clearly no one had bothered to clean the vase when the flowers were thrown out. Serena took Geraldine into the living room, sat down and gestured towards a chair. Although it looked impressive, Geraldine found it too large for comfort. When she sat back in it, her feet didn't reach the floor. Ignoring the opulent surroundings, which were somehow oppressive, Geraldine focused on the glamorous woman sitting in front of her. She had changed the colour of her hair from blonde to a soft brown, which Geraldine thought suited her. Other than that improvement to her appearance, she looked less attractive than when Geraldine had seen her last. Her face was haggard, her eyes were slightly swollen from crying, and she seemed to have aged, perhaps because her shoulders were bowed and she was wearing no make-up.

'I'm sorry for your loss,' Geraldine said gently. 'But I'm afraid I need to ask you a few more questions.'

Serena stared straight ahead without giving any response.

'When did you start working for Martin?' Geraldine asked.

'What difference does it make now?' Serena replied dully. 'What difference does anything make?'

'We want to enquire into your background so we have some context for what has happened.'

Serena wriggled awkwardly on her chair, her eyes narrowed in suspicion. 'This is about context, is it?' she enquired scathingly.

'Do you really think I don't realise this is because of her?' she demanded.

'Her?' Geraldine echoed. 'Who are you talking about?'

'She's accused me, hasn't she? You must know who I mean. I'm talking about his daughter, Daisy. She told you it was me, didn't she? She accused me of killing him to divert attention away from herself because it was obviously her. Why else would she be trying to make you think it was me? I would never have hurt him. I loved him,' she added, with a theatrical tremor in her voice that made Geraldine wonder if she was lying.

'So,' Geraldine resumed. 'I understand you only started working for him a few months ago.'

Serena nodded. 'We met almost exactly six months ago,' she said, and sighed, with a distant look in her eyes.

Geraldine pressed on. 'How did you meet him?'

Serena sighed. 'Oh very well. You might as well know. It's not like it's a big secret. We met at a business convention. We were both in the bar, on our own, and we got chatting. He told me he'd recently lost his wife, and I was on the rebound from a miserable relationship that had dragged on for far too long. We were both lonely. But it was all perfectly innocent. We just had a drink together and we hit it off. I mean, we really got on, and then we discovered we lived near each other. I liked him a lot. Anyway, after the convention he called me and took me out for dinner, and one thing led to another. We were both adults and there was no reason to wait. I was bored in my job, so when he suggested I go and work for him, I jumped at the chance.' She smiled sadly at the memory. 'I told him there was no one I'd rather have as my boss and it was true. That was when he told me his personal assistant was getting old and he thought it was time she retired. It seems she had an issue with his IT system that was causing him all sorts of problems, and he said she was resistant to the changes he wanted to make. So we started talking about change and how meeting people can sometimes change your life. And that was when we realised we had feelings for each other.' She sighed and dabbed delicately at her eyes.

'And how did you come to be living here?' Geraldine enquired. She didn't add that it seemed rather sudden.

Serena shrugged and looked slightly awkward. 'You might think it all happened very quickly, but the truth is, we fell in love. Who can explain that? I can't. All I can tell you is that it happened.' Her expression darkened. 'His children didn't like it, of course. They always resented me. He knew about that. We both did. They made no attempt to hide their feelings, even though it was making him unhappy. But he wasn't going to give me up. He said they'd come round in the end.' She paused. 'They suspected I was up to something, but if you ask me, she's the one who's responsible for what happened to him.'

'What do you mean?' Geraldine asked.

'It's obvious it was Daisy. She always hated me and she said she would do anything to stop me getting my hands on his money. That's why she killed him.' Serena smiled sadly and blinked as tears spilled out of her eyes. 'She killed him to stop him changing his will, but she was too late.'

'Are you saying Martin's daughter killed him? I understand you're upset, but do you have any evidence to support your accusation?'

Serena hung her head and didn't answer for a moment. When she looked up, her eyes were blazing, reminding Geraldine of Daisy's fury when she had spoken about Serena.

'Martin's daughter,' Serena hissed. 'She's a liar. She'll tell you how close they were, but I can tell you she's caused him nothing but trouble all his life. You've met them, haven't you? His charming children? Nigel's as self-centred as they come, and he thinks he's really clever. You must have seen that for yourself. He's a pompous spoiled narcissist who thinks only of himself. But he's nothing compared to Daisy. She's a real piece of work. She's selfish and sly and you can't believe a word she says. I don't even know if she realises when she's lying. I think she's so used to making things up, she can no longer tell the difference between truth and falsehood. She invents whatever reality she wants and changes it all the time to suit her version of the world. She's a pathological liar and she's malicious with it.' She paused for a second, her eyes dark with anger. 'It's obvious she killed Martin herself, and now she's trying to put the blame on me. Seeing me go down for her crime would be ideal, as far as she's concerned. It would be the perfect end to her mission to be revenged on both Martin and me. And all we did was fall in love. I hope you're going to question her properly.' She hesitated as though she wanted to say more but wasn't sure how to go about it. 'You need to question her,' she said finally. 'Question her again and keep questioning her until she confesses.'

Geraldine waited, but Serena didn't say any more. 'What were you doing on the Sunday night when Martin was killed?'

Serena had dropped her face in her hands, sobbing quietly, but at the question she looked up, her expression suddenly hard. 'I've already been to the police station and told them what I was doing that night,' she said. 'Do I need to go over it all again? I have nothing new to add. You know I was on my own that night and there's no one who can confirm my whereabouts. But I wasn't here. You can arrest me if you want, but I'm not the one who killed him.'

There was not much point in continuing. Reiterating her condolences, Geraldine stood up.

'Don't you think I would have arranged an alibi if I'd wanted to kill him?' Serena asked. 'I could easily have persuaded some lonely old man to lie for me.'

Serena smiled sadly and, just for a second, Geraldine glimpsed the alluring woman who had won Martin's affections. It was true, Serena probably could have persuaded a vulnerable man to lie for her and provide her with an alibi. The trouble was, it wasn't clear if she was lying now.

21

GERALDINE HAD ASKED A colleague to look into Dorothy McIntosh, Martin's former personal assistant. Her colleague told her that Dorothy had retired and had left York, but she hadn't gone far and had been traced to the nearby village of Heslington. The following morning, Geraldine recorded her intentions and went to find her. It was less than two miles to her destination so she didn't bother to call ahead. If Dorothy was out, she would try again the next day. She drove slowly, watching out for icy patches on the road. It had begun to snow, a light fall that wasn't settling, but was enough to make the roads potentially hazardous. Finding the address she wanted, she stepped carefully on to the frosty ground and made her way slowly to the front door of a small terraced cottage which opened directly on to the pavement. There were two bells, indicating the property had been divided. Clearly Dorothy had downsized from her rented house in York after losing her job, and now lived in a first-floor maisonette. Geraldine wondered how she felt about that.

A round-faced woman with greying hair opened the door. She smiled anxiously and asked how she could help. When Geraldine introduced herself and explained that she was investigating the death of Martin Reed, Dorothy's expression altered. She asked for a closer look at Geraldine's identification and insisted on calling the police station to verify a detective named Inspector Steel had been sent to see her. Only then did she invite her in. Geraldine had the impression she was nervous rather than sceptical. The front door opened into a small sitting room, with a low two-seater settee and a couple of chintz-covered armchairs. The furniture was too bulky for the room and had presumably been moved there from a larger house, but the chairs were comfortable.

When they were both seated, Dorothy told Geraldine she had worked closely with Martin for nearly twenty years.

'Were you happy working for him?'

Dorothy didn't answer directly straight away. 'He was a good man, and a good boss,' she replied instead, lowering her gaze. 'There was a complaint about him, but that goes with the territory when you're the boss. There are always people who grumble and think they can get something for nothing, but I worked with him for a long time and he was always very fair. He was always fair. Yes,' she said, finally looking up to answer the question, 'I was very happy working with him.'

'But you left your job?'

Dorothy nodded. 'That wasn't entirely my decision,' she muttered. 'Martin decided to let me go.'

'How did you feel about that?'

Dorothy hesitated. 'Well, of course I was disappointed. After years of hard work, no one wants to be thrown on the scrap heap. I was a good employee, never missed a single day. But things are different these days, aren't they? Martin wanted to change everything, to have it all done on the computer, and I wasn't able to cope. It's all so complicated. The system's supposed to do everything for you, but you have to understand how to enter the data in the right way and in the right order, and how to get it to print out the reports you need, when he asks for them, and it just wasn't for me. If I'm honest, I found it all very confusing and very stressful. It's easy for young people. They've grown up with computers, but I struggled. It's partly a generational thing and partly just my own ineptitude.' She sighed. 'I'm afraid I resisted the changes. I don't blame Martin for getting rid of me. I don't blame anyone for what happened. It's just the way it is. Things change and life has to move on. And I dare say I was beginning to lose my grip anyway. I suppose we all become complacent eventually. Set in our ways. Maybe the change was the right thing for the company, but it didn't do me much good.' She shrugged and gave a wry smile. 'I had my way of doing things that was no longer acceptable.'

'So you didn't mind him firing you? It wasn't—'

'He didn't fire me.' Dorothy was quick to interrupt her. 'He let me go. It's not the same thing. He persuaded me to give way to someone younger. The time had come, that's all. But he was a good man and I don't blame him for what he did. It was hardly his fault if I was getting too old for the job. It was the computers that finished it for me. If I could have continued doing things the way we had always done them, I would have been fine. But I couldn't manage the changes. If anyone's to blame for what happened, it's those wretched computers. But the world moves on and we can't turn the clock back.'

'You mentioned a complaint against Martin. Who complained?'

'Oh, I can't remember the details. It was nothing, really, some grunt worker who had only been with us for a matter of weeks.'

'Can you remember his name?'

Dorothy shook her head. 'I'm sorry. It's all in the past for me now.'

'Might Nigel know more about this complaint?'

'You'd have to ask him, but I doubt it very much. He was too caught up in his own side of the business to bother about what Martin had to deal with. Nigel was his son, but he wasn't much support to his father. And don't bother asking HR because the complaint was never formally lodged. It was just a storm in a teacup. These things happen. I'm sorry I mentioned it.'

Geraldine asked how well Dorothy knew Martin's children, and she admitted that she had met them, but didn't know them well.

'We only met in passing, at the office. We didn't really speak, except to exchange brief greetings. So I can't say I knew them. I'd recognise them both, of course, but I can't tell you much about them, although I did think she was a sour puss, never smiling, and he seemed quite detached from everything. He used to stand there with a snooty expression on his face, as though he found us all very dull.' She smiled. 'I suppose we were. Anyway, I didn't get the impression either of them was close to Martin.'

'Where did you meet them?'

'They came to a few of the Christmas parties but neither of them spoke to any of us employees, apart from to say good evening and to wish us a merry Christmas. He always looked as though he couldn't wait to leave, and she just stood in a corner scoffing the provisions. They were a miserable pair, the two of them, and as unlike Martin as it was possible to be. It was hard to believe they were his children. Martin's wife used to come to the gatherings as well, and she was completely different, very friendly towards everyone.'

'So you liked her?'

Dorothy smiled faintly. 'She was charming. There was nothing to dislike about her. She was always polite and seemed genuinely interested in hearing about what we were doing. She always said she didn't understand anything about the business, but I think she was more on the ball than she would admit.'

'And what about his new personal assistant, Serena? What did you think of her?'

Dorothy frowned. 'I suppose you're waiting for me to say I hated her because she took my job, but if it hadn't been her it would have been another young person more computer literate than me. What did I think of her? I thought she was young and pretty, and no doubt competent. Of course, as an older woman, you want me to say that I was unfairly passed over and he was being ageist, but Martin wasn't like that. I'm sure he acted in the best interests of the company. He explained to me that people's livelihoods depended on his success in running the company, and of course he was right. I'm terribly sorry about what happened to him and I hope you catch whoever did it. He didn't deserve to die so young, and certainly not like that.' She broke off to sigh. 'He was always very kind to me. How could something so terrible happen to such a decent man? Do you know how it happened?'

Geraldine answered her question with one of her own. 'Do you have any suspicions about who might have wanted to harm him?'

Dorothy shook her head. 'No. He was a decent man. Everyone respected him. I can't even begin to guess who could have wanted him dead. His children must be devastated. Unless—' She paused.

'Yes?'

'I don't think his children were very happy about Serena taking my place. I could be wrong and maybe it was no more than wishful thinking on my part, but perhaps they knew something about her that could help you.'

'What makes you say that?'

Dorothy shook her head. 'It's just a feeling I had. I saw Daisy looking at Serena as though she wanted to kill her. But perhaps I shouldn't be saying that, considering what happened to Martin. There, I've said too much. I won't say any more.' As if to emphasise her statement, she pressed her lips together and was silent.

Geraldine studied her for a moment. It wasn't clear if Dorothy was suggesting that Daisy might be capable of murder, but when Geraldine pressed her, Dorothy would only repeat that she couldn't imagine why anyone would want to harm Martin.

'He was a wonderful boss,' she added sadly. 'I miss him terribly.'

22

SERENA WAS WATCHING AN old spy film. She wasn't following it closely and had become lost in a convoluted story where characters betrayed each other in repeated plot twists, until it was impossible to determine who was a traitor and who was to be trusted. She kept watching in a futile attempt to distract herself from her own life. Eventually the film ended with a cryptic speech by the protagonist, which did nothing to clarify the story she had just spent over two hours attempting to follow. She switched off the television and stood up and stretched, stiff from sitting in one position for too long. Since Martin's death she had been doing her best to avoid watching anything sad or romantic, either of which was virtually guaranteed to make her cry. But at least watching television offered a temporary respite from her thoughts and gave her a fleeting illusion that she wasn't alone. If she closed her eyes, she could almost believe that Martin was sitting beside her. It was past midnight but, however tired she was, she knew she probably wouldn't be able to sleep. Usually averse to taking any kind of medication, in desperation she had gone to the doctor for something to help her through the night. He had obliged her, but the sleeping tablets didn't seem to be making any difference.

Over a week had passed since Martin was killed, and she still expected to hear his key in the lock followed by his voice calling out cheerily that he was home. Of course she knew he was never coming back, but it still hadn't really sunk in that he was gone forever, and it was hard to ignore her flashes of irrational hope.

With a sigh, she took the remnants of her supper into the kitchen. It was *her* kitchen now. A large white central island gleamed under a bright array of spotlights and rows of white cupboard doors dazzled her with reflected light. She flicked off all but the muted lights underneath the wall cupboards. She hadn't eaten much. Having scraped her leftover food into the bin, she stacked her plate in the dishwasher. Now she was alone in the house, the dishwasher was no longer full every evening. Even that struck her as unbearably sad and it brought tears to her eyes. When Martin was alive, she had filled the dishwasher every evening with their crockery and cooking pots. She could hardly believe she had only been living there with him for a few months. Her time with him felt as though it had lasted a lifetime, yet it had been over so quickly.

Having cleared up the kitchen, she washed a sleeping tablet down with a glass of water. By the time she was in bed, the pill should be starting to take effect and with any luck she would drift into a much-needed sleep. The refuse collection was due the next morning. If the sleeping tablet worked as the doctor had assured her it would, there was a good chance she wouldn't be awake and out of bed in time to empty the bins, so she went round the house filling a black rubbish bag. She still wasn't feeling sleepy. With a sigh, she dragged the bulging black bag across the hall and hoisted it up and over the door step. Reaching the bins with it, she lifted the bag in, grunting with the effort. Muffled by the hum of traffic, she almost missed a faint shuffling of footsteps behind her in the darkness, and a breath softer than a whisper carried on the still night air.

For no obvious reason, she was suddenly alert. She spun round to see an indistinct figure moving almost soundlessly towards her. As the figure passed through a shaft of moonlight, she saw a raised arm and the gleam of a knife. Her scream pierced the air as the blade leapt forwards to slice through her neck. The darkness glowed with an eerie red light and a bolt of pain shot through her. She fell, hitting her head on the nearest bin with a deafening clatter. Stunned, she struggled to pull herself up off the ground but something knocked her back again. Across a wall of pain, she was aware of something pressing against her throat, choking her. A voice hissed in her ear but she couldn't understand the words. She couldn't understand anything but searing pain. And then darkness.

23

BEFORE TOM WAS BORN, breakfast used to be a civilised affair. Ian would brew a cafetière of strong coffee while Geraldine set the cereal on the table: granary flakes for her and cornflakes for Ian, with milk in a jug and a small bowl of white sugar. Sometimes they had toast and marmalade, or fried eggs when they had time to enjoy a more leisurely breakfast. Now, they were invariably in a rush. Ian would sit, a teaspoon of baby food in one hand, a cup of coffee – not too hot – in the other, while Geraldine checked and repacked Tom's bag for the third time that morning.

'I don't know why you can't make sure you've got everything packed up before you go to bed,' Ian said.

'I do, but I like to double-check it before I go out,' she replied.

'Why can't you double-check it before you go to bed?' Ian asked, before muttering about struggling to understand how someone as organised as Geraldine could be so disorganised about something as important as her son's welfare. Geraldine ignored Ian and swept Tom up in her arms, kissing him gently on both of his chubby cheeks.

'Come on, then, little man,' she whispered. 'Zoe's waiting for you.'

She dropped Tom off and had time for only a brief chat with the childminder before heading to work. On arrival, she summoned her team to a briefing. If anything, the latest statements they had gathered only added to their confusion.

'So it seems Daisy and Serena are both accusing each other,' Geraldine said, after quoting from the two women's statements.

'That doesn't mean one of them isn't telling the truth, but it's equally possible they're both lying.'

'They must have really hated each other,' Naomi said. 'I mean, how angry would you have to be with someone to want to see them locked up for murder?'

'It's not unheard of for children to resent it when their father takes a new girlfriend,' Ariadne remarked. 'Daisy's hostility could have provoked Serena to return the feeling. But whoever started it, there was clearly bad feeling between the two women.'

'Given the circumstances, maybe that's not surprising,' Geraldine remarked. 'Family rifts are sadly all too common.'

'Especially when there's money involved,' Naomi added drily. 'And in Martin's case, there was a lot of money.'

There was indistinct muttering among the assembled officers, who all knew that Martin's estate was worth a considerable fortune.

'I have a feeling this was about more than money,' Geraldine said. 'From what she said, Daisy seemed to be obsessed with her father.'

'Are you suggesting it was a crime of passion by a daughter who felt slighted?' Ariadne asked. 'If Daisy was so close to her father, why didn't she move in with him when her mother died?'

Geraldine shrugged. 'And in any case, if Daisy is a potentially violent killer, surely she would have attacked Serena, not Martin? But whatever their motives for accusing each other, neither of them has produced any evidence, have they? Their accusations are meaningless without proof. We're talking about two women who didn't get on, for whatever reason, each trying to make trouble for the other. That's all, malicious though it is. Now, let's see what else we can find out. We need to widen the investigation to other neighbours and anyone who worked with Nigel and Daisy.'

Mid-morning, Geraldine went for a coffee with Ariadne. They were still discussing the relationship between Serena and Daisy.

'I'm guessing they were jealous of each other's influence on Martin,' Geraldine said. 'Daisy certainly seemed to be very possessive of her father. But none of this means that either one of them was responsible for killing him. All we know for now is that they want to blame each other for the murder. That certainly shows deep hatred.' She frowned. 'Do they really just want to cause trouble for each other, or is one of them trying to divert our attention away from her own guilt?'

Daisy and Serena's accusations needed to be taken seriously, but Martin could have been killed by someone else, in which case the police were wasting time exploring false leads.

'My money's on Daisy being responsible,' Ariadne said. 'She seems thoroughly obnoxious. Have you noticed how no one seems to have a positive word to say about her? She's a nasty piece of work and, before you say anything, she's had more time on her hands than is good for anyone's mental health.'

Naomi came to join them and heard the end of the conversation. 'You've seen the film *Psycho*, haven't you? Norman Bates and all that. If you ask me, there was something unhealthy about Daisy's relationship with her father. You spoke to her, Geraldine, and we've all read her statement. Unless Nigel and Serena are both lying, Daisy fabricated a story about going to live permanently with her father after her mother died. Allegedly she went there to look after him, but I wonder if she was responding to his needs or her own.'

'I thought she was just being a dutiful daughter,' Ariadne said.

'That's what Daisy said about it,' Naomi replied. 'But I think there was something twisted about her feelings for him. She may not have actually moved in with Martin as soon as his wife died, but I believe she went to see him every day, almost as though she unconsciously wanted to take her mother's place.'

'Her father was on his own after his wife died. It's natural she would want to take care of him. There's nothing unusual about that,' Ariadne insisted, reaching for her doughnut. 'I think I may have misjudged her. I think it was actually very nice of her.'

'I'm not sure nice is a word that springs to mind when we're describing Daisy,' Geraldine murmured.

'But wanting to go and live with him? I wonder what Nigel thought about that,' Naomi said. 'He might have suspected she was after getting her hands on all of Martin's fortune for herself.'

'Surely Daisy would have wanted to get rid of Serena, not Martin, if she was really so obsessed with him, and so possessive about him,' Ariadne said.

'Rage, jealousy, possessiveness – who knows what could have motivated her?' Naomi replied.

'In the meantime, we have no proof of anyone's guilt. All we know for certain is that Martin Reed was murdered and we have more than one suspect to investigate,' Geraldine said. 'Until we have more evidence to work with, we just have to be patient and keep digging.'

Geraldine finished her coffee and stood up. For all their talk, they were no closer to establishing the identity of the murderer and she was becoming frustrated with all the time they were wasting on speculation, time she could have been spending at home with Tom. Her input didn't seem to be having any impact, and she wondered whether she had made the right choice in coming back to work so soon. Still, she was committed to the investigation and couldn't back out now. Once it was over, she could review her options. In the meantime, she had work to do.

24

Jimmy liked going to the supermarket and looking around at all the items stacked neatly on the shelves. He couldn't do the main weekly trip to the supermarket on his own, of course. That involved spending a lot, and he didn't understand money. At school, they had tried to teach him about money, but no one had ever been able to explain it in a way he could understand. His parents sometimes took him with them on their weekly excursions in the car. He liked that. He liked it even more when he was allowed to go to the corner shop all by himself to buy a bar of chocolate. He asked to do that every day, unless it was raining. Passing the neighbouring house on his way to the corner shop that morning, he noticed the front door was wide open. He paused, looking around, but there was no one in the front garden. Jimmy wondered what was wrong, because it was cold outside and the house would be losing heat with the door left open like that. His mother was cross with him when he left his window even slightly ajar. Feeling uneasy, he shrugged his shoulders as he had seen his father do when he was puzzled and continued on his way.

It wasn't long since the body of their next-door neighbour had been fished out of the river, and no one had been more shocked than Jimmy and his parents when they heard about the murder on the local news. According to the reports, he had been shot right there in York. Such a terrible thing was almost unheard of. Jimmy's parents had solemnly promised him that it was extremely rare, and Jimmy shouldn't worry about it, because he and his parents were all perfectly safe. No one was going to shoot them. But, knowing the man who lived next door had been shot, he couldn't help feeling afraid.

It had been exciting as well as disturbing, because a policeman in uniform had stood on their front doorstep for ages, questioning Jimmy and his parents about their neighbour. They had nothing to say. As his mother had told the police officer, they were quiet people who kept themselves to themselves. Jimmy had known who Martin Reed was, because he had lived next door. Even though they had hardly exchanged two words with one another, Jimmy had quite liked Martin, because he was always smiling. So Jimmy was sad he had died, even though his parents told him not to worry about it. He told the policeman that Martin was a nice man.

Hurrying home with his chocolate in his pocket, Jimmy saw that the neighbour's front door was *still* wide open. That worried him. He paused. He and his parents had been told that Martin's daughter had moved into the house after the murder. She was called Daisy and Jimmy didn't like her. She always looked cross and she had told Jimmy off for walking on the low wall outside Martin's front garden.

'My mother says I can walk on here,' he had explained. 'I always walk on here and I don't fall off.'

In response, Daisy had waved her fist in the air and shouted at him that he was trespassing, and he would be in trouble if she ever saw him walking on the wall again.

'If you damage my wall, you'll pay for it,' she had yelled, her ugly face turning red. 'Get down right now! You're too old to be walking on walls. You might be an idiot but you understand when I say you're not allowed to walk on my wall.'

She had shouted at him and called him an idiot, which was bullying, and that was very bad. When Jimmy had threatened to tell his father, Daisy had laughed at him. He could tell her laughter wasn't friendly. Jimmy hadn't seen Daisy for a few weeks and his mother had told him she had gone away. The nice lady had come back but he couldn't see her, so he was bothered about the door. Cautiously, he pushed the gate open, and stepped on to the path. His mother would be pleased with him for checking that everything was in order. She liked everything to be in order. But before he reached the front door he turned back, suddenly reticent. He didn't want to invade her privacy, especially since Martin had been killed, and he was afraid Daisy would suddenly leap out and shout at him to get off her property.

He almost screamed when he saw a pair of feet in sparkly pink flip flops lying on the frosty ground next to the bins. Bare toes meant someone was still wearing the shoes. Jimmy shivered, thinking how cold they must be. At the same time, he was almost relieved because he didn't think they could be Daisy's feet. The toenails peeping out of the flip flops were painted bright pink. He didn't think Daisy would paint her toenails bright pink. He wondered if it was the nice lady.

'Hello?' he called out. 'Hello? Are you all right? What are you doing down there by the bin?'

There was no answer. He tried to think what his mother would do in such circumstances. But his mother wasn't there. He decided to run home and report what he had seen. His mother and father had taught him to tell one of them whenever anything was bothering him, like the bullies at school, or the problems he encountered in trying to find a job. No one wanted someone like him working for them, not even to do a bit of gardening.

'You're a good boy,' his father reassured him when he felt sad. 'You're just a bit slower than most people. There's nothing wrong with that. You go through life at your own pace, my boy, and don't let the bullies bother you. Rise above it.'

He wasn't sure what that meant, but he appreciated that his father was being kind. He tried to imagine what his father would do about the pink flip flops, and the person who was wearing them.

'Hello,' he called out again. 'You need to get up. It's dirty down there by the bins. You can't stay there.'

The woman didn't stir.

'Get up, get up!' Jimmy shouted, going closer to make sure the woman could hear him.

He drew level with the nearest bin and leaned forward cautiously to peer behind it, wrinkling his nose at the smell. A woman was lying on the ground. Her eyes were wide open, staring up at him with a shocked expression. Terrified that she had seen him, Jimmy backed away and ran all the way home.

25

GERALDINE AND ARIADNE DROVE to Martin's house. As usual, Geraldine was in a hurry to arrive before the body was moved to the mortuary. While Ariadne was happy to read the reports written by the officers who were first on the scene, Geraldine preferred to see the details for herself. Ian wasn't the only one who accused her of being obsessional, but she never let that put her off. There might be something about the expression on the victim's face or the position in which they were discovered that offered a faint hint about what had happened. Often there was nothing she could put into words, but she suspected her hunches were occasionally inspired by a tiny detail she hadn't consciously registered at the time. It was a question of seeing the body, absorbing what was in front of her, and waiting until it all came together, like the myriad pieces of a jigsaw that joined up to produce a picture where everything finally fell into place. She was always afraid that missing one tiny detail might delay her understanding of the whole.

This time, the street looked very different to when Geraldine had first gone there to see Serena. A white forensic tent had been erected outside the house she still thought of as Martin's property, even though he was dead and it no longer belonged to him. Several white-coated scene of crime officers were busy searching the area as Geraldine pulled on her protective clothing and followed the common approach path into the tent. The body was visible from the path, lying at the side of the area beside a large rubbish bin. As she watched, a couple of scene of crime officers concluded their scrutiny of it. One of them nodded at a third colleague in similar protective clothing who stepped forward and carefully wheeled the bin away. If Geraldine had arrived a few minutes later, she would have known the body was discovered by a bin only from her colleagues' reports. It was a detail that probably wasn't significant, but it might explain what Serena had been doing outside at night. She made a mental note to check when the bins were emptied.

She went as close as she could, careful not to let her feet land anywhere they might contaminate the scene. Reaching the body, she stared down at the dead woman who lay on her back, her arms by her sides, one of her legs stretched out while the other was bent in an awkward position beneath her. Her face was turned slightly to one side, away from Geraldine. She recognised Serena instantly, although the dead woman's expression was rigid with shock and her complexion grey, as though all the blood had drained from her face into a black puddle beside her head.

'Has the medical officer been?' Geraldine asked one of the scene of crime officers. He paused in his careful study of the ground, and nodded at her. 'So what was the cause of death?' she asked. 'There's a lot of blood.'

The officer pointed silently at the woman's head. Crouching down to take a closer look, Geraldine saw a deep gash on the far side of Serena's throat that had initially been hidden from view. There was no longer any question that she had been murdered. Geraldine straightened up, frowning.

'When did it happen?' she asked tersely.

'Some time last night,' the scene of crime officer told her. 'She was examined by the medical officer just after nine this morning. She confirmed the cause of death as probable blood loss, but couldn't rule out the possibility that the wound itself had obstructed the airway and been instantly fatal. Anyway, it looks as though the stab wound was what killed her, one way or another. We'll have to wait for the post mortem to be sure exactly how she died. She appeared to have been stabbed no less than eight hours before she was examined, but it could have been as much as twelve hours earlier. The doctor couldn't be more specific than that because the body was outside on a freezing cold night.'

'So she was most likely attacked at some time between nine o'clock yesterday evening and one o'clock in the morning?'

Her colleague grunted assent. 'That sounds about right,' he said, and turned away to continue his examination of the ground inside the tent.

Geraldine rejoined Ariadne, who had been talking to a scene of crime officer in the street. Before returning to the police station, they went to question the boy who had found the body. He lived next door. The woman who opened the door had black hair streaked with white. There were grey rings under her eyes, and she blinked nervously at them.

'Mrs Wilson?' Geraldine asked.

'This is about next door, isn't it?' she asked with an air of resignation. 'We liked Martin. He was a respectable man, and his wife always seemed very pleasant. We were all sorry to hear about her death. And his was even more of a shock. I spoke to your colleague after it happened, but there's nothing to tell you, not really. We hardly knew them. And now this. It's hard to believe there's been another murder next door. But I'm afraid we can't tell you anything about her. She seemed very nice and they were always very civil, but we like to keep ourselves to ourselves.'

A man joined them, peering out warily from beneath a mop of ginger curls.

'What my wife's trying to say is that we would like to help but we have nothing to add to what we've already told your colleague.'

'We'd like to have a word with Jimmy, if we may.'

Mrs Wilson nodded reluctantly and led them inside. Jimmy was sitting in an armchair in a comfortably furnished living room. Geraldine asked him to tell her what happened when he found Serena's body, and he launched into an account of how he had gone out to buy chocolate and had noticed the neighbouring front door was open.

'What did you do when you saw her?'

'I told her to wake up because it was cold. She wasn't wearing a coat.' He lowered his voice. 'I think it was the cold that killed her. She should have worn a coat.'

26

AT FIRST DAISY RESISTED when two police officers went to fetch her. They reported that she had physically struggled when they attempted to subdue her. She had sworn at them and run upstairs, as though she thought she could hide inside the house. She had locked herself in her bathroom, which was stupid, because of course they weren't going to go away and she had basically trapped herself. The attending female sergeant was concerned Daisy might harm herself, so young constable Sam Cullen had broken in after warning her to stand back. The sergeant reported there wasn't much else they could do, and it wasn't difficult to break open a fairly flimsy internal door. They found Daisy huddled on the floor, clutching her knees to her chest and muttering to herself. She looked up and glared at them but didn't move. In view of her obstinate refusal to accompany them, she was cautioned. Eventually she appeared to run out of energy and went with them quietly. According to the reports, she didn't react when they told her she could be a suspect in a murder investigation and it would be in her interest to cooperate fully.

At the police station, the custody sergeant offered to summon the duty brief, but Daisy preferred to call her brother and ask him to arrange a lawyer for her. After further delay, she was finally brought to an interview room and Geraldine and Ariadne prepared to conduct the interview. The lawyer Nigel had sent was a spindly old man. His hair was grey and he had thin features that seemed carved in stone.

Geraldine noticed that Daisy didn't appear surprised when she was questioned about the murder of Serena Baxter.

'So she's dead, is she?' Daisy said. 'Do you expect me to be sorry?'

She stared sullenly across the table. As usual, her hair looked greasy and there were grey pouches under her eyes. Behind her defiance there was an air of sadness, and Geraldine supposed she was still grieving for her father. When challenged about why she had resisted arrest, she merely shrugged.

'What difference does it make?' she enquired listlessly.

She seemed so feeble, it was difficult to believe she had earlier resisted being brought to the police station.

'You don't have to say anything,' the lawyer murmured.

'I know you understand what we're saying,' Geraldine said quietly. 'You are a suspect in a murder enquiry.'

Daisy shrugged. 'I never touched her,' she replied. 'But I can tell you I'd like to pat whoever did it on the back,' she added with a sudden burst of vivacity. Her cheeks flushed darkly. 'She was toxic. She was probably driven to suicide by guilt at what she did.'

'And that was what, exactly?' Ariadne asked.

Daisy's head whipped round to stare at her as though she was surprised by what Ariadne had said.

'She killed my father.'

The lawyer interrupted before Daisy could say anything else. 'My client is still very upset about her father's death,' he said, adding very quietly to Daisy that she should let him answer the police questions. 'Remember what I told you,' he told her firmly. 'Say nothing. You are not obliged to answer their questions.'

Geraldine directed the conversation back to Serena's death.

'What were you doing last night?' she asked.

Daisy shrugged and muttered that she had no comment.

'You must know what you were doing last night,' Geraldine said. 'There's no reason for you to refuse to reply to a simple question.' She turned to the lawyer. 'Doesn't that reticence suggest your client has something to hide?'

The lawyer nodded at Daisy.

'Last night?' Daisy repeated. 'I was at home. And before you ask, yes, I was alone so you'll just have to take my word for it.'

They were getting nowhere so Geraldine decided it was time to pursue a different line of enquiry.

'What makes you think Serena killed your father?' she asked.

Daisy raised her head and pulled her shoulders back with a jerk. She stared sullenly at Geraldine and insisted that it was obvious.

'Not to us,' Geraldine replied. 'Please help us understand.'

Daisy repeated her claim that Serena had manipulated Martin into naming her his sole heir, after which she killed him. 'Surely you can see what happened? She was only ever after him for his money. It's as plain as the nose on your face. She was young and attractive and she seduced him. You saw what she looked like, the way she dressed herself up. She tricked her way into his bed when he was a lonely and vulnerable old man. She waited until he changed his will and then she killed him. Ask my brother. He'll tell you she never loved him. We both saw through her straight away.'

Daisy stuck to her story despite the fact that she had no evidence to support her accusation. Eventually she refused to say anything more or to answer any more questions and the lawyer insisted on terminating the interview for the day, insisting that his client was exhausted after being forcibly dragged from her home.

'This would all have been over more quickly if your client had cooperated with us,' Geraldine pointed out sourly.

'Don't you think Daisy would have tried to set something up as an alibi if she really did kill Serena, her rival for her father's affections?' Ariadne asked after they had terminated the interview.

'Her rival for her father's money,' Naomi said.

'Unless this was a spur-of-the-moment attack,' Ariadne pointed out. 'She certainly seemed to react angrily when she was arrested, so we know she has a temper.'

They had to admit that it was possible Daisy had killed Serena in a rage, but they could no more prove it than Daisy could prove that Serena had murdered Martin. Their interview with Daisy hadn't really answered any questions.

A constable confirmed that the bins were emptied along Friars Terrace around ten o'clock on Wednesday mornings, which seemed to confirm the theory that Serena might have gone out on Tuesday night to throw her rubbish away before the collection the following morning. No one could have predicted she would do that, so someone must have been watching the house or turned up that night by a horrible coincidence, just as Serena stepped outside. It was unlikely, but nevertheless possible that Jimmy might have been responsible, although his school reports described him as docile and gentle, and he had no criminal record. But even the most unlikely suspects could be guilty, and Geraldine decided to speak to Jimmy again.

Mrs Wilson looked slightly put out to see Geraldine back on her doorstep. When Geraldine said she wanted to have another word with Jimmy, Mrs Wilson made no attempt to conceal her irritation.

'He has nothing more to say to you. Listen, Inspector, you've met my son. You can see he's simple and completely honest. He's never told a lie in his life. He wouldn't know how to. And I assure you he never keeps any secrets from me and my husband. Apart from the fact that he's very gentle and kind, if he had done anything wrong, he would have told me.'

'And you would have told the police?'

Mrs Wilson sighed. 'If I thought my son could be at risk of proving a danger to himself or anyone else, I would make sure he was taken somewhere he could be looked after and protected from himself and others. How would it help him to be allowed to wander around freely if he was capable of doing anything like that?'

'Like what?'

'The woman was dead, wasn't she? Listen, you can question Jimmy again if you have to, but I'm going to have to insist that you do so with me and his social worker present.'

Geraldine sighed. There seemed little point in speaking to Jimmy again.

'Where was your son at around 1 a.m. last night?' she asked in a final attempt to discover something that would help the investigation.

'One o'clock in the morning? He was fast asleep in bed. We all were. You can check the ring camera if you suspect he went next door and killed that poor girl. Jimmy knows he's not allowed out on his own after dark.'

27

SERENA'S PARENTS WERE BOTH dead and she had no siblings. It took the police a few hours to trace a solitary surviving relative living in Sheriff Hutton, less than half an hour's drive north of York. Having arranged for Ian to pick Tom up from Zoe's house after work, Geraldine drove out to see Serena's aunt before making her way home. The sun had not yet set at the end of a bright day, and it had been unseasonably sunny for late autumn. Had she not been engaged in so sombre a mission, Geraldine would have enjoyed the drive. Not knowing how close Serena and her aunt had been, she found it difficult to relax and put her impending visit out of her mind.

Sheriff Hutton was a small village and she found Bernice Baxter's cottage without any difficulty and parked outside. She zipped up her jacket before opening the door of the car because the bright weather was deceptively chilly and, once the sun went down, a mild autumn day could turn wintry in an instant.

A net curtain in a window beside the front door twitched when Geraldine rang the bell. A moment later, the door was opened by a diminutive grey-haired woman dressed all in grey. With her short neck, hunched shoulders and sleepy grey eyes, she looked like a tortoise. She clutched a woollen cardigan across her chest and stared up at Geraldine without speaking.

'Miss Baxter?'

The old lady nodded her head and blinked myopically at Geraldine as she introduced herself.

'Oh dear,' Bernice said in a quavering voice. 'Is something wrong? It's not Terence, is it?'

Having assured the old lady that she hadn't come about Terence, whoever he was, Geraldine suggested they went inside to talk. Bernice led her into a fussily furnished living room, with lace antimacassars on the armchairs and two-seater settee, and a host of china cats displayed on every available surface: the mantelpiece above a cast-iron fireplace, a shelving unit on one wall, and the window sill. When they were both sitting down and Geraldine had declined tea, she shared the sad news of Serena's death as gently as she could, although there was no way to hide the ugly brutality of death. To begin with, Bernice didn't seem to grasp what Geraldine was telling her.

'Serena?' she repeated. 'My niece Serena? Has something happened to her?'

'I'm afraid she's dead,' Geraldine reiterated gently.

'Dead? Serena? Oh dear, oh dear. Poor Serena. She was all I had, you know. She was the only one left. There were three of us, you know, my two sisters and me. Poor Livy died very young, and then Alice, Serena's mother, followed four years ago, and her Lenny went not long after. Serena was the only family I had left. And you're telling me she's gone too? Now it's only me and I'll be all on my own for Christmas. But what happened to her?'

'Bernice, can you think of anyone who might have wanted to harm Serena?'

The old lady gasped and her dark eyes opened so wide they almost seemed to bulge out of their sockets. She pressed a trembling hand over her thin lips and let out a muffled moan.

'Are you saying someone deliberately did this to my poor niece?' she asked in her quavering voice. 'Was it that boyfriend of hers? That Martin? I warned her he was too old for her, but she'd lost her father, you see. She had me, but there was no one to take the place of her father.'

130

Geraldine was able to assert confidently that Martin hadn't harmed Serena. She didn't add that he too had been murdered and that he had been killed first. Instead, she repeated her question. Bernice shook her head and launched into a eulogy, according to which Serena had been generous, considerate, and hard-working, and it was impossible anyone could have wanted to harm her. Geraldine sighed. All she could do was reiterate her condolences.

'I suppose I'll have to organise another funeral,' the old lady said bleakly. 'There have been too many already. My cat just died, you know. She'd been with me for fifteen years.' A solitary tear trickled down one of her wrinkled cheeks. She dashed it away with a tiny lace handkerchief and sniffed as though determined to pull herself together

As delicately as she could, Geraldine explained that Serena's aunt would not be able to bury her yet, as her death was still being investigated. Bernice frowned on hearing that.

'Investigated?' she repeated. 'What does that mean?' She drew in a sharp breath and whispered. 'So, do you think she was murdered?'

Geraldine inclined her head. 'I'm very sorry to tell you we're investigating that possibility.'

'Oh no,' Bernice replied, shaking her head vehemently. 'No, not Serena. I can't believe that.'

Ian didn't criticise Geraldine for arriving home after Tom was asleep, but she sensed his silent censure. Telling herself it was probably just her own guilt making her uncomfortable, she made no attempt to justify returning home so late. Ian had dinner waiting in the oven and while he was dishing up, she stood gazing down at Tom sleeping peacefully in his cot. She wondered how it was possible to feel so sharp a pang of nostalgia at not being able to hold him, when she had cuddled him only that morning. Although she knew that, all things considered, it had been the right choice for her to return to work, there were moments when she regretted her decision so strongly she felt as though she had been kicked in the stomach.

'I'll make it up to you, little man,' she whispered, although she knew she was the one who was missing out. Tom would have been perfectly happy to be fed and bathed by Ian. 'Once this investigation is over, I'll be able to spend more time with you, I promise.'

Tom stirred in his sleep and pursed his little lips and she sighed, knowing she had made the promise to herself alone.

28

DAISY BARELY ACKNOWLEDGED NIGEL'S arrival. Silently she led him into her living room where they sat down opposite each other. He wasn't surprised to see her face twisted in a bitter scowl. She didn't offer him anything to drink, which suited him as he didn't want to stay a moment longer than common decency demanded. Still, she was his sister, and he knew she was devastated by their father's sudden death. Apart from Nigel, she had no one. At least he had his wife for company.

'I've come to see how you are,' he murmured, already regretting having come to see her.

'How do you think I am?' she retorted. 'How would you feel if the police thought you'd killed our father?' She scowled at him as though he was to blame for the accusation that had been levelled against her.

'I'm sure they don't really suspect you,' he muttered awkwardly.

'They hauled me off in a police car and accused me of murdering him. And you've done nothing about it.'

'What do you expect me to do?' he asked, taken aback by her reproach.

Noticing a whiff of stale body odour, he squirmed uncomfortably on the chair, wondering how soon he could leave. It was always the same with his sister. He would go to see her determined to be charitable and kind, but it was never long before her needling started to irritate him.

'You're not listening to me,' she whined. 'I told you before, you need to stop the police pestering me.'

'And how do you suggest I do that?'

'I don't know, do I? You're the clever one who can do whatever you want, with your job and your wife and your nice house. Your life's all sorted. Why can't you do something for me, for a change? I can't even afford to pay a lawyer.'

'I'm paying for a lawyer for you,' he protested.

'He's useless. You're my brother. You need to get on with it.'

'What exactly do you think I can get on with?' He was almost laughing in his exasperation.

'You have to complain. Complain, and keep complaining until they stop persecuting me. I don't know, tell them I'm innocent and they'll be sued for wrongful arrest if they don't leave me alone.'

'What do you mean?' He knew it was a mistake to ask as soon as he heard himself utter the words.

'What do I mean?' she screeched, her face turning a darker shade of red. 'Are you serious? Just stop and think and tell me honestly how long you think you'd last if you were being hounded by the police like a common criminal. I know my home isn't exactly the height of luxury, not like yours, but it's my home, and I want to stay here. You know they locked me in a stinking cell like an animal in a cage. You have to tell them it's outrageous. You can't ignore what's happening. Oh, it's all right for you, you can go back to your expensive flat with a concierge and a view and stylish décor and a wife to do your bidding. You can go back to your self-indulgent life and forget all about me, but what am I supposed to do?'

Nigel looked away. He had heard Daisy's envious gripes so often he no longer paid any attention to them.

'Are you listening to me?' she persisted. 'I'm telling you, I can't stand it. The cell they put me in was disgusting. Everything was filthy. I could hardly bear to touch anything. It stank. And as for what I had to use as a toilet—' She broke off with a shudder. 'This is supposed to be a civilised country. I wouldn't lock an animal in a cage like the one I was kept in. I could have died in there and no one would know. You wouldn't care.'

She scowled when Nigel counselled her to be patient.

'You do realise I was paying rent for my flat while I was stuck there? How is that fair?'

'Come on, you were only there for a few hours. You're home now and I'm sure that'll be the end of it. You have to admit Higgs has done a good job,' Nigel said, ignoring his sister's complaints. 'He came highly recommended. He worked for Chris Robinson.'

'Who the hell is Chris Robinson? What are you on about?'

'Chris works with me and he used this man Higgs when he got himself into a spot of bother. Chris said he was excellent, well-mannered and sharp as they come. I know you wouldn't have wanted some jumped-up young know-it-all representing you.'

'So you sent me a doddery old fool who doesn't know his arse from his elbow. He must be ninety if he's a day. He's so ancient, he kept falling asleep.'

'Well, I hardly thought you'd be easy to satisfy,' Nigel replied, stung into retaliating.

'What the hell is that supposed to mean?'

As she spoke, Daisy jumped up from her chair and seized a bottle from the mantelpiece. She raised it above her head, and just for an instant he was afraid she was going to clout him.

'Sit down, for Christ's sake, and stop behaving like an idiot,' he snapped. 'You're making me nervous.'

'I'm making you nervous? Ha! Well, isn't that just typical. It's always about you, isn't it? Everything's always about you. Well, just for once, how about thinking about my feelings for a change? I'm the one who's being pursued by the police.'

Still grumbling, Daisy lowered the bottle and sat down again.

'They're hardly pursuing you,' he pointed out. 'You're back home, aren't you? So, other than him being old, how are you finding the lawyer? You have to admit he got you out in double-quick time. You haven't thanked me yet for getting him to you so quickly. It wasn't easy, you know. I do have other things to do than run around after you.'

'Thank you very much for taking a moment out of your busy schedule to make a phone call.'

'I hope you'll be very happy with him,' Nigel retorted, too angry to try and control his temper any longer.

Daisy shook her head but didn't answer. As he had expected, she was wary of going too far, knowing she needed Nigel to pay the solicitor's bill, not to mention her other expenses. He had never let her down before. After all, he was her brother and she was his younger sister. She had always known she could rely on him. Even so, he resented the hold she had over him. His wife had always nagged him to cut her loose, but Daisy was the only family he had now.

'Why don't you just walk away from her?' Carol had asked him, on more than one occasion. 'I know she's on her own and unhappy, but that doesn't alter the fact that she's malicious, and all she's ever done for you is make your life a misery. You have to put a stop to all this right now. You've put up with her whining and hectoring for long enough. All you've done is support her and what has she ever done for you? I don't want to be unkind, and goodness knows I feel sorry for her, but you need to stand up to her. You don't have to listen to her spiteful jibes. She's a miserable bitch and you owe her nothing.'

He looked anxiously at his sister now, slumped on a chair, and he felt a tremor of pity. But his wife was right. He had to stop allowing Daisy to dominate him with her constant nagging and claims of victimhood. It was not his fault her life was wretched. There was nothing more he could do for her; she needed to change.

'I just called in to see how the lawyer was doing,' he mumbled, and stood up to leave.

Daisy was on her feet again. 'No,' she said. 'You can't leave me like this. I need to know what's going to happen to me. This isn't fair. I didn't do anything.'

Nigel turned to look at her, noticing her sweaty face and fraught expression and wondered if she was telling him the truth. He did his best to control his irritation but really, he didn't know what more she expected him to do. He had spent some time on the phone persuading Mr Higgs to take on the case. Daisy was right, in a way, because the lawyer had told him he was planning to retire soon, and he had been reluctant to take on the job. Nigel had only been able to secure his services by agreeing to pay over the odds. He hadn't yet told his wife how much it was costing.

'I'm doing what I can,' he assured her.

'Well, it's clearly not enough,' she replied. 'You have to do more.'

Nigel felt uneasy. Suddenly he felt he would suffocate if he stayed a moment longer in that musty room. Muttering that he had to get back to work, he hurried away.

29

A REMNANT OF FROST remained on the ground as Geraldine left home to drop Tom off at the childminder, but the weather was milder and the roads were not icy even at that early hour. It was only November, but Ian was already talking about what they were going to do for Tom's first Christmas. Geraldine had laughed at that, because Tom was too young to have any idea what was happening, but Ian insisted they were laying down memories for him and Geraldine didn't want to spoil Ian's enjoyment of their time with the baby. Meanwhile, she was too focused on her work to have time to think about having a Christmas tree.

The only development discussed in the early morning briefing was that the VIIDO team had unearthed CCTV footage of John, captured on a security camera near Union Terrace car park at eleven twenty two nights before Martin was shot. An indistinct figure could be seen hurrying away from him. The film was being enhanced as much as possible, after which it would be subjected to analysis. Binita was impatient, but the process was going to take time, and despite the best efforts of the IT department, it might offer no clue to the identity of the woman who had purchased a gun from John.

They had sent Daisy home for the night before summoning her back to question her again.

'Perhaps a night in a cell would have loosened her tongue,' Binita said, although no one really believed that particular suspect would weaken easily. If anything, she seemed more likely to dig her heels in and complain even more stridently.

Even though they hadn't kept her, Daisy looked as though she had spent a miserable night. Her eyes were bloodshot and her skin had a grey sheen. She sat with her head held high, her expression surly, defiant rather than cowed. The lawyer sat beside her, frowning irritably, but he spoke mildly.

'Are you going to charge my client?' he asked.

'What are you talking about?' Daisy blurted out. 'You're supposed to defend me.' She muttered at him under her breath, her expression sour. 'Don't encourage them, for Christ's sake. Do you *want* them to charge me?'

'There is no case against my client,' the lawyer continued phlegmatically, ignoring her outburst. 'It seems you're trying to build a case on the fact that my client didn't get on with her father's girlfriend. It's understandable,' he went on quietly. 'Daisy told me the victim moved in with her father shortly after he lost his wife, my client's mother. Naturally she and her brother felt aggrieved. But you have no proof she has committed any crime and everything you've said so far is pure speculation.' He leaned forward. 'Inspector, you know how this works. If you have any evidence against my client, you need to state it clearly, now, and give her an opportunity to refute your allegations before this goes any further. If there is genuine doubt about her innocence, charge her formally and then we'll all know where we stand. Otherwise, you must stop this harassment and let her go.' He paused for an instant. 'There is nothing to be gained by dragging this out. We all know you have no evidence against my client or you would have charged her by now. Let her go.'

Daisy nodded and grinned. 'That's more like it. You heard what he said. Harassment, that's what this is.' She remained adamant that she had done nothing to harm Serena. 'I hated her. Of course I hated her. She was a gold-digger. She seduced my father just so she could get her hands on his money. Why wouldn't I hate her? I'm glad she's dead. But I didn't kill her.'

The lawyer was right. Unless they could find evidence that would build a plausible case against Daisy, they had to let her go. Having made no progress in the interview, Geraldine decided to look into what Daisy had been doing on the night Serena was killed. After speaking to Binita, she drove to Daisy's address off the Holgate Road. On this occasion she parked right outside the house. It was an unseasonably warm afternoon, and even though it wasn't a particularly prepossessing street, it was pleasant to be outside and she lingered for a moment to gaze at a late-flowering shrub in one of the gardens and then up at the clear blue sky. A few small white clouds drifted across the expanse of pale blue, looking like balls of fluff. Despite the bright sun having cleared the last of the frost, there was a hint of approaching winter in the air and she was glad she was wearing a fleecy jacket.

Approaching the property, she studied it from the pavement. From a certain angle she spotted a Ring security camera outside the porch and cursed herself for having missed it on her first visit. It was now somewhere between thirty-three and forty hours since Serena had been attacked. It was possible Daisy had been recorded leaving the house that night. This time she rang the ground-floor bell which displayed the name Green below Daisy's bell, and after a short delay the door was opened by a woman in her sixties, or possibly older.

'Mrs Green?' Geraldine enquired.

'Who are you? What do you want?'

Geraldine introduced herself and the woman leaned forward to squint at her identity card.

'How can I help you?' the woman asked. She seemed slightly wary but was not overtly hostile. 'And it's Miss Green. Bella Green. But you'll have to speak up.'

'I would like to ask you a few questions about your neighbour who lives upstairs. I won't keep you long. May I come in?'

'Wait a minute. I'll go and put my hearing aids on.' She closed the door leaving Geraldine waiting outside.

When Bella returned, she nodded brusquely, and stepped back to allow Geraldine to enter.

'So? What is it you want to know?'

'It's about your neighbour, Daisy Reed.'

Bella frowned. 'We don't really mix, not socially. I know who she is, of course. She lives upstairs. The police came for her yesterday, but of course you know that.' She lowered her voice, appearing to lose her reservations about talking to Geraldine. 'What has she done? To be honest, nothing would surprise me about her.'

'What do you mean?'

Bella shook her head and invited Geraldine to follow her into her living room. Her apartment was larger than Daisy's and looked relatively well maintained. It smelt fresh, and the paintwork looked new. A large grey cat was curled up on the sofa. It sprang to its feet and stalked out of the room when they sat down.

'You said just now that nothing would surprise you about your neighbour. What did you mean by that?' Geraldine asked.

Indoors, and able to speak freely, Bella seemed suddenly reticent to share her thoughts. Instead of answering the question, she shrugged and looked uncomfortable.

'It's nothing, really,' she said.

'Did you get on well with Daisy?'

'Like I said, I hardly knew her. We passed sometimes in the hall and knew each other to say good morning or good afternoon, but that was all. It was all fairly polite. Usually,' she added cryptically.

'Did you ever fall out?'

Bella shook her head. Geraldine asked her what she had been doing on Sunday evening, the night Serena was killed.

Bella looked surprised. 'I was at my Sunday night bridge game. Why?'

'What time did you come home?'

'Late. We didn't finish playing until ten, so it must have been some time after that. Maybe ten fifteen. Why?'

'So you wouldn't know if Daisy went out that evening?'

'Not if it was before ten, no. But I might have heard her if she went out later. She never usually went out in the evening, not that late, so I would have remembered if she had, assuming I'd heard her on the stairs.'

Geraldine asked for permission to access the recording on the security camera from Sunday night.

'The Ring camera? Yes, I had one installed so I can see who's at the door. It seems like a sensible security measure to me, living on my own here. Daisy didn't agree with me, of course.' She pressed her lips together in an expression of disapproval.

'Why was that, do you think?'

'She didn't want to spend the money. That's how tight she is. She wouldn't even go halves. But I went ahead with it anyway,' she said with a faint air of triumph, as though she had won an argument. 'It meant I had to pay for it myself. She could have benefited from it as well, if she hadn't been so mean. She was welcome to share it but not if she wasn't prepared to pay towards it.'

Geraldine interrupted her. 'So can I access the security camera?'

'I'm not sure I want that,' Bella replied, diffident again.

Bella's eyes widened in alarm when Geraldine told her this might help with a murder investigation.

'Murder?' she repeated, aghast. 'Murder? Did Daisy kill someone?'

She looked slightly disappointed when Geraldine explained that the police were hoping Daisy might have witnessed something that could help them in their enquiries. Geraldine was pleased when Bella told her that she subscribed to a Ring camera protection company that saved her videos for a week. Geraldine took down the contact details and left to hurry back to the police station and set the surveillance in motion.

Daisy frowned when she opened her door a few hours later and saw Geraldine on the doorstep.

'Why didn't you tell us about the security camera outside your property?' Geraldine demanded without any preamble.

Daisy didn't answer. Geraldine repeated her question.

'What? Oh, that. It's my neighbour's. The woman downstairs. Bella. It's nothing to do with me.'

'Didn't it occur to you that it might be used to establish whether or not you went out on Tuesday night, the night Serena was murdered?'

Again, there was no response and Geraldine had to repeat her question before Daisy answered.

'I forgot about it. The thing's probably packed up. Those things are all a con. In any case, knowing that cheapskate downstairs, she would have had some rubbish installed that never worked properly in the first place. Is that it?'

Without waiting for an answer, she slammed the door.

30

'SO WE'RE BACK TO square one,' Geraldine said, gazing around at the team whose faces reflected her own despondency.

They had all heard the news. A team of visual identification image detection officers had reported that after Daisy returned home at four forty-five on Tuesday afternoon, she had not left the property until ten o'clock on Wednesday morning. The only activity recorded on the Ring camera was Bella returning home at ten twenty on Tuesday evening. Unless Daisy had climbed over several garden fences, she had been at home all Tuesday night.

'So we know Daisy couldn't have gone out and killed Serena,' Ariadne said bitterly. 'She was telling the truth, and we're right back where we started, only now we have two unsolved murders.'

Once they had checked with the duty sergeant for their allotted tasks, Geraldine arranged to meet Ariadne and Naomi in the canteen for a quick coffee before getting started. When neither of them was occupied with a serious crime, she and Ian sometimes met up during their breaks, but while they were working on an investigation, they tended to stay with their teams to mull over what was happening. Geraldine found these informal conversations a useful forum for discussing issues to do with the case.

'Well, if you ask me, Serena killed Martin,' Naomi said when they were sitting down with their drinks. 'She might be dead, but she's still a suspect. Don't forget, he changed his will in her favour not long before he was killed. If that's not a clear motive, I don't know what is.'

'And then Serena was killed to avenge his death,' Ariadne added.

'That's assuming someone knew that Serena was responsible for Martin's murder,' Naomi said.

'Or her killer believed she was guilty. But they could have been wrong about that,' Ariadne pointed out.

'Don't forget, if Serena died, Nigel and Daisy would inherit his fortune, a fortune they thought they were entitled to.'

Geraldine sighed. 'This is going to make things even more complicated. Serena might well have killed Martin, but we can't question her now she's dead.'

'You don't say,' Naomi replied. 'Sorry, that was flippant, I know. I'd better get back to work.' She stood up and hurried away.

Geraldine and Ariadne chatted for another few minutes before returning to their desks but Naomi's irritable comment was bothering Geraldine. After a while she went to find Naomi to have a word with her.

'Is something wrong?' Geraldine asked quietly.

Naomi shook her head and her blonde curls bounced around her face. She looked uncharacteristically miserable. 'This is about what I said before, isn't it? I'm sorry. I shouldn't have been so facetious. It was impertinent of me and I apologise.'

Geraldine assured her young colleague that she was only concerned to know that Naomi was all right, as it appeared something was upsetting her.

Naomi nodded. 'It's just that I was convinced Serena killed Martin for his money, after ensnaring him with that end in mind all along, and somehow Daisy stumbled on the truth and killed Serena in revenge for her father's death. It all made so much sense, given how close Daisy was to her father. She was virtually living with him after her mother died. Until Serena came along, that is. It seemed so obvious she'd killed Serena, whether it was for the money or out of resentment, or both, it just made so much sense. Only now it turns out that's not what happened. Like you said, we're right back where we started. It just seems—' She shrugged. 'It sounds ridiculous to say this, but it seems so unfair, after we were so sure we had a case against Daisy.'

'You're right,' Geraldine said shortly. 'You are being ridiculous. There's no need to feel downhearted,' she added, seeing Naomi's dismay. 'Establishing Daisy's innocence takes nothing away from everything we've achieved so far in this case, and your contribution has been excellent, as always. But you mustn't allow these inevitable setbacks to affect your focus.'

'How can you help letting it affect you?'

'You have to learn to take it on the chin when your theories blow up in your face. Because they often do and we have to carry on regardless.'

'What if I can't be that detached?'

'Then you're in the wrong job. You're an excellent detective,' Geraldine went on quickly, seeing Naomi's deflated expression. 'But we all have to guard against the trap of believing in hypotheses that haven't yet been proved beyond doubt. Theories are useful, but evidence is essential. And when the evidence disproves our theories, we just have to take a step back and think again. And there's another thing. Daisy isn't a particularly likeable person, but we mustn't let our personal responses influence us. Now, let's get back to work. Come on, you can drive me to the hospital. It's time to talk to the pathologist.'

Arriving at the mortuary, for once Geraldine didn't pause to chat to Avril but strode straight past her to the examination room.

'Ah, I see you've brought a colleague with you,' Jonah said, waving a hand in greeting. 'Please, introduce me to this goddess,' he added with an exaggerated bow.

'He's like this with everyone,' Geraldine told Naomi, laughing. 'He's incorrigible. And he knows perfectly well who you are. Jonah, stop being such a flirt. You're going to land yourself in trouble one of these days. Not everyone appreciates your questionable sense of humour.'

'I hate to disappoint you, but I'm afraid I have a wife at home,' Jonah replied, winking at Naomi across the table. 'Of course, there's always room for one more in my heart.'

'Just ignore him,' Geraldine said. 'Jonah's a happily married man, although how his wife puts up with him is a mystery. I mean it, you need to be careful,' she went on, turning to Jonah and speaking seriously. 'Not everyone's going to find your banter amusing. One day you'll make someone uncomfortable and before you know it, you'll be facing a charge of sexual harassment.'

'If that happens, I hope I can rely on you as a character witness,' he replied solemnly.

'Absolutely not.'

'It's just a bit of fun,' Jonah assured Naomi. 'Working here, I have to seize any chance I can get to lighten the mood. We can't rely on her to cheer us up, can we?' He gestured at the body.

'But she may be able to help us find out who killed her,' Geraldine said. 'So, what can you tell us?'

Suddenly brisk, Jonah nodded and turned to the body. 'She was in her twenties or possibly early thirties if she took care of herself. She was a good-looking girl. That is to say,' he added with a teasing glance at Geraldine, 'she was what some people might consider attractive: tall, slender, with symmetrical features – good bone structure with pronounced cheekbones, although she wasn't underweight, and a clear complexion. Good muscle tone suggests she worked out or took regular exercise. I'd say she must have been fit and healthy in life. Of course, it makes no difference if a victim is young and beautiful or old and decrepit, except that at her age she still had so much life ahead of her, so much potential future stolen.' He sighed, momentarily saddened by the victim's fate.

Geraldine told him that Serena Baxter had been twenty-six years old when she was killed. She was the girlfriend of Martin Reed whose body Jonah had examined only a week and a half earlier. Jonah whistled and enquired whether the two murders were related.

'That's what we're trying to find out,' Naomi replied.

Geraldine explained briefly how they were progressing.

'So it wasn't Martin's daughter who killed our girl here,' Jonah said. 'That's a pity. For you, I mean. It would have wrapped the case up neatly, with two strong motives: money and revenge.'

'That's just what we thought,' Naomi said, a hint of bitterness in her voice. 'It all seemed to fit together so nicely, but that's not what happened.' She scowled.

'Yes, well, it's true we were disappointed, but it's time to move on. So, what can you tell us?' Geraldine asked, nodding at the body.

Serena was lying on her back, her arms at her sides, both legs outstretched. From where Geraldine was standing, she could see the gash in Serena's neck. Now that it was bloodless, the extent of the wound was visible. It looked about six centimetres long.

'Either the assailant knew what they were doing, or it was a lucky strike, because the carotid artery was severed, probably straightaway. This was one deep stab, not a frenzied slashing, so we're looking at a broad blade about two centimetres across at a point five centimetres from the tip. She was struck from the front and slightly to the right-hand side. She must have seen her attacker, but there are no defence wounds, so it must have been quick. Perhaps the killer closed in on her silently, whipped out a knife and stabbed her before she realised what was going on or had a chance to resist.'

'It would have been dark,' Geraldine said thoughtfully. 'It's possible her attacker crept up on her without her noticing him until it was too late to react.'

'Or her,' Naomi added. 'We don't know the killer was a man.'

Jonah nodded. 'She'd been drinking, but we'll have to wait for the tox report to find out if there was anything else in her bloodstream. It looks like she might have been caught unawares.'

'What was the exact cause of death and can you tell us anything else about the murder weapon?' Geraldine asked.

Jonah paused before telling them that Serena had died from blood loss after her carotid artery had been severed with one blow.

'So the killer must have been strong,' Naomi said. 'Which suggests it was a man.'

'Or it could have been someone wielding a very sharp blade,' Geraldine pointed out.

'It was razor sharp,' Jonah agreed. 'Look closely at the wound. Actually, it's not obvious to the naked eye, but under magnification it's apparent that the edges are perfectly straight. A blunt blade would have made a more ragged cut. So that means the killer could have been powerful but wasn't necessarily so. I'm afraid that doesn't narrow it down very much for you, does it?' he added with a faint shrug. 'Hopefully, knowing it was sharp might at least help to eliminate some other knives you find.'

'Assuming we find any,' Geraldine muttered.

Jonah's findings were potentially helpful, but so far they hadn't found any potential murder weapons to check against his measurements.

31

As Daisy hadn't killed Serena, Geraldine turned her attention to Nigel. He lived in a tall block of flats in Leeman Road, near the station. The exterior of the building was pale stone, and most of the windows had balconies. Apart from the fact that it was a smart-looking building, its location would have added to the value of the apartments, as it was close to the station. Having admired the block from the outside, Geraldine rang the bell and a concierge buzzed her in. Black and well built, he was seated comfortably behind a narrow counter. He greeted her with a broad grin, a man content with his position in life. Geraldine held up her identity card and he leaned forward to scrutinise it before nodding at her. She told him she was there to see Nigel Reed, and the concierge gave her the number of the flat without even having to check his list.

'I know all the residents here, some better than others, of course,' he told her when she complimented him on his efficiency.

'What can you tell me about Mr and Mrs Reed?'

'Not a lot,' he replied easily. 'Some of the residents like to chat on their way in and out, but the Reeds never stop. So I can't tell you anything about them, really, except that they're both in. They're quiet, keep regular hours, are no trouble and don't have a great deal of post delivered. Who shall I tell them is here?'

Geraldine wondered whether he might have been more discreet if he had actually had anything to tell her. As it was, his openness was disarming.

'There's no need to announce me,' she replied. 'I'll find my own way there.'

'Third floor,' the concierge called after her as she walked away.

She found the lift and made her way to the right flat. Nigel's wife, Carol, opened the door and looked enquiringly at Geraldine as she introduced herself.

Carol smiled anxiously on hearing that Geraldine was a police officer. 'Have you found out who killed my father-in-law?'

'We have nothing definite yet, but we're working on several leads,' Geraldine replied, slightly untruthfully. 'Is your husband at home?'

Saying she would fetch him, Carol disappeared into the apartment, leaving Geraldine waiting on the doorstep. Dismissing a fleeting fear that Nigel might try to slip away, she waited. They were on the third floor and there was unlikely to be another way out of the flat.

A few moments later, a man appeared and stood framed in the doorway. One of Geraldine's colleagues had informed Nigel of his father's death, and this was the first time Geraldine had come face to face with him. Older than his wife, he was pale, with a bald pate bordered by a thin ring of dark grey hair. His head was oddly long and narrow, and his chin seemed to merge into his neck without any lower jaw bone. His features gave an impression of weakness but his dark eyes were steely and somehow relentless. As he gazed at Geraldine without blinking, she thought there was something almost reptilian about him.

'Nigel Reed?' she confirmed, displaying her identity card again.

He coughed and cleared his throat. 'Is this about my father?'

Geraldine asked to go in and he stood aside to let her enter. The apartment was decorated in blue and cream, and expensively furnished with stylish wooden furniture. Through an open door Geraldine glimpsed a gleaming white and chrome kitchen. Nigel took her into a study with an impressive roll-top desk and space for several chairs. Green velvet floor-to-ceiling drapes hung at two long windows that overlooked a landscaped garden. He took a seat at the desk and Geraldine sat down facing him.

'I can't give you long,' he said, with a casual glance at his watch. 'I have to leave for a meeting in fifteen minutes.'

Geraldine needed to gain the initiative quickly, so instead of hurrying at Nigel's prompting, she waited a moment before responding. 'This will take as long as it takes,' she replied, raising her voice slightly. 'If we're finished in time, you'll be free to go ahead. If not, you'll have to postpone your meeting.'

'I'm afraid that won't be possible,' he said in his lazy drawl, staring at her without blinking.

'You might prefer to conduct this interview at the police station,' she said. 'In any case, we're going to need you to come and give a statement at some point. I can easily arrange for you to come in now.'

Nigel shifted in his chair and started to pull himself to his feet. Geraldine took out her phone and he sat down again, shaking his head to indicate that it wasn't convenient for him to go to the police station just then.

'Very well,' he said. 'Let's get this over with, shall we?'

Ignoring his patronising tone, Geraldine asked him about his relationship with his father and he assured her they had got on as well as any father and son might. Nigel explained that he ran a division of his father's company that operated independently. Even though he technically worked for his father, he said they rarely met at work.

'I'm in charge of my area,' he said. 'My father never interfered. He trusted me to run things in my own way.'

'You worked for your father,' she began but Nigel interrupted her.

'We worked together,' he said irritably. 'He wasn't my boss.'

'You worked with your father,' she conceded patiently. 'Can you think of anyone in the company who might have had a grudge against him?'

Nigel shook his head and repeated that he rarely saw his father when he was working.

'Your father's former PA told us there was a complaint made by an employee.'

Nigel frowned. 'There was one man, but it's probably nothing.'

Geraldine waited.

'My dad fired him for a misdemeanour,' he said slowly, as though he was struggling to remember what had happened. 'He'd only been working with us for a few weeks so he had no protection, no redundancy or anything. He was just out. Gone. But he didn't go quietly.' He grimaced. 'He kicked up a hell of a fuss. It was utterly ridiculous. He threatened to cause all kinds of trouble for us. He was particularly angry with my father. He seemed to think it was personal.' He broke off with a shrug.

Geraldine asked for the disaffected ex-employee's name and address. Nigel scrolled through the records on his laptop and found the details she wanted. His demeanour didn't alter when she asked about Serena.

'Serena?' he repeated coldly, possibly playing for time while he decided what to say. 'Of course I knew her. She was my father's personal assistant. She met him after my mother died, and moved in with him very shortly after he offered her a job.'

'How did that make you feel?' Geraldine asked, watching his reaction carefully.

A disdainful frown crossed Nigel's face. 'It didn't make me feel anything at all,' he replied. 'Why? What should I have been feeling?' His voice was faintly sarcastic, his face expressionless once again. 'And now I'd like to prepare for my meeting, and I'm not sure you are in a position to stop me leaving.'

Geraldine nodded, and she thought Nigel looked relieved. 'I would like to continue this at the police station after you've finished your meeting,' she said, concealing her satisfaction as his expression darkened again.

'Very well,' he agreed. 'If you insist, I'll be with you in about two hours. But I can assure you that you'll be wasting your time. I know nothing about Serena, other than that she worked for my father and went to live with him after my mother died. I have no doubt she helped him to cope at a very difficult time.'

'How did you feel about their relationship?'

Nigel shrugged. 'I can't say I had any strong feelings one way or the other. She was an attractive young woman and what my father chose to do in his own time made very little difference to me.'

That wasn't quite true. Had he not embarked on a relationship with Serena, Martin would almost certainly have left his entire fortune to his children. Geraldine wondered if Nigel was being deliberately disingenuous, but she didn't challenge him. Somehow he had managed to keep taking control of their exchange. She hoped the dynamics would alter once he was facing her in an interview room at the police station. She didn't point out that Serena was not the only suspect in his father's murder.

32

DAISY WAS FEELING UNSETTLED, if not downright angry, and with good reason. It was all right for her brother, who could walk away any time he wanted, but Daisy had been trapped in that foul-smelling cell again. The police could keep her locked up but they couldn't force her to answer their endless questions, and they weren't going to trick her into saying something she would regret later, however many times they interrogated her. If they tried to question her again, she would complain. Despite her decision to say nothing more to the police, the injustice of her situation had provoked her into speaking as soon as the inspector entered the cell.

'What the hell do you want with me now?' she demanded crossly. 'I've got nothing more to say to you, and I'm not saying another word without my lawyer present. If you think you can catch me out while I'm here on my own, you can think again. You know as well as anyone that this is irregular, you coming to talk to me like this. It's victimisation and you can be sure my lawyer's going to hear all about it.'

She had folded her arms and glared up at the inspector, with a determined expression on her face. Prepared for another interrogation, she was taken aback when the inspector told her she was free to go. She said it just like that, without any preamble. Daisy smiled to herself, because it was clear the police knew they were beaten and didn't have the bottle to keep on bullying her. They had treated her so badly; if it wasn't actually illegal, it must at least be a case of professional misconduct. Mr

Higgs had probably already lodged a formal complaint. He had to do something to earn his money. The smug inspector would be given an official reprimand, if Daisy had anything to do with it. She might even be demoted.

'How am I supposed to get home?' she had grumbled. 'Can I at least call my brother to come and pick me up?'

Before escorting her out of her cell to collect her shoes and bag, the inspector warned her not to leave York.

'What are you talking about?' Daisy countered angrily. 'Why can't I leave? Have we become a police state while I was locked up in here? I haven't committed a crime. As an innocent citizen, not to mention a victim of your misconduct, I'm free to go wherever I want and you can't stop me.'

'We might want to talk to you again, so we have to ask you not to leave York just now.'

That sounded ominous, but all at once Daisy had felt too drained to protest. Mumbling that she didn't appreciate being threatened, and would make sure the inspector came to regret her unprofessional behaviour, she had stumbled out of the building and was relieved to see her brother's car waiting for her outside. For once, he was being helpful and had arrived on time. She had fully expected him to keep her waiting. She clambered into the car, trembling with relief that her ordeal was over, and was put out to see that it wasn't her brother, but her sister-in-law, who had come to pick her up.

'So they've let you go,' Carol said, pointlessly. She always was stupid.

'You don't understand anything,' Daisy replied sourly. 'Of course they let me go. They never should have taken me there in the first place. I expect it will be your turn next,' she added spitefully.

It was true the police had released her, but they hadn't done so willingly. She didn't intend to waste her breath explaining the situation to Carol.

'Why didn't Nigel come to get me?' she asked instead.

'He's at a meeting.'

'So his meeting is more important than his own sister, is it?'

'He sent me, didn't he?' Carol countered with a question of her own. 'You seem to think he has nothing else to do all day but run errands for you. You do know he has a job?'

Daisy grunted but didn't bother to answer.

'Nigel is a very busy man,' Carol went on, as though she was speaking to a child, 'and you're not the most important thing in his life,' she added unkindly.

'And I suppose you think you are,' Daisy sneered.

'What I think is none of your business.'

Daisy didn't reply and they drove the rest of the way in silence.

'Aren't you going to thank me?' Carol asked as they turned into Daisy's street.

Daisy grunted and swore under her breath. She had hardly slept for the past two nights, and now her sister-in-law was being typically inconsiderate, only thinking about herself. She didn't care how Daisy might be feeling after being locked up in a stinking cell.

'Why is everybody so damned selfish?' she growled as she climbed out of the car.

Daisy slammed the door without saying goodbye and Carol drove off, tyres squealing on the road as she sped away. Entering her building, Daisy was further irritated at encountering her neighbour from downstairs in the hall. Hearing the street door shut, Bella turned from opening her own front door.

'What are you looking at?' Daisy snapped.

'Oh my goodness,' Bella blurted out, her eyes wide and her eyebrows raised. 'What on earth happened to you? You look terrible.'

'You're no picture yourself,' Daisy retorted. 'Don't go sticking your nose into things that don't concern you. I don't have to answer your questions.'

'There's no need to be rude. I only asked if you are all right.'

'And I told you to mind your own business. Who do you think you are, questioning me like that?'

Daisy took a step towards her neighbour who hurriedly pushed open the door to her own flat and vanished inside.

'And good riddance,' Daisy shouted as Bella's door shut.

She had spent more than enough time being questioned by interfering busybodies. She wasn't prepared to be interrogated by her nosy neighbour now she was finally home. She stomped upstairs, making as much noise as she could. Back in her own flat, she showered and changed. It felt good to scrub herself until she was clean, after spending so much time in that grubby cell. At last she began to relax and realised she was starving. Checking in the kitchen she found the fridge was empty apart from a piece of rock-hard sweaty cheese and a pint of sour milk. It was disappointing, but she refused to let anything ruin her good mood at being home. Those wretched police had nothing on her and the nightmare was over. She regretted having snapped at the woman downstairs and resolved to be civil the next time they saw one another. She would explain that she hadn't been herself. It wasn't a good idea to be on bad terms with her nearest neighbour.

She needed to get to the corner shop for a few supplies, but just as she was preparing to go out, her bell rang. She swore. If this was the police chasing her again, she would give them a piece of her mind. She was tempted to ignore her caller and just wait indoors until they went away. It was frustrating, having to hide in her flat like this, when she wanted to go out, as though she was imprisoned all over again. She was beginning to hope the caller had given up and gone away when the bell rang for a second time. Whoever was calling on her was not going to give up.

33

TRUE TO HIS WORD, Nigel turned up at the police station exactly two hours after Geraldine left him. She wondered if he had waited in his car until the agreed time, he arrived so promptly. Recalling his patronising air, she decided to keep him waiting and sent the young constable, Sam Cullen, to keep an eye on him. If she had been hoping the delay would rattle him, she was disappointed. Nigel seemed perfectly calm when she entered the room ten minutes later. Resisting an impulse to apologise for keeping him waiting, she noted he had changed into a smart navy suit and tie, and his shoes had been polished. She told Sam to stay. He was intelligent and keen to learn, and she told herself it would be a useful experience for him to observe her questioning Nigel, who was a possible suspect. Even if he was innocent, he might prove useful as a witness. But she had an uneasy feeling her real reason for asking Sam to stay was that she wanted to intimidate Nigel. If that was her intention, it didn't appear to have much effect, because outwardly Nigel remained as impassive as ever.

Before she had a chance to speak, Nigel demanded his lawyer be present. Waiting for the solicitor caused a further short delay, and Geraldine wondered if Nigel was carrying out some puerile retaliation for having been kept waiting himself. As it turned out, Mr Higgs arrived within half an hour of being summoned, and at last they were ready to begin. Looking at Nigel, Geraldine thought how different he and his sister were: one smart, businesslike and unemotional, the other unkempt and seeming to lack all restraint.

'How would you describe your relationship with your father?' she asked.

'My relationship with my father?'

'Yes. How would you describe your relationship with your father?' she repeated, with slightly exaggerated patience.

'It was normal.'

'What do you mean by that?'

'It was unremarkable.'

With Nigel refusing to be drawn, she changed her approach, addressing him in the same even tone.

'You worked for your father.'

'I worked with my father, yes, that is correct.'

'How did that feel?'

He shrugged as though dismissing the question. 'It felt like a job.'

Out of the corner of her eye, Geraldine saw Sam watching, and she felt irritated because Nigel was giving nothing away. She wished she could come up with something clever to penetrate his defences, but he persisted in giving laconic answers. At Nigel's side, Mr Higgs was leaning back in his chair, his posture relaxed, his eyes alert. He certainly seemed more engaged than he had been when Geraldine was questioning Daisy, and she wondered if that was because Nigel was the one paying the legal fees. They were making no progress, so she decided to change tack once more and asked Nigel directly where he was on the night his father was killed. Nigel frowned and said he couldn't remember. Showing no sign of discomposure, he offered to check, and took out his phone. Nonchalantly, he scrolled through his calendar, reading his entries aloud in a barely audible murmur.

'Surely you can't have forgotten what you were doing on the night your father died?' Geraldine asked, imbuing her voice with as much scepticism as she could.

The lawyer stirred, but he didn't intervene.

'I didn't know anything about it at the time the attack took place,' Nigel pointed out, reasonably enough. 'I didn't know my father had been murdered until I was informed of it the next morning. So at the time it happened, as far as I was aware it was just a normal evening, like any other evening.' He looked up from his phone. 'I wasn't doing anything particular, and I didn't see my father that evening.' His emotionless response was somehow chilling.

'Where were you when your father was shot?' Geraldine asked bluntly.

'I was at home with my wife.'

Had Geraldine blinked, or lost focus for an instant, she might have missed the barely perceptible tremor in his voice, and the faint flush in his gaunt cheeks. These signs of discomfort vanished almost as soon as they appeared, but Geraldine had been studying him closely and was convinced his composure was a carefully controlled mask. The fleeting alteration in his demeanour could have been a response to the mention of his father being shot. Equally, it might indicate he was hiding something from her. She pressed on even though, apart from that one faint wavering, he remained composed, and she didn't hold out much hope she would be able to catch him out in a lie.

'Let's take a step back,' she said. 'What did you do during the day?'

'We always do our weekly food shopping on Sundays and, as far as I was aware at the time, that Sunday was no different to any other Sunday. So we went shopping in the afternoon, and would have arrived home at around six, after which I wouldn't have left the house again until I went to work on Monday morning. We like to stay in after dark. I'm sure you'll be able to check my credit card records to see what time I paid for the shopping, and after that I was home all evening and all night.'

'It's surprising you want your lawyer to be present when we just wanted to ask a few questions,' Geraldine said quietly.

'You seem to expect to be regarded as a suspect. I wonder why. Unless you have something to hide?'

Nigel stared at her without speaking.

'There's nothing unusual in a member of the public exercising their right to have a lawyer present when they're being questioned by the police,' Mr Higgs replied for him. 'In fact, it's a sensible precaution for clients to have legal representation, as you well know. To suggest he wants me here because he has something to hide is an unpleasant insinuation, Inspector, and entirely baseless. It may be he wants me here because he doesn't trust the police, and can you blame him for that? You locked his sister up on a spurious charge, and now you've been forced to admit you had no evidence for apprehending her, you're turning your attention on him, again without producing any evidence he has committed a crime. I suggest you do your job and find out who carried out this heinous murder, instead of wasting everyone's time interrogating the members of Martin's family, who are grieving his loss. You've already upset Daisy. Unless you have any evidence against my client, this interview is over.'

'This is neither an interrogation nor an interview, as you well know,' Geraldine answered mildly. 'We merely wanted to ask your client a few questions. I pointed that out to your client, when I invited him here.'

She turned back to Nigel and asked him whether anyone could corroborate that he had been home all night between midnight and 4 a.m. on Sunday morning, on the night his father was shot.

'You can ask my wife. She'll tell you we were both at home all evening. This is my father you're talking about,' he burst out suddenly. For the first time, Geraldine saw his mask of composure slip and his voice rose in sudden consternation. 'Why would I want to kill my own father?'

Geraldine could think of a number of possible answers to that question, but she kept them to herself. This was not the time to start indulging in fanciful theories.

'Now, if you don't mind, I need to get back to work.'

Geraldine didn't mind. In fact, knowing Nigel was going to work suited her plans perfectly.

34

ASSURED THAT NIGEL WOULD be at work, Geraldine drove straight to his house where she hoped his wife would be at home on her own. She was right. Carol looked well-groomed, with her hair stylishly cropped. She was wearing a blue and white tracksuit, as though dressed for the gym. She looked faintly puzzled on seeing Geraldine on her doorstep.

'My husband's not here,' she said when Geraldine held up her identity card.

'I know.'

'Oh, I thought you were here to see him. Is this about my father-in-law?'

'Yes, but it's you I want to have a word with. Can I come in?'

Carol hesitated. 'I've got an appointment with my physical trainer in—' She glanced at her dainty gold watch. 'In an hour.'

'This won't take long.'

Carol led her into the spacious white and chrome kitchen which Geraldine had glimpsed on her previous visit, where everything looked new and gleaming, from the stainless-steel sink and sparkling white worktops to the polished tiled floor. There wasn't a used plate or a dirty fork in sight. Geraldine took a seat on a white and chrome chair at a white-topped table, and declined an offer of tea or coffee. She hadn't expected hospitality; this wasn't a social visit. Carol sat opposite her and eyed her cautiously.

'How can I help you?' she asked, with an anxious smile.

'Tell me about your father-in-law.'

'He's dead,' Carol replied quietly.

'Yes. I'm sorry.' Geraldine paused. 'Can you tell me what kind of person he was?'

'He was nice enough. I can't say we were close, but he was always civil to me. He was like that with everyone, very pleasant. I know he was very upset when Ann passed away. They'd been married for years. He didn't talk about her much, but you could see he was devastated.'

'I understand Serena moved in with him quite soon after his wife died.'

'It was about six months later.'

'How did you and your husband feel about that?'

'I can't answer for Nigel, but I was glad when Martin told us he'd met someone else,' Carol said, almost fiercely, as though she expected to have to defend her opinion. 'I know she was a lot younger than him, but that doesn't really matter, does it? If two people are happy together, that's better than them both being unhappy separately, isn't it?'

'What did your husband think about Serena moving in with his father?'

'We hardly talked about it, but he didn't seem to mind. Why would he? If anything, I think he was pleased to see Martin was happy again. Like I said, my father-in-law was devastated by Ann's passing, and Nigel was worried about him. We both were.' She hesitated, before adding that Daisy didn't feel the same way. 'She hated that Martin was seeing someone else. She seemed to feel her mother had been supplanted, even though Ann was dead and Martin was lonely. Daisy made a great show of complaining that Serena was too young for Martin, but they were both adults. According to Daisy, it was obscene for him to be seeing someone so much younger than him, younger than her and Nigel, but if you ask me, she was jealous. She idolised Martin and was unnaturally possessive over him. That is to say, the way she behaved didn't seem natural to me. Not that she did anything wrong, but after Ann died, Daisy was round at Martin's house every day. She said she had to cook for him, even though he could have managed perfectly well without her. *She* was the one who wanted *his* company, if you ask me, not the other way round. He had always been the man in her life.'

'Daisy must have been upset when Serena moved in with your father-in-law,' Geraldine murmured.

'Well, once Serena arrived, Daisy could hardly go on claiming that her father needed her visiting him every day. There was nothing she could do about it. In a strange way, I think Daisy felt rejected.'

'How did Martin react when Daisy objected to Serena moving in with him?'

Carol smiled ruefully. 'He never paid much attention to anything Daisy said. She was always complaining about something. If it wasn't one thing it was another. She was never satisfied. Honestly, I think he and Ann put up with a lot from her. He was always too indulgent towards Daisy, but he was a kind man, kind to everyone. He was kind to me too, not in any way I could point to specifically, but just in general. He tried to make me feel welcome in the family. It's terrible, what happened to him. Do you know who killed him?'

'Do you?'

If she was surprised by the question, Carol didn't show it. 'It must have been some horrible tragic mistake. Martin was such a nice man. I can't believe anyone could have wanted to kill him. Do you have any idea who it was?'

'We're following several leads and hope to find the answer to your questions very soon.' Geraldine paused before asking, 'How well did you know Nigel's mother?'

Carol shook her head. 'Not well. We met a few times and she came to our wedding, but we didn't have much to do with each other. There were no hard feelings,' she added quickly. 'There was just no reason for us to see much of each other.' She glanced around before continuing. 'Nigel wasn't particularly close to her. She was a very private woman.'

'What about Daisy? Was she close to her mother?'

Carol frowned slightly. 'Daisy was always more attached to her father. I don't think her mother minded, but I'm not really the right person to comment on Daisy's relationship with her parents. From what I could see, Daisy and her mother got on well enough.'

Geraldine had contacted a forensic gait analyst, and he arrived shortly after she returned to the police station. George Goodwin was an avuncular red-faced man, nearly bald, with a genial air and a broad smile. They hadn't worked together before, but Geraldine immediately felt comfortable with him. Having explained the situation in outline, she showed him the footage of a sketchy figure who was suspected of buying a gun from John. The tenuous identification was based purely on the time the figure appeared and left, assuming John had been correct in placing the transaction at eleven fifteen at night. Comparing the stranger's height with John's, they were able to ascertain that the woman he had met was too tall to be Daisy, but looked too short to be Serena. None of their assessments were conclusive; all they had to work on was grainy CCTV footage from a security camera, which showed an indistinct figure hurrying away from the car park.

The analyst examined the short CCTV film and compared it with a film of Serena that had been retrieved from Martin's phone. The security camera had caught no more than a fleeting grey image. On Martin's phone, there was a shot of Serena laughing and walking along the golden sands of a beach in bright sunshine. George stared at the two video clips closely for a few minutes before scrolling through the images frame by frame. Each film lasted no more than a matter of seconds and they were very different.

'I'm afraid it's not much to go on,' Geraldine said. 'But anything you can suggest might be useful.'

'Don't worry. It's enough to enable us to reach some kind of conclusion,' he replied. 'I wouldn't be able to definitely confirm a positive identification from what you've given me, but I can tell you these two clips don't appear to show the same person. Forgetting the height discrepancy, which could be due to the woman stooping or wearing risers inside her shoes, the gait doesn't match exactly, although they look extremely similar.'

'The way they're walking looks exactly the same to me,' Geraldine replied. 'But we need to be sure.'

He nodded. 'You do know gait isn't the same as walking? Gait analysis is looking at the manner in which a person walks. For example, each step an individual takes differs in kinematics – the branch of mechanics concerned with the motion of objects,' he added, seeing Geraldine's puzzled expression. 'No two steps are completely identical. That said, examining the length of stride, the foot line and the ankles, you can feel fairly confident when two clips are of the same person.'

'Can you be confident these clips match?'

'In a court I couldn't admit to being completely sure when we're looking at the same person in different clips. But off the record, between you and me—' He paused, frowning. 'My point is, these two videos haven't been randomly put together, have they? So it would be an unlikely coincidence for two people whose gait is this similar to both attract your attention in the same context at the same time. I mean, what are the odds of that? But I can't say I'm certain it's the same person, and they certainly don't match exactly.'

Geraldine sighed and thanked him for his time.

35

THEY MIGHT HAVE BEEN mistaken in focusing all their attention on Martin's family, when it was possible his murderer wasn't related to him at all. Perhaps they had been misled by the fact that he was wealthy, and the killer's motive had nothing to do with his money. Nigel had given Geraldine the name of the employee who had fallen out with Martin after being fired by him and it was important not to overlook that lead, tenuous though it was. Not knowing what to expect, she took PC Sam Cullen with her. The young constable's eyes lit up at being invited to accompany her. She smiled, appreciating his zeal for the job. Some of her more experienced colleagues grumbled about the amount of administrative tasks they were expected to carry out, recording every decision they made and entering every iota of data on to the centralised system, but she had never lost her passion for her work and she warmed to the young constable's enthusiasm. He drove her to Markham Crescent and they found the house.

Beside the door, a line of bells advised them that the property was split into four separate apartments. Each bell had a name beside it, one of them Fellows. At her side, she was aware of Sam straightening his jacket and pulling his shoulders back. She nodded at him. At her signal, he darted off to watch the back entrance of the house. Geraldine gave him a moment. Reaching for the bell, she took a deep breath, conscious that she could be about to question a killer. A frowsy-looking girl opened the door. With a turned-up nose and wide-eyed stare, at first glance she didn't look older than about sixteen. She moved and a shaft of sunlight briefly lit her face, betraying lines on her forehead and crow's feet that showed she was no longer a teenager. Catching sight of Geraldine's identity card, she started back in alarm.

'Hello,' Geraldine said, doing her best to sound friendly and signal that this was an informal visit. 'Don't look so worried. This is just a routine enquiry and nothing to be concerned about.'

'The police come to my door and tell me it's nothing to worry about,' the girl mumbled. She seemed jittery.

'We're not the drug squad,' Geraldine hazarded.

Her guess was correct because the girl appeared to calm down.

'What do you want then?'

Geraldine spoke very gently, concerned not to cause her interlocutor to panic again. 'No one here is suspected of any wrongdoing,' she lied.

'What do you want then?' The girl repeated the phrase like a mantra.

'We think Andy Fellows may be able to help us with an enquiry into a crime he may have witnessed. Could you call him, and maybe don't tell him who's here to see him. We don't want to scare him.'

The girl's eyes narrowed and for a moment Geraldine thought she was going to slam the door, but instead she turned and bawled, 'Andy! Police!'

Geraldine sighed. That was predictable. She hoped Sam had found his way around the back and was in position at the rear of the property, in case Andy decided to scarper rather than face her questions. But a stocky man appeared in the hall behind the girl. He was frowning.

'What's this about, then?' he demanded.

The girl shrugged. 'She's police,' she said. 'You don't look it,' she added. Geraldine assumed her comment was intended as an insult, although it could equally well have been meant as a compliment.

She turned her attention to the man. He had short curly ginger hair and coarse features, with a blunt flat nose and thin wide lips. His small eyes held her gaze levelly, as though to assure her he had nothing to hide.

'Are you Andrew Fellows?'

'Who's asking? And it's Andy. No one calls me Andrew.'

'I told you, she's filth,' the girl said.

'Shut up, Kylie,' the man said, not unkindly, before asking Geraldine what she wanted.

'We're investigating the death of Martin Reed.'

'Martin Reed?' He frowned, looking baffled, then his expression changed. 'That crock of shit.' He glowered at Geraldine. 'I'm not sorry.'

He looked as though he was going to shut the door so Geraldine continued quickly. 'You worked for Martin Reed.'

'What of it? So did a lot of other people.'

'Why did you fall out with him?'

'Would you be on good terms with someone who fired you for no good reason?' He snorted derisively. 'I was late to work a couple of times and he fired me, and if that wasn't bad enough, the bastard refused to give me a reference. Two weeks of hard graft and then out on my ear with nothing to show for it, just for turning up late a couple of times. He was a bastard, all right. If you ask me, he got what was coming to him.'

Without taking her eyes off Andy, Geraldine summoned Sam. Seeing a uniformed officer sprinting around the corner of the property, Andy's eyes widened in panic, but he made no attempt to run.

'I'd like you to accompany me to the police station to answer a few questions,' Geraldine said quietly. 'It won't take long.'

'Bloody hell. What now? You do know it's nearly five years since he kicked me out?' Andy replied, but he went with her quietly enough.

With Sam beside him, he didn't really have much choice.

36

'This is like bloody Goldilocks and the three bears,' Naomi grumbled. 'We know we're looking for a woman who bought a gun, but it seems Serena's too tall, and Daisy's too short. So we need to find someone in the middle. A woman of middling height. What are the chances of finding the right suspect from that description? And we can't even be sure it *is* a woman. And if we *do* find her, she might not be our killer anyway.'

'The video clip hardly narrows it down,' Ariadne agreed, her black eyes troubled. She scowled at Geraldine as though it was her fault that the forensic gait analyst had virtually ruled out their main female suspect in the investigation into Martin's murder.

'The killer could have sent someone else to buy the gun,' Geraldine said. 'We don't know that he was killed by whoever bought the gun.'

'Meaning it could have been anyone at all who shot him – man, woman, tall, short,' Naomi said. 'So that's helpful. At least we can agree a person did it, or are we going to consider a trained chimpanzee as a possible suspect?'

'Whoever organised the murder must have had a motive, assuming it wasn't a random attack,' Geraldine said. 'And that means Serena, Daisy and Nigel are all still suspects. And Nigel's married, isn't he? We should add Carol to our list of credible suspects. It's worth checking her out, isn't it? So far we haven't even looked closely at her but if Nigel lost his inheritance to Serena, that would affect her as well, wouldn't it? And she isn't particularly tall or short, is she?'

'Do we have any footage of Carol's gait?' Ariadne enquired, although she didn't sound very convinced.

'We need to follow that up,' Geraldine replied.

Leaving Ariadne to hunt for holiday videos of Nigel and Carol on social media, Geraldine organised a team to question everyone who had known Serena before she met Martin. She went to Serena's former place of employment herself. Before she worked for Martin, Serena had a job in an estate agent's office in Fossgate. Geraldine entered to find a young woman with streaks of pink in her short spiky hair sitting behind a desk. She was wearing a lurid green and blue shirt and she smiled up at Geraldine. Her expression barely altered when Geraldine introduced herself and explained that she was looking for information, not lodgings. The girl shook her head when she heard what Geraldine wanted, and said that she had never worked with anyone called Serena. Geraldine showed her a photo and the girl frowned.

'Wait a minute,' she said, suddenly animated, her spiky hair joggling as she nodded. 'I saw her just the other day. I swear it was her. She phoned first and then turned up. It must have been about a week ago. I'm sure it was her.'

'What did she want?'

'She was looking for a job. She seemed pretty desperate. I told her we weren't recruiting at the moment and she went away.'

The girl, who worked in lettings, repeated that she knew nothing about Serena. A young man who worked in sales had been there longer, and he remembered his former colleague. With his boyish features and slender build, Ronny looked about eighteen.

'She joined us about a year after I started,' he explained. 'She was only here for a few months, maybe three or four. I could find out for you if you like. Anyway, she left to go and live with some old guy. I can't remember his name. It might have been Mark. I can tell you he was loaded. I mean, I'm not insinuating anything. She seemed very happy. I haven't heard from her since she left, so I'm afraid I can't help you if you want to find her now. Is she in some kind of trouble?'

He was shocked to hear that Serena was dead and asked what had happened.

'We don't know,' Geraldine replied, which was partly true.

'But how did she die?'

'I'm afraid I can't talk about it.'

Ronny nodded as though he understood, although he looked faintly disappointed. He repeated that Serena had been employed at the estate agents for a matter of months. As far as he was aware, she had been reliable and steady and had neither experienced nor caused any trouble in the time he had known her. They hadn't socialised outside the office and he admitted that he knew very little about her personal life, other than that she had left when she had gone to live with her boyfriend. He had nothing to add to what Geraldine already knew about her, and didn't think he had ever heard Martin's full name.

The manager of the agency wasn't in the office that day but Ronny called her to say the police were enquiring about Serena. She agreed to come in straight away, and arrived within ten minutes. Lisa was a smartly dressed woman of about fifty. She was wearing a business suit with a knee-length navy pencil skirt and a matching fitted short jacket. Her face was heavily made up with kohl-ringed eyes and red lipstick. On a less vigorous woman the effect might have been vulgar but Lisa was dynamic enough to carry it off.

'Now, Inspector,' she said. A woman accustomed to being in control, she took charge of the conversation. 'Tell me how I can help you.' She smiled, revealing a smudge of lipstick on her top teeth which somehow blunted her professional image.

'I'm here to find out what you know about Serena Baxter.'

'I only just heard that she died. I'm sorry. Was it very sudden?'

Geraldine repeated what she had told Ronny, and Lisa frowned.

'Tell me what happened,' she said in a voice of quiet command.

Stifling a sigh, Geraldine explained that she couldn't discuss an ongoing investigation.

'You can trust me,' Lisa said, lowering her voice to a conspiratorial murmur. 'I'm the manager here. Now, please, tell me everything.'

Ignoring the entreaty, Geraldine continued to question her, but Lisa couldn't tell her anything she didn't already know about Serena. Returning to the station, she learned that Ariadne hadn't managed to find any holiday videos of Nigel and his wife online. According to Naomi, who had gone to their house to enquire, Nigel had reacted quite aggressively, wanting to know why the police would be interested in watching their holiday films. On the face of it, the request did seem a bit odd, and she had come away with nothing. Since they had put Nigel on his guard, Geraldine decided to bring him in the next morning for further questioning.

In the meantime, she had left Andy Fellows waiting to be interviewed. He was aware that he was being held as a possible suspect in a murder enquiry, and by now he had been fretting in a cell for long enough to be seriously unnerved. They couldn't hold him indefinitely without evidence, but hopefully he would panic and give himself away, even if unintentionally. She just had to find the right pressure point to make him lose his self-control.

37

THEY HAD BEEN DOING their best to follow up every possibility, but somehow Andy Fellows had escaped their notice until Nigel had mentioned his name, almost in passing. Geraldine remembered Dorothy had mentioned an employee complaining about Martin, and kicked herself for not paying more attention to the comment at the time. Binita was quick to pick up on the oversight, although it had only been a passing reference from Dorothy which no one else had noticed either. In addition, as far as they knew, it was five years since Andy had last had any contact with Martin. It was hardly surprising that they had failed to look into his dismissal. Geraldine didn't protest that she would probably have followed it up at the time, if Serena's body had not been found the day after Dorothy made her statement. There was no point in making excuses. The fact remained: she hadn't investigated a possible lead when it first came up. She reread Dorothy's statement but it was too vague to be any help, so she paid her a visit to ask for more information.

Dorothy was clearly vexed to see Geraldine on her doorstep. She didn't invite her in and moved to block her from coming inside. When Geraldine explained the reason for calling, Dorothy shook her head and insisted she couldn't remember anything about the employee who had complained.

'Could it have been someone called Andy Fellows?' Geraldine asked, determined to follow up this new lead rigorously.

But Dorothy just shrugged. 'It could have been. I'm afraid I can't remember.'

With nothing definite to corroborate her suspicions, Geraldine returned to the police station and had Andy Fellows brought to an interview room. An ex-employee with a grudge against his former boss, he was a likely suspect and she was hopeful they might have found Martin's killer. He strode into the room, glaring around so aggressively that Geraldine could well imagine him lashing out when provoked.

'What am I supposed to have done?' he demanded as he sat down. 'I insist you tell me what this is about. You can't just haul people in here and bang them up for no reason. I'll have you for this.'

Having issued that vague unsubstantiated threat, he leaned back in his seat, crossed his arms and glared across the table at Geraldine. She opened indirectly, delving into Andy's time at Reed Construction.

'Reed's?' he repeated suspiciously. 'I worked there for a while. Shit job. But that's not a crime, last time I looked. They're the ones you should be locking up, not me.'

'Why should anyone at Reed's be locked up?'

'Not just anyone. Martin Reed. The boss. He's the one should be sitting here, not me. But it's always the same, isn't it? The top brass get away with murder while the rest of us are persecuted for nothing. Like I told you, I'm not going to lose any sleep over it if he's dropped down dead. Serves him right.'

His air of hostility vanished as soon as he heard that Martin had been murdered. His jaw dropped and he looked frightened.

'What's that got to do with me? What happened?'

Geraldine didn't answer. Instead she asked him to account for his movements on the night Martin was murdered. Andy shook his head, while his eyes flicked around the room as though looking for an escape.

'Sunday night?' he repeated. 'Two weeks ago?'

His face cleared and he banged his right fist in his left palm, making a sharp thud. 'Sunday night,' he repeated, 'two weeks ago. You're talking about Sunday night? We were in Middlesbrough, Kylie and me. We were staying with her sister. She had a mad party.' He grinned. 'You want witnesses? Ask anyone. Kylie and me were there for a week. A bunch of us stayed over after the weekend. Only the locals made it home on Sunday.'

Concealing her disappointment, Geraldine made a note of Kylie's sister's details, before returning Andy to a cell where he wouldn't be able to contact anyone to ask them to confirm his alibi. Once she was sure he couldn't communicate with anyone, she called the police station in Middlesbrough with detailed questions for Kylie's sister. She explained the background to the enquiry and sent through an image of Andy. Not until she was confident her colleague in Middlesbrough understood what was needed, and appreciated the importance of the enquiry, did she ring off. She didn't have to wait long to hear that Andy's alibi checked out. Her colleague rang to tell her Kylie's sister had hosted a party that had started on the Friday night and several guests, including Andy, had stayed until Tuesday or Wednesday.

'We didn't only speak to his girlfriend's sister,' Geraldine's colleague in Middlesbrough assured Geraldine. 'Your suspect was definitely in Middlesbrough that Sunday night. We have confirmation from three witnesses. I'll send you through their statements.'

Listening to her, Geraldine sighed quietly. It seemed they had been right to focus all their attention on Martin's family. Perhaps money was behind the murder after all, as they had initially suspected. It was time to turn their attention back to Martin's heirs.

38

THE FOLLOWING MORNING, TWO constables were sent to fetch Nigel and Carol. They had been instructed where to park in the police station car park, so that they would have to walk some distance to the door. Meanwhile, Geraldine had invited the forensic gait analyst to watch their approach from the doorway. George stood perfectly still as the two suspects walked from the police car to the police station. It was raining and cold as they hurried towards the entrance. Once they were safely indoors, Geraldine and George went inside and she asked him whether Carol's gait, or even Nigel's, might match the one he had studied on the CCTV footage.

George shrugged his broad shoulders. 'It's definitely not the man. He's too tall. He would have had to be stooping so much it would have been apparent, even on such a poor quality video. It could be the same woman, but I really can't say with any degree of confidence.' He gazed down at his phone where he had recorded Carol's approach from the car park. 'For a start she was hurrying, and she was hunched over because of the rain, all of which would have affected her gait. But let me upload this and make a detailed comparison of the two clips and then I'll see if I can confirm it either way. But for now, I have to say I really don't know.'

Geraldine hid her disappointment. 'How soon will you have an answer?'

He shrugged. 'It's going to take time. I know it's only a couple of very short clips, but I'll need to look at them closely several times.'

'Well, let me know as soon as you can.'

He nodded. 'Of course.'

Geraldine prepared to question Nigel and Carol. She started with Nigel, thinking that he was going to be difficult to unsettle however they approached him, whereas spending time in a cell might shake Carol's composure. It took some time for the lawyer to arrive, but finally Geraldine and Ariadne were seated facing Nigel across a table in an interview room once again.

Nigel leaned back in his seat and folded his arms. 'Well,' he prompted them with a sneer. 'Here we are again and I have nothing more to tell you than when you last questioned me. You can keep me here for as long as you like and I'll still have nothing more to tell you because there is nothing more to say. I've already told you I was at home with my wife when my father was killed.'

The lawyer stirred, but Nigel held up a pale manicured hand to silence him.

'I was at home with my wife,' he repeated. 'She'll tell you the same thing. And anyway, do you really think I would want to kill my own father? It's a monstrous accusation and one I take great exception to.'

Geraldine didn't answer his question.

Having achieved nothing by attempting to press Nigel, they tried Carol. She sat herself down and smiled at Geraldine, patting her neatly layered brown hair and looking perfectly comfortable.

'This won't take long, will it?' she asked. 'Only it's just that I have a hair appointment this afternoon. It's not a problem, but I wasn't sure whether to cancel it and I decided not to, but now I'm wondering if I should have cancelled it after all. I didn't realise you were going to keep me waiting so long. Not that I'm complaining,' she added quickly, 'I appreciate how busy you are and I know this is important, but I would like to know when I'm going to be able to get away.'

Geraldine assured her she only had a few questions, and those were soon dealt with. In fact, the only real question was where she had been on the night of Martin's murder. That was easily asked and answered without any hesitation.

'Oh, yes, of course,' Carol replied. 'I've already told one of your colleagues that Nigel and I were both at home that night.' She smiled a little shrewishly. 'I appreciate you would like to blame my father-in-law's death on my husband, but I can assure you that Nigel is innocent. He was very close to his father. They worked together.' She glanced at her neat little gold watch. 'May I go now?'

While Geraldine was talking to Nigel and Carol, Naomi had been checking out Dorothy's social media contacts. When the interviews were over, she came to find Geraldine to discuss her findings.

'We didn't make any headway at all with Nigel or Carol,' Geraldine told her. 'It was a complete waste of time. So, what have you discovered about Dorothy?'

'She isn't active on social media but she does have a Facebook page where she interacts with younger family members. There's a niece living in Brighton who she keeps in touch with. Most of Dorothy's activity is posting inane comments on her niece's posts, or giving them a thumbs-up, and sending out routine messages on birthdays and at Christmas. She never posts anything original but sometimes shares what other people have written – inspirational memes, that kind of thing. I get the impression her activity on social media is fairly tentative and she's only really there to keep in contact with her niece.'

'Nothing that's of any use to us then,' Geraldine replied.

'Wait,' Naomi said. 'There is something. A couple of years ago, Dorothy visited her niece in Brighton, and her niece posted some photos and videos of them. In among the selfies and videos, which were mainly of her own children, there's a short clip of Dorothy walking along the promenade by the sea.'

'I'm on it,' Geraldine said, reaching for her phone.

Once again, the analyst was unsure whether the brief clip of Dorothy walking with her niece's dog matched the gait of the figure suspected of purchasing a gun from Neil's informant. He didn't think it was the same person but needed more evidence before he could be make a confident assessment. Geraldine asked him to accompany her to Dorothy's house. Dorothy seemed surprised to see Geraldine standing on her doorstep yet again. She hesitated for a second, looking agitated, and Geraldine thought she was going to slam the door in her face, but then Dorothy seemed to think better of her impulse and smiled warily.

'Hello, Inspector,' she said, pleasantly enough. 'How can I help you?'

Geraldine smiled. 'I'd like you to accompany me to the police station.'

Dorothy took a step back and looked past Geraldine to where George was waiting in the car. He had moved into the driver's seat before Geraldine rang the bell, and looked as though he was there as her driver.

'Why would I do that?'

Geraldine assured her it was just routine.

'You say it's routine, but I don't seem to have a choice in the matter. What will happen if I refuse to go with you?'

'Is there any reason why you would be unwilling to talk to us?'

Dorothy shook her head. 'Of course I don't have any objections to talking to you, it's just that you're wasting my time quite a lot. I don't see why we can't just talk here.'

'I'd prefer it if we talked at the police station. It won't take long.'

'Oh, very well. Wait here while I get my bag.'

Geraldine took a deep breath as Dorothy closed the front door. She needed to distract Dorothy so she didn't notice George filming her as they walked down the path.

'That's a lovely shrub,' Geraldine said, gesturing to what was obviously a rose bush.

Dorothy nodded but didn't answer and they walked to the car in silence. They drove to the police station where George waited in the car, so he could observe Dorothy walk away. Geraldine left Dorothy with Naomi, who asked her a few innocuous questions before letting her go, still grumbling about the police wasting her time. Once she had left, Geraldine turned to George.

'Could she be the same person?' she asked. 'Could she be the woman who bought the gun?'

Everything about George looked shiny. His forehead had a slightly glossy sheen, and his teeth gleamed in a grin as he answered, 'It's certainly possible.'

'I need you to be sure.'

'It's not possible to say for certain, but I can tell you that the length of the stride appears to coincide, which is one indication that this could be the same woman. The gait comparison could be useful as supporting evidence if a charge comes to court, but on its own it's never going to be enough to build a case on. Leave it with me for now. I'll do some work on it and see what I can find.'

As she thanked George, Geraldine wondered whether his input might be used to persuade Dorothy to confess to buying the gun that had been used to shoot Martin. After giving it some thought she decided to question Dorothy again. She was also going to request a reexamination of Dorothy's fingerprints. There was a slim chance they had missed a match to unidentified prints on the gun they suspected had been used to shoot Martin.

39

GERALDINE WAS WAITING IMPATIENTLY to hear from George. Meanwhile, she had a day off and Ian was also free. They both overslept and only stirred when Tom began bawling for his breakfast. After doing their shopping and a few household chores, they drove out of the city. It was a lovely sunny afternoon so they decided to take a chance on the weather staying dry and drove to the gardens at Allerton Castle, which they had been planning to visit for a while. That night, Ian was due to start an undercover job that would keep him away for a few days, so they were both keen to spend some time together before he left. He couldn't tell her where he was going and she would be unable to contact him while he was gone, but he had been assured the job would last no more than a week. He had been away like this before, working undercover, and she always hated being out of touch with him. At least he had promised her this job was not dangerous, and she had to be content with that.

'My days of taking risks are well and truly over,' he had assured her, glancing at Tom.

Geraldine stifled a sigh as she secured Tom in his car seat. They had spent a fortune on baby equipment, but she wondered whether working to pay for the most comfortable and most expensive equipment for him was a poor excuse for surrendering the responsibility of his daily care to a stranger. If she was truly a responsible mother, she would give up work and devote her time to her infant, regardless of her personal wishes. Tom would be just as happy in a cheap car seat. He chuckled and reached for her with his tiny fingers as she withdrew and shut the door. It was no good tormenting herself like this. She told herself Tom was fine. He would probably be less contented stuck at home with a miserable and frustrated mother. It was better for him this way. Her underlying feeling of guilt was just something she had to live with; she had chosen the best option for Tom as well as for herself.

Scanning through the report on Dorothy as Ian drove them to Allerton Castle, Geraldine read that Dorothy had remonstrated when her fingerprints had been taken, but she had finally cooperated. She hadn't really had any choice in the matter. It hadn't taken long to confirm that Dorothy's prints were not on the gun that had been found, nor did they match any on record, and there was a plausible explanation for Dorothy's DNA in Martin's car. Stifling a sigh, Geraldine focused on enjoying the day out and for an hour or so she managed to forget about work as they admired the outside of the sixteenth-century castle with its Gothic turrets and chimneys. They walked around the landscaped gardens, where a few late flowers still bloomed in sheltered walkways, even though it was November. As the afternoon wore on, the sun dipped and the temperature dropped and they decided it was time to leave.

The following morning, Geraldine was at work early, and it wasn't long before her patience with the gait analyst was rewarded. She had been expecting a phone call from George, but he came to see her in person. This time his eyes were shining.

'I'm pleased to say I have more positive news for you this time,' he told her, with an air of triumph.

He went on to explain that he had run the two clips Geraldine had given him through a sophisticated computer programme designed to compare different gaits.

'There is still room for doubt,' he warned her. 'You can't reach any firm conclusions based on what I'm telling you. This kind of analysis can be used to eliminate suspects, but we can't positively identify individuals without any significant margin of doubt. So all I can tell you is that it's possible this is the same woman. Hopefully this will help with your investigation.'

'It certainly will,' Geraldine replied. 'You've just told us she might have committed a murder.'

George whistled. 'Remember this is not clear cut,' he said. 'You can use it to support other evidence, to aid the probability of your conclusions, but by itself it gives you no more than an indication.'

The evidence might not be incontrovertible, but at least they now had a lead to pursue. Geraldine sent a constable to bring Dorothy in for further questioning. She was found at home and within an hour she had been brought to the police station. Unaware that new evidence had been gathered against her, she refused the offer of legal representation, hoping to leave as soon as possible.

Geraldine had her taken straight to an interview room where she sat staring at Geraldine, blinking nervously.

'What are you talking about?' Dorothy gasped, when Geraldine began to question her. 'You seem to be labouring under the misapprehension that I was involved in what happened to Martin.' She sniffed, making an attempt to look confident. 'Surely you can't think I had anything to do with it? He was my ex-boss, that's all. I had nothing to do with what happened to him.'

'What did happen to Martin?' Geraldine asked.

Dorothy raised her eyebrows in a show of astonishment, but Geraldine sensed that beneath her apparent surprise, she was frightened. 'You know more about that than I do. I only know what I read on the news. He drowned, didn't he? I read that he was fished out of the river.' Stifling a sob, she hid her face in her hands.

'You were careful to wear gloves,' Geraldine said quietly.

'What are you talking about? I don't know what you're talking about. Am I being accused of something?' Dorothy looked up, her expression altered to one of alarm. 'I'd like to leave now.'

'We found your DNA in Martin's car.'

'Yes, well, of course. I told your colleague about that. Martin sometimes gave me a lift to the bus stop. That's why my DNA was there. I don't know what you're implying, but it was perfectly innocent.' She glared at Geraldine, seemingly struggling to retain her self-control.

'That's what we thought, but there was another journey in his car, wasn't there? On the night he died.'

As Dorothy listened, her cheeks flushed red and then she turned very pale. 'What do you mean?' she stammered, looking genuinely shocked by the accusation. 'You can't possibly be serious. I worked for Mr Reed, that's all. He was my boss.'

'You worked for him for twenty years, and then he passed you over without any recognition of your years of service. He got rid of you in favour of a younger woman.' Geraldine watched Dorothy closely as she was speaking. 'That must have been hard to accept.'

Dorothy shook her head and hesitated, fiddling with the edge of the table. Geraldine waited patiently to hear what she had to say.

'I was ready to retire,' Dorothy answered at last, speaking very stiffly. 'It was entirely my choice to leave. Twenty years is a long time. Mr Reed was a good boss but, if you want to know, I'd had enough. I was tired. I'm not a young woman, and I've not been well. I wanted to stop working. When Mr Reed raised the possibility of getting me some help, an assistant to work the computer side of things, I took the opportunity to tell him I was ready to hand in my notice. I can assure you that Mr Reed was very sorry to see me go. It was all very amicable but my time had come to an end. That's all.'

Geraldine went slowly through Dorothy's movements on the night Martin was shot.

'You have no alibi for that night,' Ariadne pointed out quietly.

'Of course I don't have an alibi,' Dorothy replied tetchily. 'I live by myself. No one living alone would have an alibi. How can that make me a suspect? What you're suggesting is ridiculous. I would never kill anyone.'

Geraldine took her time answering. She began by asking Dorothy if she still refused legal representation, given the case against her.

'Case? What case?' Dorothy protested. 'I've told you, I was at home when Mr Reed was killed.'

Speaking slowly and carefully, Geraldine told Dorothy they had further evidence that indicated Dorothy was responsible for Martin's death. She said nothing specific about the findings of the forensic gait analyst; she was not confident the results of George's tests would stand up in court. To make sure of a conviction, she had to press for a confession, but Dorothy had recovered her composure.

'With the information we have in our possession, there's no use continuing to deny what you did,' Geraldine concluded firmly, if not quite truthfully. She leaned forward in her chair and urged Dorothy to confess everything. 'You need to tell us why you killed your former employer. You must have hated him very much.'

'Hated him?' Dorothy repeated, her voice rising. 'Hated Martin?' She burst out laughing. Nearly hysterical, she went on. 'No,' she spluttered. 'No. You think you're so clever, but you couldn't be more wrong. Martin and me, we were a team. We worked closely together for twenty years. I would never have done anything to hurt him.'

'What did you think was going to happen when his wife died?' Geraldine asked, suddenly spotting a different possibility.

'I told him he could rely on me. He was a wonderful man. You have no idea. How could you?' Dorothy stared defiantly at Geraldine. 'You never even met him.'

Geraldine nodded. 'A wonderful man who replaced you with a younger woman.'

'You don't understand,' Dorothy said. 'It was more than a job. You can't imagine what it was like. For twenty years I worked for him and in that time we grew really close. Closer than a husband and wife. We spent all day together, and I learned to understand his moods and anticipate his needs. I understood him better than anyone. He should have turned to me when his wife died.'

'You loved him,' Geraldine prompted her softly.

Dorothy pressed her lips together.

'What did you think was going to happen after you killed him? What were you hoping to achieve? Or was it just an act of revenge?'

Again Dorothy said nothing.

'Very well,' Geraldine sighed. 'If you won't speak to us, perhaps it's time you talked to a lawyer. But it seems to me that you felt betrayed by the man you loved and so you killed him. Do you deny it?'

Breaking down in tears again, Dorothy didn't deny the accusation. Geraldine was convinced she was guilty but without a confession it was going to be difficult to make a charge stick. Meanwhile, there remained the question of Serena's murder.

'Not content with killing Martin, you then killed his new girlfriend.'

Dorothy insisted she knew nothing about the second murder.

Although she denied murdering Serena, she had not refuted the first accusation Geraldine had levelled at her, but neither had she confessed, and they had no conclusive evidence. Tired, Geraldine and Ariadne agreed they had done enough for one day, and they agreed to leave further questions until the next day. Dissatisfied, Geraldine went to collect Tom.

'I was expecting Ian,' Zoe said.

'He's away for a couple of days,' Geraldine replied and then regretted having mentioned his absence. If she hadn't been so tired, she would have been more careful, but it didn't really matter. Zoe would probably have realised he wasn't around anyway, especially if he was gone for more than a few days.

'He's just woken up,' Zoe said quickly, with a smile.

Geraldine took Tom from her and held him close, elated by his obvious pleasure at seeing her.

'See you tomorrow,' she called out to Zoe as she turned away. Zoe didn't answer.

40

THE FOLLOWING MORNING THE interview resumed, but this time Dorothy was accompanied by a lawyer. He suggested it was unnecessary to interview her again, since she had already provided an explanation for the presence of her DNA in Martin's car.

'We would like to go over it again to confirm why you killed him,' Geraldine said. 'Stop me if you would like to add anything.'

'My client denies the accusation,' the lawyer protested.

Dorothy was unresponsive as Geraldine suggested how Dorothy might have felt when Martin had pushed her out in favour of a younger woman. Furious at being scorned, Geraldine went on in her own words, Dorothy had killed him.

'No, no,' Dorothy interrupted Geraldine's recitation. 'I didn't kill him. It wasn't me who pushed him in the river. It wasn't me.' She brushed a stray strand of her short grey hair off her forehead and smiled grimly. 'There it is then,' she said.

'My client has cooperated fully with your investigation,' the lawyer added. 'It is time to stop this interview and let my client go home.'

Ignoring Dorothy's denial, Geraldine proceeded to accuse her of killing Serena.

'Why would I have wanted to kill *her*?' Dorothy asked. 'She was nothing to me. Nothing. I didn't even know her.'

'You were jealous of her relationship with Martin,' Ariadne replied.

'You resented Serena taking him away from you after his wife died,' Geraldine added. 'You thought you would step into his wife's shoes. And perhaps you would have done, if a younger woman hadn't come along and ousted you. But the truth is, you had no right to assume that Martin would turn to you for comfort. You had no right to expect anything from him.'

'No right?' Dorothy repeated, stung into responding. 'No right, after I'd given him twenty years of my life?'

'He employed you and he paid you for your work. That was all there was between you. He'd given you a job for twenty years, but you wanted more than that. And when he made it clear he didn't reciprocate your feelings, you killed him and his new lover.'

Dorothy scowled and shook her head.

'My client has denied killing anyone,' the lawyer interrupted firmly.

Geraldine placed a photo of Martin, taken at the scene of the crime after he had been pulled from the river. His sightless eyes seemed to be gazing directly at the camera. Dorothy stared at it, transfixed with horror, as Geraldine explained what was happening for the benefit of the tape. Dorothy was shaking and mumbling. She reached out with a trembling hand to touch the picture but Geraldine whisked it away.

'Please speak up,' she said.

'I didn't mean to do it,' Dorothy cried out. Her confession seemed to reverberate off the walls. 'I didn't mean to do it,' she repeated in a whisper, and burst into tears.

'What did you do?' Geraldine pressed her, scarcely registering that the lawyer was agitating for a break.

'I pushed him. I pushed him in the water. I'm sorry. I didn't mean to hurt him,' Dorothy wailed.

'You admit to killing Martin Reed?'

'Yes, yes, it was me, it was me. I didn't mean to do it,' Dorothy sobbed.

Geraldine nodded and terminated the interview for a short while.

'The attack was clearly carried out while my client was temporarily not in her right mind,' Dorothy's lawyer announced when they reconvened after a break of twenty minutes. 'This can only be described as a crime of passion, which she now bitterly regrets.' His tone hardened. 'She firmly repudiates your cynical attempt to attribute a second death to her. You don't have a shred of evidence to support the charge. The second murder has nothing to do with my client.'

'I didn't kill that young woman,' Dorothy burst out angrily. 'Why would I, when I didn't even know her?'

'Revenge is a powerful motive,' Geraldine said.

'Even if that's true,' Dorothy replied, 'why would I want her out of the way once Martin was dead? I don't even know when she was killed.'

Ariadne told her that Serena had been fatally stabbed on the previous Tuesday, between nine in the evening and one the following morning. Dorothy's eyes narrowed and then she muttered urgently to her lawyer.

He spoke very rapidly. 'My client wasn't in York at that time. She was visiting her sister in South East London. Her sister will confirm her alibi. We can supply her contact details.'

The lawyer's words were a blow. Geraldine could only hope they would prove false. It was frustrating, but Dorothy insisted she had not harmed Serena and had been visiting her sister at the time of the murder. Her lawyer pointed out they had only to check her alibi to discover the truth. Geraldine had Dorothy returned to her cell. She had confessed to killing Martin, but she had come up with an alibi for the time of Serena's death. If her alibi proved robust, then the investigation into Serena's death would continue.

There were more questions for Dorothy. Purchasing a gun and taking her victim from his house at gunpoint while his girlfriend was away would have taken premeditation and careful planning, so hardly a crime of passion. But they had a confession, and that would suffice for now. Dorothy wasn't going anywhere. The next round of questions could wait while Geraldine prepared the next interview. She was on her way back to her desk, worrying about Dorothy's alibi for the time of Serena's death, when Naomi intercepted her. Geraldine felt a flutter of excitement, hearing what her colleague had come across. Naomi had been looking into Serena's history. They already knew that she had been living in London before she met Martin. It turned out that she had been living with a physically abusive partner called Barry Cooper. Naomi had been in contact with the Met, but so far no one had been able to locate Barry; there was a chance he had followed Serena to York. They needed to find him urgently.

Leaving Naomi and Ariadne to search for Barry, Geraldine went to collect Tom. To her surprise, no one answered when she rang the bell. She checked the time and after waiting for ten minutes, she phoned Zoe. There was no answer. Assuming that Ian had come back early, she hurried home, eager to see him. But he wasn't at the flat. She tried calling him but he didn't answer. Convinced he wouldn't have picked Tom up without letting her know by now, she tried Zoe's number again, but there was still no response from her. Geraldine returned to Zoe's house, but once again no one came to the door and Zoe didn't answer her phone. An hour had passed since Geraldine had been due to collect Tom, and still there was no word from the childminder. She told herself Zoe must have gone out and been held up somewhere, but it was difficult to see where she might be that could prevent her from contacting Geraldine. It was possible she had mislaid her phone, but it was hard to believe she wasn't able to find some way to get in touch with Geraldine. It was becoming increasingly likely she had met with an accident. If that was the case, perhaps Tom was hurt. In desperation, Geraldine went home and called all the local hospitals and doctors' surgeries, but no golden-haired woman had been seen that day, with or without a six-month-old baby. She was wondering whether it was time to report her concerns to the police, when her phone rang. She snatched it up.

'Hello? Zoe?' she gabbled. 'Where are you? What's happening?'

'Geraldine?' The voice sounded oddly hoarse and Geraldine had the impression the speaker was disguising it.

'Yes, yes. Who is this?'

'How does it feel?' the caller asked.

'What do you mean?'

'How does it feel to lose someone you love?'

A thrill of terror shook Geraldine, and a wave of nausea swept through her. Even with all her training, it took all of her energy to keep her voice steady as she forced out a reply.

'Who are you?' she demanded. 'Where is my son?'

As the caller continued, Geraldine grabbed a scrap of paper and a pen and tried to jot down everything she heard.

'If you want to see Tom again, you're going to do exactly what I say,' the voice continued. 'If you tell anyone, you'll never see your baby again. Do you understand? You speak to no one about this. No one. If you talk, I'll know. I'll be watching you wherever you are. You aren't safe anywhere. I have eyes inside the police station.' There was a curious note of triumph in the voice, as though the speaker was gloating. 'You thought there were people you could trust but now you know the truth: you can't trust anyone, not even those closest to you. Wherever you go, whoever you talk to, I'll be watching. And I'll know if you talk. The slightest interference by your people and you sign your child's death warrant. Do you understand?'

'What do you want? Tell me what I have to do.'

As she began issuing threats about what would happen to the caller if Tom was hurt in any way, she was conscious of a curious gurgling sound, and realised the caller was chuckling.

'You'll have to wait until you hear from me again.' With that, the caller hung up.

Terrified, Geraldine could do nothing but wait. She had never felt so helpless. In the course of her work she routinely dealt with the most appalling tragedies, but this was different. This was personal, and she was emotionally involved in a way that sent her thoughts spinning out of control into dark places. And there was nothing she could do. It could be no coincidence that Tom had been kidnapped while Ian was away. Even her colleagues at the police station would not have been told about his absence, but clearly someone knew he was not around and had chosen that moment to strike.

41

GERALDINE NEVER SLEPT WELL when Ian was away working under cover, but this was completely different. Every time she closed her eyes, she relived the conversation with her anonymous caller. In the end she abandoned any attempt at sleep, and clambered groggily out of bed, still undecided what to do. The slightest outward change in her behaviour might provoke the kidnapper, yet she wondered how she could possibly get through the next day without breaking down and blurting out what had happened. If she believed the kidnapper, to do so might compromise Tom's safety.

It was almost impossible to believe she couldn't trust her colleagues, not to mention her friends, Ariadne and Naomi. Yet someone must have informed the kidnapper that Ian was away from home and no one outside the station would know about his absence. It was standard practice, not to mention common sense, not to advertise when an officer was going away to work undercover, but Binita must have known about it, and other colleagues would have noticed his absence. Or perhaps someone else entirely had been watching Geraldine's flat and had been aware that Ian had not come home on Sunday night.

Experienced in dealing with stressful situations, all her training seemed to have deserted her and she was too tired and panicky to think clearly. She brewed herself a cafetière of strong coffee and almost broke down when the aroma reminded her of Ian.

However his absence had been spotted, Geraldine was convinced it could be no coincidence that Tom had been kidnapped just when Ian had gone away. She shuddered. Just thinking of the word 'kidnap' somehow made what had happened seem more real. Tom had been kidnapped and she might never see him again. Struggling to control her emotions, she pressed her lips together, refusing to cry. She would have to carry on outwardly as though nothing had happened. Unable to eat, she poured herself another coffee, and tried to think. The flat felt horribly empty, and she had to restrain herself from hurrying into the nursery to check on Tom. Eventually she gave in and immediately regretted entering the nursery where, at the sight of the empty cot, she broke down in tears. She picked up the little blanket and held it to her lips, inhaling the familiar smell of talcum powder, with just a hint of sour milk.

After a few moments, she pulled herself together and returned to the kitchen. Sipping her coffee, she told herself that, sooner or later, the kidnapper was bound to contact her again. It made no sense for her son to be seized without any follow-up message. She pulled out the crumpled piece of paper she had scribbled on while listening to the kidnapper. Flattening it on the table, she studied it, hopelessly searching for clues that might suggest where Tom had been taken. The caller had prefaced their instructions with the words: 'If you want to see Tom again, you're going to do exactly what I say and stay silent.' They had continued by telling Geraldine that if she spoke to anyone, she would never see Tom again. The speaker had concluded with a warning that if Geraldine involved the police, she would be condemning Tom to death. Monstrous though the threats and warnings were, Geraldine was reassured by the number of times the speaker had used the conditional construction 'if'. Each repetition suggested that Tom was still alive, and he would survive as long as Geraldine did as she was instructed.

It occurred to her that this might be a revenge attack perpetrated by a disaffected criminal she had arrested in the past. It could be someone recently released from prison, perhaps a violent offender. That line of speculation was plausible, but it was too distressing to dwell on for long. The kidnapper must have an objective other than to harm Tom and when that became clear, Geraldine would negotiate his release, if necessary offering herself in his place. She consoled herself with thinking that the kidnap must be intended to hurt her, not her son. Whatever happened, she would save him, whatever it took. If she had to sacrifice her own life to save Tom, she would do so willingly. Comforting herself with that prospect, she finished her coffee and rinsed her cup, her actions automatic, her thoughts whirling.

In the meantime, she did not intend to wait idly for the kidnapper to contact her again. Her last contact with Tom had been at the childminder's house. Whether Zoe had been an accomplice in the kidnap or had been bribed or frightened into handing Tom over made no difference at this stage. What mattered was that Zoe was the one person who might have had contact with Tom's kidnapper. If he had been snatched on the street, Zoe would be able to tell Geraldine exactly where it had happened, and there might be CCTV recording of the incident. She drove to Zoe's house and rang the bell. She was not altogether surprised when no one answered the summons. As she had drawn up outside the house, she had a vague suspicion she might have mentioned Ian's absence to Zoe, but she was too confused to remember clearly.

Uneasily conscious that her unknown enemy might be watching her, she drove straight from Zoe's house to the police station, following her usual route. Her mind seemed to have seized up and she couldn't think of anything beyond slavishly following the instructions she had received. She had no difficulty keeping herself emotionally detached from her work and was shocked to discover her training and experience didn't extend to her private life. Seated at her desk, she tried to behave professionally, only she wasn't investigating Serena's murder, but pursuing a clandestine hunt for Tom's kidnapper.

She balked at suspecting Zoe. Her DBS Certificate had looked genuine but, on reflection, Geraldine realised that she had only seen it very briefly. Zoe had held it up and told her it was up to date and Geraldine had accepted what she was told without reservation. As for the testimonials from other parents, Zoe could have written those herself. When Geraldine had spoken to a couple of them, it could have been Zoe who took the calls on cheap pay-as-you-go phones. Geraldine hadn't checked the numbers to make sure they were genuine. In her work, she would never have been so trusting. It was hard to believe her instincts could have let her down so badly in something so important. She was usually exceptionally perceptive in her judgements of other people, but she had evidently been naïve in expecting her work skills and experience would apply in all areas of her life. What made it worse was that she couldn't remember whether she had mentioned to Zoe that Ian was going away. She seemed to have morphed into a different and totally dysfunctional person, nothing like her familiar self. She drew in a deep breath and tried to focus.

She started by looking into Zoe's background. There was a lot to cover. Everyone Zoe had associated with needed to be cross-referenced against the police database. With a team to help her, the work could have been completed in a relatively short time. Working alone, it might take weeks, and she didn't know how long she had before the kidnapper contacted her again. Realistically, she knew the task was hopeless. She anticipated the kidnapper would call her again that night. That gave her less than a day before she heard from them again. If she failed to come up with a lead within twenty-four hours, she knew she would have to speak to the detective chief inspector. Even though there was no knowing who else might realise she had spoken about it, she had to accept that alone there was little she could do. But before she revealed the situation to anyone else, she was determined to do whatever she could to find her son, while outwardly following the kidnapper's instructions.

Putting her case notes on Serena to one side, she began searching through everyone named Zoe Pike. It was a fairly common name, but along with an address and a rough idea of Zoe's age, she managed to piece together a little of her history. The puzzling thing was that the Zoe Pike living at the childminder's address had no husband and no children. It made no sense, unless the childminder had lied about having a family. The realisation that she had failed to check into Zoe's credentials carefully enough made Geraldine feel physically sick, but at the time there had been no reason to suspect Zoe was deceiving her. It seemed the women who had given the childminder glowing testimonials had also lied. Looking back, Geraldine recalled meeting just one mother who had sent her child to Zoe. The other referee had only spoken to her on the phone. The fact that Tom was Zoe's sole charge should perhaps have made Geraldine suspect something was wrong. But this was no time for self-recrimination. She had to focus on finding Tom.

Zoe's status as a childminder was questionable, but Geraldine's next discovery was petrifying.

42

GERALDINE FORCED A SMILE. 'I told you, there's nothing wrong. Now, I need to get on, and so do you.'

Ariadne returned to her own seat, looking worried. For a second, Geraldine caught herself wondering whether Ariadne was concealing an ulterior motive for showing an interest in her affairs. Realising she didn't know whether she dared trust anyone, even her closest friend, she shivered. She had never felt so alone before. She missed Ian so much it was like a pain in her gut. If only he would return, or at least contact her, but she knew that wasn't going to happen. She had to deal with the situation by herself. Glancing around to make sure no one was watching her, she turned back to her screen. What she had discovered there was devastating.

Looking into Zoe's history, Geraldine had experienced a stab of fear as she realised why Zoe's name had given her a faint tremor of unease when she had first heard it. A few years earlier, in the course of another investigation, Geraldine had arrested an armed robber named Ronny Pike. He had been sent down for four years. It could have been a coincidence, her childminder sharing a surname with a criminal she had arrested. It was a common enough name. But Ronny had been released two weeks before Tom was kidnapped, and now Zoe had disappeared. Geraldine suspected Zoe's abduction of Tom had been deliberately carried out when Ian was away in retaliation for Ronny's arrest and subsequent incarceration. It was a horrific scenario, but possible. Certainly it made sense of what was happening.

While she was waiting to hear from the kidnapper again, she was determined to look for Zoe. If the alleged childminder had left York, there was no way Geraldine would be able to find her without the support of a team. She wondered if she was a fool to think she could hunt for Tom by herself. But the kidnapper's words seemed to reverberate in her head: 'If you talk, I'll know. I'll be watching you wherever you are. You aren't safe anywhere. I have eyes inside the police station.' Meanwhile, Geraldine had given herself a day to find Tom.

Zoe's mother lived in Whitecross Gardens near Haxby Road, so Geraldine decided to start there. If only she had a surveillance team, it would have been easy to watch the house, but she was working alone, and Zoe could be anywhere. If Geraldine's hunch that Zoe was hiding at her mother's house was wrong, then she would have wasted a day when she could have been using police resources to look for Tom. But she might also have protected him by not telling anyone about what had happened. She dared not alert any suspicion at the police station in case someone there was communicating with the kidnapper. After mentioning to Ariadne that she was going to Heslington to question all of Dorothy's neighbours, she logged her false trail for the day and then set off in an unmarked car to watch Mrs Pike's house.

Settling down as low as she could behind the steering wheel, she opened her iPad and set to work reviewing Serena's case. It was difficult to focus while keeping an eye on the house, watching for a sign that Tom was there. Several hours passed and she was beginning to feel physically uncomfortable. Nearly in tears of desperation, she was ready to give up and return to her desk at the police station, when the front door opened and Zoe emerged from the house. Geraldine froze, but Zoe scurried away in the opposite direction without glancing across the road where a car had been parked all morning, seemingly empty. Zoe was on her own, and Geraldine suspected she had left Tom with her mother.

She had to act fast. It was a slight gamble calling a colleague, but even in her state of exhaustion and panic, she knew it was far-fetched to suspect Ariadne of conspiring with Zoe to punish Geraldine for having arrested a felon four years earlier. Trembling, she made the call.

'Whatever you do, don't draw attention to yourself,' she said, speaking as quickly and clearly as she could through her chattering teeth. 'Step outside without anyone noticing and call me back immediately.'

'I don't understand—'

'Just do it. And act normally. You mustn't let anyone suspect something's wrong.'

She hung up, not daring to say more in case Ariadne reacted and betrayed what was happening to anyone who might be watching. Time seemed to stop, although in reality it was only a couple of minutes before her phone rang. As calmly as she could, she summarised the situation.

'Slow down,' Ariadne interrupted her. 'I can't understand what you're talking about.'

Geraldine could hear the concern in her friend's voice. It could have been disbelief. Crouched behind the steering wheel, she shivered, while outside it began to rain, a light steady shower that obfuscated her view through the windscreen. But she had already seen Zoe. Carefully she repeated her account.

'I don't understand,' Ariadne repeated. 'You say Tom was taken yesterday and you heard from the kidnapper last night. Why didn't you say anything before now? What's going on, Geraldine?'

Geraldine tried to explain that she had been too frightened to tell anyone what had happened. She hesitated to admit that she hadn't known whom she could trust. Fear flickered through her even now, as she shared what was happening.

Ariadne understood what lay behind the words. 'You could have told *me*!' she burst out indignantly.

Geraldine did her best to make her position clear. Not only was it difficult to be sure no one was listening, but any change in behaviour at the police station might have been noticed. She couldn't discount the possibility that one of their fellow officers was communicating with Zoe.

'If I reported it, there was a chance Zoe might have been warned. I couldn't afford to take that risk. But now I think I know where Tom is, there's no reason to wait any longer. I have to act. Now. And I can't risk doing this alone. The kidnapper's dangerous. They could be armed.'

Ariadne responded to Geraldine's urgency and agreed to bring a few officers to Whitecross Gardens as discreetly as she could, without explaining where they were going.

'I could bring a van?' she suggested but they agreed that would be impossible to arrange without attracting attention. 'Wait there and keep me posted if there's any change,' Ariadne said. 'I'll be there as soon as I can and I'm going to bring an armed response team. Don't worry, I'll make sure we arrive discreetly. I'll have to tell Binita, but no one else will know what's going on. I'll fill the team in on the way, once we're away from the police station. We'll be there as soon as we can and I won't tell anyone who doesn't need to know.'

'Make sure no one talks,' Geraldine said, as Ariadne ended the call. And then there was nothing she could do but wait for her colleagues to arrive, and hope that they managed to rescue Tom before he could be harmed. She couldn't entertain the thought that the worst might already have happened. He had to be alive.

43

TEN MINUTES LATER, ARIADNE and a hand-picked team of armed and unarmed officers arrived in unmarked cars which they parked a few doors along the street. Ariadne had brought Naomi, Constable Sam Cullen and two more burly officers whom Geraldine deployed to cover the back of the building in case anyone tried to slip out that way. They had to move swiftly before Zoe returned or anyone inside the house noticed unusual activity in the street. Approaching the front door with Sam beside her, closely followed by Ariadne and Naomi, Geraldine had to force herself to keep walking. Despite her determination to maintain her composure, she could feel herself shaking with fear. Summoning all her reserves of energy, she rang the bell and after a moment the door was opened by a middle-aged woman. Her faded blonde hair was shot through with streaks of grey, but her resemblance to Zoe confirmed her identity.

'Are you Mrs Pike?' Geraldine asked.

As the woman looked apprehensively at Sam, who was in uniform, Geraldine nodded at him to position himself beside her.

'I've come to collect Tom.' Geraldine was amazed at how calm she sounded, when her thoughts were churning with powerful emotions.

'I don't know what you're talking about,' Mrs Pike replied but she looked scared.

She made a move to close the door but before she could do so, Sam had put his foot over the threshold, and she had to content herself with folding her arms across her chest and glaring at Geraldine. The belligerence of her stance failed to conceal her alarm. 'There's no one called Tom here,' she blustered. 'You've got the wrong address. Now get out of the way,' she added, scowling at Sam whose foot remained firmly planted in the doorway.

She tried to close the door and was again thwarted by Sam's large black boot.

'Tom is the name of a baby who's gone missing,' Geraldine said, trying to sound disinterested and maintain an appearance of professionalism.

The woman's lips stretched out in a sour grin. 'Do I look young enough to have a baby?' she hissed. 'Now get lost, all of you. There's no babies here and there haven't been for many years.'

As if on cue, somewhere in the house a baby began to cry. Geraldine thrilled at the sound. She had never believed other mothers when they swore they could recognise the sound of their own babies crying, but in that instant she knew she was listening to Tom. Behind her, Naomi let out an expletive, very softly.

'You must know you can't get away with kidnapping a baby. The house is surrounded,' Geraldine said carefully, trying not to provoke Zoe's mother. 'You can see I didn't come here without back-up. So let's end this peacefully, and no one needs to get in trouble. All you have to do is return the baby right now, without any fuss, and this will all go away.'

'I can't do that—' the other woman began.

The baby's cries grew louder. Geraldine shoved the woman to one side and barged her way into the house, leaving Sam to guard the door while Ariadne and Naomi dealt with Zoe's mother, who was looking around with an air of desperation. Without warning, she darted forwards. Ariadne promptly seized her by both of her arms and snapped handcuffs on her wrists.

'We'll wait inside, shall we?' Geraldine heard Ariadne say pleasantly.

Mrs Pike cursed and remonstrated, but her resistance was pointless. Leaving the kerfuffle behind, Geraldine entered a small square hall cluttered with a jumble of shoes, boots and an untidy pile of letters and local newspapers that appeared to have been discarded but not yet thrown away. In front of her was a carpeted staircase that climbed upwards between dull mushroom-coloured walls. The paintwork was chipped and had been rubbed away in patches, as though furniture had been dragged up and down there. The baby's cries had stopped, but Geraldine was sure they had been coming from upstairs. As she was about to ascend, a figure appeared in the shadows above her. Gaunt and unshaven, he was barely recognisable as Ronny Pike, the man she had arrested five years earlier. His eyes glittered malevolently at her but, before either of them could speak, a commotion broke out behind Geraldine. She turned to see Zoe had returned and was standing in the doorway, her mouth open, her eyes stretched wide with fright.

'You!' Zoe shrieked accusingly at Geraldine. 'What are you doing here?'

'I've come to collect Tom,' Geraldine replied.

Behind her, she was aware of movement. Looking over her shoulder, she saw Ronny was halfway down the stairs. Had she seen him in any other setting, she might not have recognised him, even at such close proximity. She remembered a stalwart figure, with a florid complexion and shrewd eyes, who had towered over her when she arrested him for withholding evidence in a murder investigation. He had been lucky to escape with nothing worse than a conviction for aggravated burglary, which was the only charge that could be proved against him, even though Geraldine had testified that he had been armed. He seemed to have shrunk since she had last seen him. His once ruddy cheeks looked pale and gaunt, and his shoulders were bowed. He stared at her dully and pushed past her without a word. She suspected he was high.

'Look at him. Go on, look at him!' Zoe screeched. 'Look what you did to him. Do you know what four years locked in a cell does to a person? Do you have any idea? He's a broken man. Broken.' She began to weep.

'Whatever happened to your brother, he brought it on himself,' Geraldine replied as she turned on her heel and raced up the stairs.

Four doors led off the landing. All were shut. Geraldine opened the first door. Tom wasn't there, nor was he in the second room. In the third room she found him lying on the floor beside an unmade bed, his tear-streaked face flushed. He wasn't moving, and for a terrible instant she was afraid she had arrived too late to save his life, despite the colour in his chubby cheeks. As she held out her hands towards him, his eyelids fluttered and she let out an involuntary gasp. His eyes opened and he let out a piercing wail of protest. She scooped him up, her fingers grasping the warmth of his firm little body. Greedily, she clutched him close to her, ignoring the tears streaming down her face. Snuggled into her neck, snuffling and smacking his lips, Tom stopped crying, comforted by her familiar voice as she murmured gently to him.

Hugging Tom tightly, Geraldine wiped her eyes and made her way downstairs to the hall, where her colleagues were waiting for her. Zoe and her mother were both handcuffed and seething. Ronny was also cuffed, but he was standing with his head lowered, cowed and silent.

'Take these things off at once,' Mrs Pike ordered. No one took any notice of her outraged bleating.

'You'll pay for this,' Zoe hissed, glaring at Geraldine. They both knew those were idle threats. Her attempt to take revenge on Geraldine had failed and she wouldn't try again. Meanwhile, Ronny remained silent, subdued by the commotion around him.

Geraldine wondered if he had even been aware that her son had been kidnapped. He gazed around, without seeming to register anything.

'If prison was so horrible, why did you want to send your brother back there?' she asked Zoe, who glowered in response.

Geraldine turned to Ronny. 'You realise what you've done? You and your sister and mother have all just committed a serious crime.'

Ronny shrugged and gazed at her with the blank eyes of a man who could no longer understand anything. It was not Ronny who had masterminded the abduction, but Zoe. Clutching Tom tightly, Geraldine left. She had a murder investigation to pursue, but first she needed to take care of Tom who was soiled and hungry, and crying again.

44

TOM APPEARED NONE THE worse for his abduction. Once Geraldine had fed him and bathed him, he gurgled happily at her, waving his little fists in the air and chuckling with delight when she tickled him. She played with him until he fell asleep and didn't wake when she put him down, merely grumbling and fussing before he settled, without crying to be picked up. In fact, he showed no signs that he had been at all bothered by his recent experience. He had a generally cheerful nature, except when he was hungry, and seemed as happy as usual. Of course, he had no idea he had been kidnapped. He was familiar with Zoe, who knew how to take care of him, and he would have been asleep for most of the time anyway. Now he was home, it was hard to believe he had ever gone missing. Nevertheless, that night Geraldine slept on the floor of the nursery, waking up intermittently to check that Tom was all right even though it was obvious that, while she had been driven almost insane with worry, he remained oblivious to the danger he had so narrowly escaped. Zoe had been looking after him every day, so nothing had actually changed for him. He had probably not even noticed that he had spent the night in an unfamiliar house.

By the next morning, Geraldine had started to recover from the trauma of Tom's disappearance, but she couldn't think about the murder investigation yet, and called the police station to say she would be off for a few days. She had bought herself a little breathing space, but she couldn't shake off the feeling that she had come close to solving the mystery of Serena's death. There was something off about Nigel and his wife, and she needed to discover what it was. Perhaps she was deluded, but she thought if she could only concentrate on the case for a few more days, she might be able to wrap it up. She couldn't walk away from it now. As long as the killer remained at large, she was going to have to find someone to take care of Tom so she could return to work.

Holding Tom on her lap, and rocking him backwards and forwards, she considered her limited options. She didn't want to use an agency. Apart from the expense, she couldn't consider leaving Tom with a stranger again. After her recent experience, she was apprehensive about leaving him at all, but she wanted to return to work and would need to focus without being distracted. The question was, whom could she trust? She had a twin sister in London, but Helena had no experience with babies and, besides, she smoked. Even if she could be relied on to look after a baby, Geraldine knew Ian wouldn't be happy if Tom was left in her twin sister's care.

The only other solution that immediately came to mind was to ask her adopted sister, Celia, to come and stay until a replacement for Zoe could be found. Geraldine had only learned as an adult that she had been adopted at birth. Although she had grown up with Celia, she had never felt close to her when they were younger, but since discovering she had been adopted, somehow she and Celia had grown close. Celia's daughter was a teenager and old enough to be left at home with her father for a short time, while Geraldine looked for another childminder. If her sister was unavailable at such short notice, Geraldine wasn't sure what she would do.

Celia answered the phone straight away. 'Geraldine, how lovely to hear from you. It's been a while, hasn't it? Too long. How are you? And how are Tom and Ian?'

After exchanging news for a few moments, Geraldine broached the reason for her call, explaining that their childminder had let them down unexpectedly. She didn't go into any details over the phone. She couldn't trust herself to talk about it without breaking down.

'I wouldn't ask, only I'm right in the middle of a complicated murder investigation and I really don't want to abandon it.'

To her relief, Celia immediately agreed to come and look after Tom, as long as she could bring her own toddler with her. Celia declared she would be happy to stay for a week to begin with, after which they could review the arrangement, and Geraldine promised to start looking for a permanent childminder first thing the following morning, while she was waiting for Celia to arrive.

'I'll ask around,' Geraldine said. 'I'm in touch with a few mothers from a local toddler group and I can contact my health visitor and see if she knows anyone. I really appreciate you dropping everything to help me,' she added. 'I don't know what I would have done without you. We're in the middle of an investigation and it would disrupt everything if I quit right now.'

Celia didn't answer but Geraldine could imagine what she was thinking. *'Oh yes, your all-important police work, that takes precedence over everything else, even caring for your own child.'* Celia had given up any hope of a career when her first child was born and had seemed genuinely happy to stay at home, insisting that being a wife and mother was career enough for her. She had been predictably critical of Geraldine's decision to return to work so soon after Tom was born. In many ways, Geraldine envied her. She wished she could be satisfied with her role as a mother. But being a detective was her passion. She knew she was good at her job, and she needed to work to feel fulfilled. She was relieved that Celia refrained from finding fault with her now. She was already struggling with guilt and fighting to dismiss the uneasy feeling that she was responsible for Tom's kidnap. As a mother, she should have been taking care of him herself; as a detective, she ought to have researched his childminder more carefully. She had failed on both counts, and he was so little and so reliant on her. If Celia had launched into criticising her decision to spend time at work when she could have been at home with Tom, Geraldine's resolve might have weakened.

But Celia asked only whether Ian would mind having another a second infant in the flat. 'Or me, for that matter.'

Geraldine explained that Ian was away for a few days, prompting Celia to enquire whether everything was all right.

'Yes, everything's fine. Couldn't be better. He's just away for a few days with work. How soon can you get here?'

Gazing down at Tom sleeping peacefully in his cot, she hoped she was doing the right thing. But Celia would only need to look after Tom until a new childminder could take over. Geraldine hoped Ian wouldn't arrive home while she was at work and wished there was a way she could contact him to warn him in advance that Celia and her little boy were coming to stay. In the morning, she would have to start looking for a replacement childminder, but for now she was busy preparing for Celia. While she was making the bed in the spare room, she received a message that Barry had been traced. He had moved to Leeds and would be brought in for questioning the following day. Celia had to travel all the way from Kent, so she wouldn't be in York until early afternoon. As soon as she arrived, Geraldine would go to work.

Lying in bed that night, Geraldine's thoughts drifted to Serena, and she wondered whether Barry was guilty of murdering her, or if a member of Martin's family was responsible. Something about Nigel was bothering her, but besides him there was no shortage of suspects. She sighed and promised herself she would take time off once the investigation was over to review her priorities. But right now she was impatient to get back to work.

45

NEXT MORNING CELIA SET out early and arrived in York before midday, bringing her infant son with her. Geraldine and Tom were waiting for her at the station. It was cold and they spoke little, apart from rushed greetings, as they bundled Celia's bags and toddler into the car and joined the traffic crawling out of the station. Once they were back at Geraldine's flat, they hugged and greeted each other, and exchanged news briefly as Geraldine was impatient to leave. She expressed her regret that a proper chat would have to wait until later. Once Geraldine had shown her sister where everything was and they had succeeded in opening a two-seater baby stroller Geraldine had borrowed, Celia wanted to hear about Tom's routine.

'What about his bedtime? You need to tell me everything about him. Everything. I don't want to disturb his routine.'

Geraldine smiled. 'There's no need to look so worried. You know what to do. You've had two children yourself. Feed him if he cries and put him in his cot when he's tired.'

'You sound very relaxed about it all.'

Geraldine shrugged. 'I just make it up as I go along and hope for the best. So far we seem to have muddled along okay. He's an easy baby and he doesn't fuss much.'

As she spoke, Tom's little lips puckered and he began to cry.

Celia laughed and picked him up. 'I'm happy to make it up as I go along, but I think it might be best for Tom if I keep to his routine.'

Geraldine shrugged. 'He's very flexible.' She didn't like to add that she wasn't altogether sure what Tom's daily routine was during the week. 'I just need someone I can trust absolutely, and who better than my own sister? I'm hoping to find a new childminder very soon, but now I really have to get to work. You can call me at any time. I'll keep my phone on at all times and I won't be far away.'

She wrote down her number and her doctor's number and watched as Celia stored them both on her phone. Then she left with strict instructions that her sister was to call her if she had the slightest concern about Tom. In the hall, she reminded Celia yet again that she would never be far away and she would keep her phone on her at all times.

'Don't worry, he's going to be fine,' Celia said, smiling. With a shiver, Geraldine remembered Zoe had used the same words. 'It'll be lovely for the two cousins to spend some time together,' Celia added.

'Call me any time.'

'Just go and stop fussing. And yes, of course, I'll call you if I need to.'

With Celia's reassurances ringing in her ears, Geraldine set off to question Serena's ex-boyfriend. Barry was a dapper man in his thirties. His ginger hair was cut quite short, but still long enough to show his curls. Clean shaven, with an open expression on his youthful features, he looked like an oversized boy scout, but Geraldine knew only too well that a guileless appearance was no guarantee of innocence. She remained stony-faced in response to Barry's tentative smile.

'Can someone please tell me what I'm doing here?' he enquired, with just a touch of asperity that made him look his age. 'All I've been told is that I've been brought here for questioning, but no one's actually told me what this is about. Why am I here?'

'We'd like to talk to you about Serena Baxter.'

'Serena?' He shook his head. 'I haven't seen Serena for—'
He held out his hands in a gesture of helplessness. 'At least six
months. She dumped me,' he added, with a faint grimace.

'That must have upset you.'

'Well, I wasn't best pleased,' he admitted with a rueful
laugh. 'She went off with some old rich guy. I could hardly
believe she was so shallow. I mean, I'd thought we were happy
together.'

'You must have been very angry with her. It would be
understandable.'

'Angry? Not exactly. More disappointed. But at least I
discovered what she was really like before it was too late.'

'Too late?'

'What I mean to say is, we weren't married, nothing like that,
and there were no kids to worry about. It was easy enough for
both of us to walk away. We weren't even living together. To be
honest, I've not really thought about her lately. It all seems like
a long time ago. I've moved on. I was very fond of her, but it's
all water under the bridge now. So what's this about? If she's in
some sort of trouble and you're looking for someone to give her
a character reference, you're asking the wrong person. I can't
say I feel inclined to help her out, although I can tell you she's
not one to go breaking the law. She's honest, even if she did start
seeing someone else behind my back. But that's hardly a matter
for the police. I'm surprised she's got herself in trouble. What
has she done?'

Barry looked genuinely shocked when he heard that Serena
was dead.

'Dead? What happened?'

'We think you know.'

'What do you mean? I told you, I haven't seen or heard from
Serena for months. What's going on? Are you suggesting she
was—'

'Unlawfully killed, yes.'

'Killed? Oh my God. I hope you've got the bastard who did it. Serena may have broken up with me but she was a sweet girl. Harmless. Why would he do that?'

'Who are you talking about?'

'The old guy, her new boyfriend, partner, whatever he is. The new man in her life. It was him, wasn't it?'

'It wasn't him.'

'Then who? Surely you don't think I had anything to do with it?' He gasped audibly as he realised the import of Geraldine's questions.

Somehow Geraldine didn't think he had killed Serena, but after her terrible blunder in placing her trust in Zoe, she no longer trusted her instincts about people. She needed to look into Barry's movements at the time of Serena's murder.

'Where were you between nine in the evening and one in the morning last Tuesday night?'

Barry frowned. 'Tuesday? I'll need to check my calendar.' He took out his phone and scrolled through the dates, frowning. 'Okay,' he replied after a moment. 'I was out with a group of friends on Tuesday evening.'

'What time did you meet?'

'We met for drinks after work, at around seven, and had a table booked for eight thirty.'

'And what time did you leave?'

'I can't remember exactly, but I'd say it was about one when we split up.'

'So you were alone at one?'

'No. One of my friends dropped me home.'

'And after that you were alone?'

He shook his head. 'No, after that I spent the night with my girlfriend. I was upset about losing Serena, but I wasn't going to sit around moping for the rest of my life,' he added, sounding a trifle defensive. 'I told you, I'd moved on with my life.'

Geraldine asked Naomi to look for contact details of Barry's girlfriend and the friends he claimed to have spent the evening with. She decided to leave him to wait, while she researched his history. She was half hoping that her instincts about Barry had been correct, even though it would be more helpful to establish him as a possible suspect. While she was waiting, she gazed around at her colleagues. Although Ian's undercover work was never talked about and not even Geraldine knew where he had gone, many of her colleagues were aware that he had been temporarily posted to a different area. She felt uneasy, remembering that in her desperation she had suspected one of them had betrayed her when she had now remembered that she was the one who had told Zoe Ian was away. Before she had Tom, she had seemed to possess an almost infallible instinct about people. Now, it seemed she could trust no one, least of all herself.

Suppressing an unfamiliar stab of apprehension, she wished Ian would come home. She had never before realised how emotionally dependent on him she had become and the realisation frightened her. She wondered how he might react were they ever to split up, and how long he would sit around moping before finding a replacement for her. Shaking off her gloomy musing, she began to look into Barry's history. There was no formal record of his being accused of any violent activity. He was apparently innocent of any wrongdoing, but she was determined to confirm his alibi before releasing him.

46

NAOMI SOON FOUND DETAILS of Barry's new girlfriend, which she passed on to Geraldine. Paula Johnson lived in the nearby village of Askham Bryan, and she worked in the offices of Knavesmire racecourse in York. The racecourse was only two miles from the police station, so instead of sending a constable to question Paula, Geraldine decided to go there and check on Barry's alibi herself. With any luck, his girlfriend wouldn't corroborate his story, and on hearing that his alibi had been discredited, he would crumble and confess to having killed Serena. But Geraldine knew that the case was unlikely to be resolved so easily. It was twenty to five, and she hoped to still find Barry's girlfriend at work. Leaving him to fret at the police station, she set off. Driving along Fulford Road, she crossed the River Foss, then on to Skeldergate Bridge and over the Ouse along Bishopthorpe Road to York racecourse.

A steady drizzle had begun to fall, obscuring the grassy expanse of the racecourse in a fine mist. By the time she arrived at the administration building, the rain had become torrential. She decided not to wait in the car until the rain eased off in case she missed Paula. Yanking up her hood, she scurried for shelter, accidentally stepping in a deep puddle that splashed the bottom of her jeans. Ignoring the chilly dampness around her ankles, she hurried indoors and cursed under her breath as the rain let up just as she reached the door. At the entrance, she asked for Paula and was directed to an office at the end of the corridor on the top floor. It was nearly five o'clock and she walked quickly to the lift, keen to find the room she was looking for before Paula went home.

In a room at the end of the corridor, four women were working on computers in a large office furnished with enough terminals for twice as many people. Through a window that reached right across the wall opposite the door, there was a wide view of the racecourse. Three of the women continued working in silence when she entered the room, but a stout middle-aged woman who appeared to be in charge looked up and asked her what she wanted. At the sound of her voice, the other women looked up from their screens.

'I'm sorry, we're just about to pack up for the day,' the woman who seemed to be in charge added. She didn't sound very apologetic.

When Geraldine explained what she wanted, a slim blonde-haired girl rose to her feet, shuffling a few documents on her desk as she stood up.

'That's me. My name's Paula Johnson,' she said softly.

At first glance, the blonde girl's resemblance to Serena was striking; closer scrutiny revealed that her beauty was less showy. She looked as though she wasn't wearing make-up and, unlike Serena, her hair colour looked natural. While Serena's slightly brassy good looks would have attracted attention wherever she went, Paula seemed self-effacing. She was dressed in a light grey jumper and black jeans. Quietly, Geraldine introduced herself and enquired whether there was somewhere they could talk privately. With a quick nod, Paula led the way out of the room and along a corridor, her heels tapping lightly on the polished wooden floor. She took Geraldine to a small office that was empty.

'I suppose we can use this,' she said. 'No one's going to be coming in here at this time.'

Paula didn't seem curious about her visitor until Geraldine explained the purpose of her visit.

'You're asking about last Tuesday? Last week? Yes, I remember,' Paula replied without any hesitation. 'Barry was out last Tuesday evening.'

Geraldine hoped Barry's alibi wouldn't hold.

'What time did he come home?'

'Around one. He goes out with his friends every Tuesday. One of them dropped him home last week. They take it in turns not to drink,' she added quickly, 'and it wasn't Barry's turn to drive. Not that he drinks much anyway. It was probably after one by the time he got in. After that, we went straight to bed because it was late. There was nothing out of the ordinary, as far as I can remember. But what's this about, please? Is he suspected of robbing a bank or something?' She gave a tentative laugh, but Geraldine could see she was scared. 'Has something happened? I'm sure it wasn't Barry's fault. They might get a bit rowdy, him and his friends, but they'd never break the law, nothing like that. They just like to have a bit of fun. It's harmless, really. Has someone complained?'

Without answering the question, Geraldine took her leave, satisfied that Paula was telling the truth and her story confirmed what Barry had already told them. But as she drove away, she felt a flicker of unease that had become all too familiar over the past couple of days. For years she had believed she could tell when someone was lying, but since her disastrous experience with Zoe, she was no longer sure she could trust her own judgement. Until Barry's friends had confirmed his alibi, she had to admit it was possible he was lying and his girlfriend was covering up for him. Naomi had taken contact details and arranged for them to be questioned. There was nothing more Geraldine could do.

Resolved to put the case out of her mind and enjoy a pleasant evening with Celia, she went home. Celia insisted on preparing supper for them, since Geraldine had been at work.

'You've been working too,' Geraldine protested. 'Looking after a baby and a toddler can't be easy, and you're not even in your own home. They must be far harder work than questioning adults.'

'Oh, they're no trouble,' Celia replied, laughing. 'We've had fun. Now, why don't you go and put your feet up while I make us something to eat?'

Geraldine was relieved that Celia looked so well and seemed to be enjoying herself, and was only too pleased to go and sit in the living room and close her eyes, and before long she dozed off. Celia woke her gently and for a moment Geraldine felt slightly confused.

'Celia? What are you doing here?' Waking up, she laughed apologetically. 'Sorry, I was fast asleep.'

Over a plate of pasta and a glass of chilled white wine, Celia asked Geraldine about her day, and she answered in as much detail as she could. Much of her police work was confidential, but she was happy to share with Celia whatever the media had already discovered and reported. Celia's eyes grew wide with alternating excitement and alarm as Geraldine recounted what had happened to Martin and Serena, and she leaned forward in her chair, her hands clasped, when Geraldine told her about Dorothy's confession.

'She was in love with her boss all along,' Celia murmured when Geraldine had finished. 'She served him faithfully for twenty years and at the end of it he just threw her over for a younger woman, after she had given him the best years of her life.'

Geraldine hesitated, seeing Celia's eyes glistening with tears. 'Are you all right?' she ventured, recalling that Celia and her husband had gone through a rocky patch in their marriage before Celia had fallen pregnant with their son.

'What? Yes, of course. I'm fine.' Celia wiped her eyes on the back of her hand, laughing apologetically. 'It's really sad, that's all. I suppose you get used to hearing stories like that. People must confide all sorts of things to you, while you just keep everything to yourself and won't admit anything to anyone, like where Ian's disappeared to.'

On the point of explaining that she couldn't tell Celia where Ian had gone, she was overwhelmed by relief at the realisation that no one at the police station could have informed Zoe of Ian's whereabouts.

'Geraldine? Are you all right?' she heard Celia ask.

'I'm fine,' she replied, more fervently than she had intended. 'I just realised something.' She broke off, unable to explain. 'It's complicated,' she added lamely.

'Are you sure you and Ian are okay?' Celia enquired earnestly. 'You can tell me.'

'We're fine,' Geraldine assured her. 'It's just work.'

'It always is with you,' Celia replied, with a tolerant smile. 'I know, I know, someone has to protect us from the criminals roaming the streets and keep us safe. I just don't know why it always has to be you.'

'Because I'm good at my job,' Geraldine replied without thinking.

Having uttered her thought aloud, she realised she hadn't lost faith in her abilities after all. Admittedly, her confidence had taken a knock, but it had been a temporary setback, that was all. She was ready to take on the task of tracking down Serena's killer and she wouldn't fail.

47

NIGEL CAME HOME FOR an early lunch as he always did on weekdays. He glanced in the kitchen. The oven wasn't on and the table hadn't been laid. He looked around, but there was no sign Carol had prepared anything, which was strange. He checked his watch to see if he was home for what he thought was an early lunch and saw that he was on time. Puzzled but not yet alarmed, he wondered if she was feeling unwell, and went upstairs to look for her. She wasn't resting in the bedroom. He found her sprawled comfortably on a sofa in the lounge, engrossed in studying travel brochures. She looked up with a lazy smile when he entered the room.

'I didn't hear you come in,' she said.

'You know what time it is?' he asked irritably, taking a seat opposite her.

He didn't add that she bloody well ought to know, having recently splashed out and bought herself an expensive watch. It had cost her housekeeping allowance for at least a month and he had been forced to give her extra that month. He often wondered how she managed to get through so much money. She never did anything, other than spend a fortune on clothes and make-up and facials and hairdos, although she never looked any different for all the pampering. Thanks to his extravagant wife, he had ended up supporting a local beauty salon without ever setting foot across its threshold.

'What's all this?' he asked, gesturing at the pile of brochures lying on the coffee table and suppressing his irritation that she had forgotten to prepare his lunch.

'I'm looking at holidays,' she replied breezily.

'Holidays? Really?' He forced a smile to conceal his rising anger, telling himself it did no harm to look. She knew perfectly well he was not prepared to waste money on pointless jaunts. But that didn't explain why she had forgotten to make lunch.

'What about something to eat before I go back to the office?'

'It was going to be a surprise,' she added, with a little laugh. Ignoring his question, she picked up one of the glossy brochures.

Nigel's smile faded. 'A surprise? What are you talking about?' He perched on an armchair and stared at her. 'What's going to be a surprise? What's going on?'

'What's going on is that we're going away together, far away from here, somewhere exotic and luxurious. Somewhere sunny where we can laze around on a beach, and swim in a warm ocean, and drink cocktails by the pool all day—'

'Stop talking nonsense,' he interrupted frostily.

'Oh, don't be such a stick-in-the-mud. Everyone goes away. Why shouldn't we? We're going on holiday. We can afford a luxury cruise now. Or maybe a fortnight in the Canaries. With your inheritance, we can do whatever we want, go wherever we want, whenever we want. Don't you get it? We're loaded, and that means we're free to do anything we like!' She laughed and clapped her hands foolishly.

'Stop being ridiculous,' he snapped. 'You're behaving like a spoiled child.'

'You're the one who's being ridiculous,' she retorted angrily. Her cheeks grew bright pink. 'What's the point of getting our hands on such an eye-watering amount of money if we don't spend it? We might as well not have bothered, if we're not going to enjoy ourselves once in a while.'

A curious chill seemed to settle in the air and Nigel lowered his gaze, unable to look at her.

'What do you mean, we might as well not have bothered?' he

asked quietly. 'Not bothered with what?'

Out of the corner of his eye, he saw his wife shrug.

'Tell me what you meant,' he repeated.

Without answering, she picked up a brochure from the table and began leafing through it. He repeated his question once again, desperately hoping he had misconstrued her words. It seemed almost incredible that he would be harbouring any such suspicion of his own wife. Almost.

At last she looked up and stared at him defiantly. 'Well, you weren't going to do anything, were you? We had a small fortune coming to us, and she was getting her hands on it. All of it. We couldn't let her get away with it. That was your money, your inheritance, yours and mine, and she was snatching it away from right under our noses. There was nothing else for it. She had to go.'

His words came out in a strangled squawk. 'You're talking about Serena?'

'Of course I'm talking about Serena. Who else? We had to get rid of her. You must have realised that too. I thought you'd be pleased with me for sorting out the mess your father made of everything.'

'Sorting it out? Are you saying you – you killed Serena?' he struggled to put the terrible question to her.

She dropped the holiday brochure she was holding and carefully selected another one from the pile in front of her.

'What if I did?' She looked up, her eyes wide, pleading with him to understand. 'Somebody had to do it,' she snapped impatiently when he didn't answer. 'If you were any sort of a man you'd have dealt with the situation yourself.'

'Dealt with the situation?' he repeated, aghast. 'What do you mean, dealt with the situation?'

'Don't look so indignant. I did it for us. For you. You wanted it more than me. I did it for you. Don't you see? Serena meant nothing to us. Less than nothing. She wasn't even family. You never liked her. Think about it. What's right is right. You're Martin's son. Doesn't that mean anything to you? You deserve to inherit his estate. All of it.'

'Not all of it,' he corrected her automatically, unable to take in the enormity of what she was saying. 'Daisy gets half of everything my father left.'

'We'll have to wait for a while before she has her accident, or people might start to suspect.'

Nigel shuddered, barely able to suppress a cry. He wondered how long Carol was planning to wait before he met with an accident too.

'Oh, stop pretending to be shocked,' she said. 'You never had a good word to say about your sister. You know perfectly well what she's like. She's a snake. She doesn't deserve anything. Why should she have an equal share of his fortune? It ought to come to you, all of it. Don't you understand? Listen, you know she wouldn't share it with you if she got her hands on everything. Well, that's never going to happen. Leave it to me and we'll end up with the lot.' She came and sat on the arm of his chair and leaned in tantalisingly close to him. He could see her cleavage, her breasts thrusting forwards inside her jumper, and smell the faint odour of her body beneath her delicate perfume. 'Nigel,' she murmured, 'you're not thinking clearly. This is about you and me.' She began caressing his temples with her fingers. 'Our future happiness. Together. Just think how wonderful life is going to be now we have enough money to do whatever we want. You'll be able to stop work and we can be together all the time.'

She looked at him so tenderly that, just for a moment, he was almost seduced by her words. Then the reality of what she had done sank in and he rose unsteadily to his feet, no longer able to contain his horror. With one wave of his arm, he swept the holiday brochures to the floor before sinking down on the chair again. In a voice that shook with emotion, he ordered her to go to the police. She couldn't undo what she had done, but she could at least confess her crime. If she didn't come clean, he said, guilt would destroy her.

'We'll say it was self defence,' he blurted out. 'We'll say she attacked you first. She did, didn't she? That was what happened. We'll get you the best defence team, the best lawyer. You won't go to prison. You won't be convicted. I won't let that happen. Temporary insanity. We'll get you off.' He dropped his head in his hands and began to sob. He barely heard her furious insult as she left the room.

'You always were feeble,' she yelled at him. 'Feeble and stingy. I thought you had some balls. I wish I'd never met you! I should have followed my instincts and gone after your father. He was a real man.'

48

BY LATE MORNING THE following day, Barry's alibi had been corroborated by the six people he had been out with on the night Serena was murdered and he was released. He didn't appear particularly upset at having been kept in a police cell overnight. When Geraldine warned him not to leave the area or its surrounding villages, he merely shrugged before sauntering out of the cell to collect his shoes and possessions.

'We may need to speak to you again,' Geraldine said.

'You know where I am,' he replied breezily.

Despite her misgivings about her own judgement, Geraldine found it hard to believe that such an easygoing man would commit a murder. Back at her desk, she reviewed what they knew so far. Dorothy was known to be capable of murder, but she had an alibi for the time of Serena's death, as did Barry. They had to return to questioning Martin's children, both of whom had a motive for killing Serena. Geraldine decided to start with Nigel and sent a constable to fetch him. The officer reported that Nigel had seemed reluctant to accompany him, insisting that he had already been extensively questioned about his father's shooting and the subsequent stabbing of Martin's girlfriend. By the time Geraldine joined Nigel in an interview room, his usual air of insouciance had vanished and he was red-faced with irritation.

'What the hell is going on?' he blurted out as soon as Geraldine and Ariadne entered. 'I can't believe you're still pestering me. You do realise I have work to do?'

The two detectives sat down without responding to his outburst. Geraldine noticed the change in him straightaway. He was dressed in a different suit, this one dark grey and clearly expensive but, apart from his smart outfit, he was almost unrecognisable from the man she had questioned previously. Something had rattled him. It could have been that the reality of his father's death had finally sunk in, but she suspected there was more to it than that. He looked frightened.

'Well?' he enquired, one eyebrow raised with a hint of his earlier haughtiness. 'Haven't you finished with me yet?'

Geraldine barely hesitated in replying that they were nowhere near finished with him. She realised her mistake straightaway. A shutter seemed to come down and Nigel's eyes fluttered with hostility. Taking a deep breath, Geraldine pressed on, hoping to see his composure shaken again.

'Let's go through your relationship with Serena once more.'

'What relationship?' he retorted. 'I barely knew the woman. All I know about her is that she moved in on my father and persuaded him to part with every last penny of his fortune. He was leaving everything to my sister and me until Serena came along and talked him into changing his will in her favour. It was obvious from the start what she was after, but he was too infatuated with her to see what was happening. She was young and glamorous, and he was a lonely old widower. There's nothing difficult to understand about that. He wasn't the first man to be duped by a woman and I don't suppose he'll be the last,' he said bitterly. 'Surely even you can grasp what I'm saying,' he added, with a resurgence of his earlier sneering tone. 'But I didn't kill her.'

'That's not how Serena described her relationship with your father,' Ariadne pointed out mildly.

'That woman was a liar,' he replied, his pale cheeks flushed. 'You can't believe a word she said. That was my father's mistake and look what happened to him. He never should have got involved with her. She was evil and he let himself be completely taken in by her lies. That was his undoing.' His implication was clear.

'You've already been informed that your father's death wasn't Serena's doing. His former PA has already confessed to killing him. It had nothing to do with Serena. But we're now investigating her murder and that's why we're here,' Geraldine said, adding quietly, 'You seem to have been very angry with her.'

Nigel scowled and appeared to retreat into himself. Geraldine suppressed a sigh. They weren't getting anywhere. She was almost relieved when Nigel demanded his lawyer be present before he would agree to listen to any more questions. It took a while for the lawyer to respond to Nigel's summons, and when he arrived they reconvened in an interview room. Mr Higgs settled himself beside Nigel with a grunt, his bony features impassive, and Geraldine resumed the interview.

'This isn't about your father, Nigel. Where were you last Tuesday evening?'

'At home with my wife,' Nigel replied stolidly. 'We watched television and then went up to bed at eleven, as we do every night. We like to keep to our routine. Really, Inspector, you're wasting your time with me. My answer isn't going to change, however many times you put the question. The fact is, I'm a creature of habit, so it's never any problem for me to remember what I've done in the evening. Like every day, I went to bed at eleven, having spent the evening with my wife, and slept until morning.'

'Are you a sound sleeper?'

Nigel nodded. 'Actually, since my father died, I've been sleeping better than ever. I'm sorry if that disappoints you.'

'What about your wife?' Geraldine enquired, with a sudden flash of interest.

'What about her?'

'Did she sleep all night?'

'She has never had any problems sleeping so yes, you can write in your report that we both slept well all night. I doubt whether you can say the same. I'm not sure what you're getting at here but, as I've already told you, this is a complete waste of my time, and yours. Now, I take it I can go? And you won't bother me again?' He glanced at the lawyer who gazed at Geraldine without speaking.

'We'll drop you home,' Geraldine said.

Nigel glared at her, but he couldn't refuse. Besides, it was pouring with rain. Muttering crossly, he trailed after Geraldine to the car. Soon the pale block of flats where he lived came into view and Geraldine followed Nigel inside. The black concierge looked up and nodded at them.

'Afternoon, sir,' he called out and smiled tentatively at Geraldine. 'Good afternoon, Inspector.'

Nigel turned and thanked Geraldine with a dismissive air.

'While I'm here, I'd like to have another word with your wife,' she said.

They went up to his flat together. Nigel opened the front door and called out to his wife, but there was no answer.

'Well, there it is. I'm afraid she isn't home,' he announced.

'Does she often go out at this time without telling you?' Geraldine asked. She had a strange sensation that he was hiding something from her.

Nigel glanced at his watch. It was ten past six. 'My wife is free to come and go as she pleases,' he replied tersely. 'I'm not her jailer. She's probably out getting her hair done,' he added.

'Can you call her and find out when she's coming home?'

Nigel grunted and tried Carol's number. He let it ring until her answerphone message kicked in and then he nodded curtly at Geraldine. She noticed he looked worried, and somehow deflated. She couldn't be sure, but she suspected he might have had a row with his wife. She wondered what it could have been about, but there was no point in asking him.

'Please tell Carol to come to the police station first thing in the morning,' she said, since there was nothing more she could do.

'Very well,' he replied, his features taut with suppressed anger. 'Now, if that's all, I'd like you to leave.'

Deep in thought, Geraldine drove home through the rain to where Celia was waiting with a hot dinner in the oven. Grateful that she wasn't going home to an empty house, she thought about Nigel and wondered where Carol had gone.

49

IT HAD TAKEN ALL his forbearance not to break down when the dark-haired detective announced she was going to accompany him home. Not content with that, she had insisted on following him inside his block of flats and coming up in the lift with him, right to his own front door. It was infuriating that the concierge had seen the inspector going upstairs with him. As if that wasn't bad enough, he had recognised that she was a detective. Nigel hoped the concierge would be discreet. He didn't want all his neighbours to suspect him of being under investigation by the police, of all things. He was relieved when the intrusive detective left soon after she had arrived with him. He felt as though a weight had lifted from his shoulders as he watched her walk away and disappear into the lift without anyone else seeing her with him. He didn't want to think about the other reason why he was worried about talking to the police. He had tried to convince himself he had misunderstood what Carol had told him, but there had been nothing ambiguous about her admission.

Once he was convinced the detective had gone, he turned his thoughts to his wife again and began to fret in earnest. Initially he had been relieved she wasn't at home when the police had come looking for her. At least she wouldn't have to answer any more of their questions. That feeling was ousted by concern about what might have happened to her. After what she had done, he supposed she must be feeling desperate. He tried phoning her again, but still there was no answer. He wasn't used to being in the flat by himself. Carol was always there whenever he came home; he had never liked her going out without him. Disconsolately, he went into the kitchen and made himself a cup of tea. When he was at home with Carol, they used loose leaf tea in a pot, but on his own he was satisfied to make do with a tea bag. He wasn't sure it tasted any different, but Carol said tea bags weren't 'properly brewed tea'. Drinking his tea on his own, he felt her absence painfully.

He forced himself to wait until he finished his tea before calling her again. Waiting for her to pick up, he wandered into the bedroom where he noticed a faint vibrating noise that stopped immediately her answerphone message began. He called her mobile again and the buzzing resumed. Following the sound, he found his wife's phone in the drawer of the cabinet on her side of the bed. He swore, discovering she had left her phone at home; he had no way of reaching her. There was nothing to do but wait for her to return. He didn't know where she could be and had no idea what he was going to say to her when she reappeared.

When his phone rang, thinking that Carol was finally contacting him, he hurried to answer it. He wasn't sure whether to be relieved that she was safe or angry with her for leaving her phone at home and failing to let him know where she was.

'Where the hell are you?' he yelled. 'Anything could have happened. Don't you know I've been—'

'Nigel? Is that you?'

His relief was cut short as his sister's voice interrupted him. 'Daisy?'

'What the hell are you on about? Where do you think I am? I'm at home, of course. Where else would I be at this time?'

'Do you know where Carol is?'

'Carol? No. Why? What's up? Nigel, what have you done?'

Nigel drew in a deep shuddering breath. He didn't want his inquisitive sister to know what was going on. Any marital difficulties he and Carol might experience would stay between the two of them. It was no one else's business. As for what Carol had done, that was certainly going to remain a secret from everyone else until he had decided what he was going to do about it. He wasn't even convinced it was true. That was to say, he was struggling to believe it. Even if it was true, Daisy was the last person with whom he would want to share his terrible secret.

'Nothing's up,' he replied quickly. 'Nothing at all. I just wasn't sure what time Carol would be home, that's all.'

Whatever happened, he was determined to conceal his unease from Daisy. He hoped Carol would soon be home and he would look like a fool if he revealed his fears to his sister, even without mentioning her confession. Knowing Daisy, she would probably jeer at him for being hysterical.

'What do you want?' he asked, without thinking. He had no interest in hearing her answer.

Daisy launched into a familiar complaint about her financial difficulties. She had no income of her own and had been relying on her inheritance from her father to pay her outstanding rent and settle her credit card bill. Cut adrift from her expectations, she was growing desperate. Nigel sighed. He was fed up with Daisy constantly begging him for money. Until they had heard their father's will, she had always promised Nigel that she would repay him for his generosity as soon as she inherited half of Martin's considerable fortune.

'It's only temporary,' she had assured him. 'Once Dad's not around, I'll pay you back whatever I owe you. And if I die before Dad, you'll be getting my share as well as yours anyway, so either way you can't lose.'

Her argument had been reasonable, and Nigel had always been willing to bail her out before. Carol had remonstrated that Daisy wasn't their responsibility but, taking care to keep a careful note of whatever he had lent his sister, Nigel had been confident the debt would be repaid once their father died. But now circumstances had changed and it wasn't so straightforward. Daisy was no longer going to inherit a small fortune. At best, it might take the lawyers a while to sort out the mess their father had left. In the meantime, Daisy was broke and she had no prospects, and she already owed him a serious sum of money which he might never recover.

Listening to Daisy's splenetic diatribe about her landlord, her fuel bills and the rising cost of living, Nigel's attention wandered back to his wife.

He interrupted his sister abruptly. 'I need to get off the phone. I have to keep the line open. I'm expecting a call.' With that, he rang off without any further explanation.

His phone rang again almost at once. This time, he checked the screen before picking up and saw that Daisy was calling him again. Furious with her, he ended the call without answering. All his pent-up fear and rage against his sister seemed to explode. He had told Daisy he needed to keep the line clear. She had no business calling him again so soon. Carol was right. He owed his sister nothing. On the contrary, she was indebted to him. Meanwhile, he waited. Daisy didn't call again and he heard nothing from Carol. It occurred to him that she might have met with an accident so he called the local hospital to find out if she had been admitted. They had no record of her. He didn't know what else to do. Another hour went past and he finally began to wonder if Carol had actually left him. It was hard to believe she would simply walk out on him without a word. He had no idea what she was playing at and his perplexity gradually gave way to another fit of anger. He spent a while thinking about what he was going to say to her when she finally turned up, but that didn't help. More time passed and still he heard nothing from his wife.

50

GERALDINE AND CELIA WERE sitting chatting over a glass of red wine. The two little ones were asleep in the study, which had been turned into a makeshift nursery while Celia was sleeping in Tom's room. There was a child's bed in there, ready for when Tom was old enough to be moved out of his cot. The bed was too small for an adult, but Celia assured Geraldine she was happy to sleep there for a few nights. She had only been in York for one night so far, and Geraldine was busy looking for a childminder who was available to take in another infant at short notice. Difficult though it was for Geraldine to countenance trusting another stranger, she knew she had no choice. Celia wouldn't be able to stay and look after Tom indefinitely. Geraldine had arranged to meet one woman who had been recommended and was going to introduce her to Tom the following evening. After that, she would have to make up her mind about whether she wanted to engage her. It was going to be a difficult decision, but one she couldn't postpone indefinitely. She would have preferred to hold out until Ian returned to give herself a little breathing space, but she didn't know how much longer he would be away from home.

On her second glass of wine, Celia began to unwind and talk about her own family. As far as Geraldine was aware, her sister's marriage was reasonably happy. Some years earlier Celia had confessed that her brother-in-law had been unfaithful, but now she seemed confident that her marriage was no longer in trouble. As Celia chattered cheerfully, Geraldine's thoughts drifted to Nigel. His wife had been out when she had taken

Nigel home. What had struck Geraldine was that he had been expecting to find Carol waiting for him. Listening to Celia talk about her husband led Geraldine to speculate about what might be happening to Nigel's marriage, and whether that might have any bearing on the murder investigation.

'How about you?' Celia asked. 'What's happened to Ian? Come on, you can tell me. Where is he at the moment?'

With a rueful smile, Geraldine admitted that she had no idea. 'This is strictly confidential, but he's on an undercover job, so for his protection there's no contact with him and I don't know where he is.' She didn't add that by now everyone at the police station would have guessed he was working on an undercover job. 'It's okay,' she added, seeing Celia's frown. 'He's been away undercover like this before. He's been gone for five nights and he promised me he would be away for less than a week, so he should be home soon. I expect he'll be back tonight.' She smiled in expectation of seeing him again soon.

Although she didn't complain, Celia was tired, having been woken in the night, so she went to bed early. Geraldine sat up reviewing her case notes and had dozed off when she heard the front door close and a voice calling her name. For a moment she thought she was dreaming, then she leapt off the sofa and ran to the kitchen where she found Ian humming to himself as he waited for the kettle to boil.

'Geraldine!' he cried out, turning to her with a broad grin. 'It was so quiet here, I thought you were asleep.'

'Not yet. I wasn't tired,' she fibbed. 'How are you? It's so good to see you.'

Breathless in her happiness, she hugged him and for a moment they held each other close without speaking. At last, Geraldine pulled away and studied his face.

'You look shattered,' she said. 'Tell me all about it.'

'I'll tell you everything, but not right now.' He smiled. 'I haven't slept properly for four nights. Let's have a cup of tea and I'll give you a summary before we turn in. And that'll have to do for now. But first, I'll look in on Tom. I take it from the silence that he's asleep.'

Geraldine gazed at him, wondering how to tell him what had happened with Zoe. She would have preferred to wait until the morning, but she couldn't hide the fact that her sister was staying with them.

'It's not been exactly quiet here,' she said. 'Let's make that tea. I've got something to tell you.'

'It can wait until I've seen Tom. I won't wake him up.'

'No, it can't wait. Celia's staying with us,' she said cautiously. 'She's here looking after Tom, just temporarily.'

'Is Zoe unwell?'

She shook her head. 'Not exactly,' she admitted. 'It's complicated. Let's talk about it tomorrow.'

They took their tea into the living room and sat down. Ian leaned back in his armchair and put his feet up, grinning with pleasure and murmuring that it felt good to be home. Geraldine sipped her tea and said nothing.

'Now,' Ian said, sitting forward with sudden resolution. 'Tell me what's been going on here.'

'It can wait until tomorrow. You're tired.'

'Tell me what's been going on,' Ian repeated doggedly. 'Something happened while I was away. What?'

Geraldine hesitated before telling him Zoe was no longer looking after Tom.

'What? Why? I'm sorry, but this is all a bit sudden. Couldn't you have waited until I got home? Tom's used to Zoe. Do we really want to have to start all over again, looking for a childminder? Surely we should work this out together. What makes you think anyone else will be any better? Better the devil you know and all that.'

'Not this devil. Zoe's no longer available,' Geraldine said grimly.

'What do you mean? Is Tom hurt?'

'Tom's fine, but Zoe's been arrested for kidnapping an infant.'

Ian looked shocked. 'Kidnapping an infant?' he repeated in surprise. And then his eyes widened in horror. 'Not Tom?'

Geraldine spoke quickly. 'Tom's absolutely fine. Everything's been sorted out and Celia's here until we find another childminder. Tom's perfectly safe and well.'

'What happened?'

As concisely as she could, Geraldine explained what had happened. Ian let out an expletive when she described how Tom had vanished and she had been contacted by the kidnapper.

'Why didn't you report it at once?' he asked.

'I was scared. The kidnapper threatened to harm Tom if they suspected I had told anyone.'

'I don't understand. How could you let yourself be intimidated like that? You should have told Binita. You should have reported it officially. What were you thinking?'

'I wasn't sure whether it was a coincidence that Tom was taken while you were away. I was afraid one of our colleagues might have been in contact with Zoe and her family, and as long as it was possible they had let her know you weren't around, I didn't dare talk to anyone. Not even Ariadne. Because as long as I could keep the dialogue going with the kidnapper, there was a chance they wouldn't harm Tom.'

Ian's jaw dropped but he said nothing.

'I had a lead,' Geraldine continued. 'Zoe had disappeared too. It wasn't as though she had come to me in a panic to let me know Tom had been taken, so it seemed she was complicit. I did what I thought was best at the time. But if I hadn't traced him within a day, I was going to report it. I just didn't want to do anything to provoke the kidnapper if I could possibly help it.'

Ian sat staring gravely at his tea, and Geraldine was worried he was furious with her. He would be justified in thinking she had risked Tom's life by wanting to act on her own. She wondered if she had truly been motivated by fear, as she claimed, or by her own ego driving her to try and save Tom by herself. She held her breath as Ian began to speak.

'I should have been here,' he said at last, his voice husky with emotion. 'I should have been here.' He looked up and she saw that he was trembling. 'I won't go away like that again. Never again.'

He reached out to her and she flung herself into his embrace, sobbing. 'It's all right,' she said. 'Everything's all right now.'

Ian held her in his arms. 'I can't begin to imagine what you went through,' he murmured. 'You shouldn't have had to face that ordeal alone. I'm sorry. And I'm sure you did the right thing at the time. You always do. I should have been here.'

'No, no, you did nothing wrong. It was me. It was all my fault. There wasn't an informer. It was me. I told Zoe you were away.'

'Now you've lost me, but you're all right and Tom's all right so let's leave it at that for now and we can talk it through tomorrow when we're not both so shattered.'

Geraldine sighed. 'It's so good to have you home.'

51

NIGEL HAD EXHORTED HER to go to the police and confess what she had done. He had been insistent, but there was no way she was going to give herself up. The more she thought about it, the more gutted she felt that Nigel would even think of suggesting it. When even her own husband hadn't understood her reasons for what she had done, there was no chance the police would view her actions sympathetically. The truth was, she had behaved perfectly reasonably in seeking to thwart a miscarriage of justice. The police were too obsessed with solving crimes and locking people up to see sense, but her husband should have known better. He was a huge disappointment.

It was all clear: Martin's money belonged to Nigel and she was Nigel's wife. All she had done was try to ensure the inheritance went to its rightful heir, not to some jumped-up trollop who had leapt in at the last minute and tried to grab it for herself. What Serena had done should have been illegal. It would have been, if the justice system wasn't so screwed up. Any sensible person would appreciate that Serena had received her just deserts; only Nigel was too small-minded to see that his wife had done the right thing by acting in his best interests. He was being so stupid it was hard to believe she hadn't seen his true nature before this. Once she had seen how weak he was, she knew she couldn't stay with him. She wasn't even sure she could trust him to keep his mouth shut. He had actually advised her to tell the police what she had done, when he must have realised that was bound to result in her going to prison. So much for Nigel taking care of her.

As soon as he left, she ran to the bedroom and packed a small bag with a few necessities. It was difficult to know what to take, but she didn't have time to deliberate. Money, toiletries and clothes were the limit of what she could cram into the bag. It was a pity but she would have to leave her phone behind so she couldn't be traced, but she needed to frighten Nigel into believing she had gone for good. She needed to convince him she was serious about leaving him if he refused to comply. Twenty minutes after Nigel left, she was out of the house, long before he was due to return. Their routine had been disturbed and, for all she knew, he might come home early. She used to think she knew him, but she would never have predicted his dismay when she returned his stolen inheritance to him. Far from showering her with gratitude, he had seemed perturbed. More fool him.

She hurried along the street, looking anxiously around as she went. It began to rain and she took shelter in a café, the kind of place Nigel would never set foot in. She felt safe in there, and if the floor looked grubby and the tables were sticky, at least she was dry and the coffee was relatively cheap. Warming her hands on a chipped mug, she sat down at a corner table, wondering what to do. Everything had been so straightforward until she had spoken to Nigel. It was her own fault. She ought never to have told him what she had done. His reaction had taken her by surprise and, what was worse, she didn't know if she could trust him to be discreet. It had been a mistake to say anything to him. She had always suspected he was spineless, but she hadn't realised quite how contemptible he was. She couldn't believe she had been so deluded as to think he loved her. If that were the case, he would never have suggested she go to the police. He would have defended her liberty to the death.

It was all well and good Nigel saying she wouldn't go to prison if she confessed, but he couldn't be sure of that. No one could. Not even his stooge, the lawyer Higgs. The fact that she had committed a murder meant that prison was almost inevitable if she was convicted. The truth had to remain hidden from everyone. She didn't actually believe Nigel would betray her to the police but if he did, she would deny it and denounce him in turn, claiming he was accusing her to avoid the risk of being blamed himself. It would be no less than he deserved, if he was condemned for a crime his own wife had committed. As for the victim, there was no question in Carol's mind that Serena had got exactly what she deserved. She had no right to barge into their lives, grabbing what was rightfully theirs. She was no better than a thief and Carol had done nothing wrong in fighting for Nigel's inheritance.

For now, she had more pressing concerns to occupy her than whether Serena had deserved to die, or if Nigel would keep his mouth shut. The truth was bound to come out eventually. The police would subject the crime scene to forensic scrutiny and come up with a tiny fleck of dandruff, or a skin cell, that would suggest she had been present when the murder was committed, but they couldn't prove she had killed her. In any case, before that happened she planned to be far away, somewhere she could never be traced. As soon as Nigel got his hands on what was rightfully his, she would take her share and be gone, with or without him. But for tonight, she had to find a place to hide where no one would think of looking for her, so Nigel would believe he had lost her for good. Once he was convinced she was prepared to leave him, Nigel would do anything she wanted.

She wasn't used to roughing it and couldn't possibly countenance sleeping on the street. Fortunately she had possessed the foresight to transfer some of the joint funds into her own private account before she had confided in Nigel. As soon as he discovered the transaction, he might reverse the process. She wondered if she should act quickly and withdraw some of the money, but it was probably too risky to try and access it; the police might already be searching for her. She had been careful enough to take out five hundred pounds in cash. It wasn't much – nothing compared to what she could have had – but it would be enough to get her out of the country if Nigel let her down. She was still fairly confident he would cave in when he realised he risked losing her, but she had to be prepared for the worst. Once she was safely away from the UK, she would assume a different identity and start again. She was still young enough to find another husband, and this time she would target a man who possessed wealth of his own, not someone who was waiting to inherit a fortune. That had been a blunder.

She would need a passport, and while she was making preparations to escape she had to avoid the police. They were bound to question Nigel and she wasn't convinced she could trust him. In the meantime, she had to stay out of sight somewhere he wouldn't expect her to go. She sipped her coffee and considered her options, which were looking bleak. Glancing around anxiously, she noticed a man at the next table watching her. For a moment, his attention made her feel uneasy and then it crossed her mind that she might ask him for help. But if she couldn't rely on her own husband to look out for her, she couldn't risk relying on help from a stranger. She turned away from the man and tried to make it obvious that she was ignoring him. A few moments later he was joined by a woman, and Carol realised she must have been mistaken in thinking he was interested in her. She wasn't sure if she felt relieved or disappointed.

The café wasn't busy, but she couldn't stay there forever. The man behind the counter seemed to be watching her suspiciously, so she pretended to study the menu and went up to the counter for another coffee and a cheese and tomato sandwich. Taking her order back to her table, she realised she was ravenous. The sandwich was dry and tasteless, the bread stale and the cheese slightly hard, but she bolted it down; she hadn't eaten anything since breakfast. As soon as she finished, she regretted having eaten so quickly. The hard bread and cheese were difficult to digest. The coffee was now cool enough to drink and gulping it down helped. She ordered another coffee, but she knew her time there was running out and she would be forced to move on soon.

As day turned to night, the café closed and she had to leave, but she had finally thought of a good hiding place. She hardly expected a warm welcome, but at least no one was going to find her where she was going. Having checked her knife was in her bag and readily accessible, she gathered up her accoutrements and set off, trudging wearily along the street. It was going to take her the best part of an hour to reach her destination on foot, but she didn't dare risk boarding a bus, which was bound to be riddled with security cameras. The police must be looking for her. Nigel had probably already reported her missing. She had been a fool to run off without making up some story to account for her absence to keep him quiet for a few days, but it was too late now. She had left him and there was no going back, even if she wanted to.

52

'I'VE NO IDEA WHAT you're talking about,' Daisy grumbled. 'Can't you talk sense for once in your life?'

As her face twisted in a sour expression, Nigel thought how unpleasant she was. It wasn't just her physical appearance he found disagreeable; her eyes seemed to glitter spitefully. In another era, she might have been condemned to death as a witch. For a fleeting instant he thought that would have served her right. She might be his sister, but she was a bitch. He had done what he could to support her both emotionally and financially, but he couldn't feel anything other than a dull aversion towards her. As children they had squabbled incessantly, their animosity cooling in adulthood to mutual dislike. It was typical of her to misconstrue what he was saying. But it was possible there was a more sinister reason for Daisy's claim that she didn't understand him.

'I'm talking about Carol,' he replied impatiently. 'Haven't you been listening to a word I said? She's not here.'

'So you keep saying. So where is she?'

'That's exactly the point I'm trying to make, if you'd only listen for one moment. I don't know where she is. She's not at home and I don't know where she's gone. I was hoping you might be able to tell me where she is.'

'Me? Why would I know where she is? She's your wife, not mine. If you don't know where she is, what makes you think I would know?' She shook her head, her eyes gleaming peevishly. 'I've no idea where she is and, what's more, I couldn't give a toss.' He wondered if she was being unusually strident in her protest.

With a sigh, Nigel tried to explain the reason for his concern. Carol had not been home when he had returned the previous afternoon. As far as he knew, she had been missing for a day. She had never gone out without telling him where she was going, and she had certainly never stayed out all night before. He was afraid something had happened to her. He had contacted the hospital when she went missing, but they had no record of her.

'Do you really think she's had an accident?' Daisy asked. She didn't sound convinced.

'Are you suggesting you think she's left me?'

'I wouldn't blame her,' she replied spitefully.

'What's that supposed to mean?' he asked, stung by her words.

'Well, she is a lot younger than you and, let's face it, you're not exactly a great catch. Has it really never occurred to you to wonder whether she married you for the money you were expecting to inherit? All I'm saying is that if that *is* why she married you, she must be feeling pretty let down. I mean, it's not as if you have much to offer. Now we're going to have to wait for our inheritance, if we ever get it at all, and in the meantime there won't be any more handouts from our father. Let's face it, he was always pretty generous, wasn't he? Maybe your loving wife is starting to feel a bit impatient. If you ask me—'

'I didn't ask you,' Nigel replied, and abruptly turned and left, slamming her front door as violently as he could on his way out.

He had always found his sister difficult to deal with, not least because, while he disliked her, he also felt sorry for her. Not only had she not married, but as far as he knew she had never even had a boyfriend. Come to that, she had never had much of anything in life. Unable to hold down a job, she had no friends that he knew of and had lived in their father's shadow. When their mother had died, Daisy had appeared to blossom, even while she was mourning. Learning that Serena had moved in with their father, they had both been shocked, but Daisy's feelings had clearly been complicated. She had seemed to resent their father for becoming independent and living his own life without her, and she had scarcely been able to control her hatred for Serena.

Nigel had always known Daisy was envious of his relationship with Carol, but he had never realised quite how vindictive she was. Now, in addition to losing his father and his money, it seemed he might have lost his wife as well. Perhaps none of them had ever really been his to lose. Hearing about his misery, all Daisy could do was make nasty comments and try to aggravate his suffering. He had never felt close to his father and was convinced the old man hadn't cared for him, and while he had been led to expect he would inherit half of his father's fortune, that might have been nothing but wishful thinking on his part. He had genuinely believed his wife loved him, but he supposed it wasn't possible to actually know how another person was feeling. He could have been taken in by an appearance of affection that had never reflected Carol's true feelings towards him. But there was no pretence with Daisy. She had always resented him.

At least his sister had never tried to deceive him with a false show of affection, but she was going to be disappointed if she expected him to help her out again when she couldn't pay her rent. She was still young. It was high time she got off her backside and found herself a job, instead of scrounging off other people. Now their father was no longer around to bail her out, and she had lost Nigel's goodwill, she would have to learn to fend for herself. It was hard to believe she had been stupid enough to alienate him when he was the one close family member she had left, and the only person she could turn to for support now their father was gone. It was equally hard to believe she might have physically harmed Carol but the more he thought about it, the less inclined he was to trust his sister. He wondered if she, and not Carol, had killed Serena.

As he was musing wretchedly to himself, all alone, the doorbell rang. Carol had gone off without making any attempt to contact him. Nevertheless, he resolved to listen to her explanation before losing his temper with her. There might be a perfectly good reason to explain why she had disappeared like that without a word. Taking a deep breath, he went to let her in. Only as he reached the door did it occur to him to wonder why she wasn't using her key, so he was not altogether surprised to discover that it wasn't Carol, but the detective, standing on his doorstep. All at once, his repressed emotions threatened to overwhelm him, and he only controlled his rage with an effort.

'What do you want?' he demanded. Aware that he sounded aggressive, he struggled to sound calm. 'I've already answered your questions, again and again. Isn't it time you accepted that I've told you everything I know? What do you hope to achieve by this constant harassment? I've told you all I can, and there's really nothing more to say.' He drew himself up to his full height, before adding, 'I refuse to speak to you again without my lawyer present to witness the way I'm being hounded in my own home.'

He started to close the door but the detective stopped him.

'I haven't come here to question you, Mr Reed. As you point out, we've already questioned you more than once and you've told us everything you know. It's your wife I'm here to see, not you. I'd like to speak to her, please.'

'You can't. She's not here,' he replied shortly.

'Then can you either tell me where she is or let me know what time you're expecting her home?'

'No, I can't, because I don't know. She's missing.'

The detective's voice betrayed no emotion at all, but her eyes widened almost imperceptibly in her otherwise blank face. 'Missing? Since when?'

Nigel sighed. 'You'd better come in.'

Without another word, he led the dark-haired detective in to the living room.

53

GERALDINE CONCEALED HER ALARM when Nigel told her his wife had gone away without a word of explanation. He was clearly upset and admitted he was afraid she might have had an accident. Geraldine enquired gently whether he thought it possible she had left home deliberately.

His answer was emphatic. 'No. She doesn't go out, not without telling me.'

'I wasn't exploring the possibility that she had just gone out,' Geraldine replied carefully. 'I wondered whether she might have decided to leave and not return.'

'My wife's happy with me,' he replied, his tone slightly aggressive. His narrow chinless face seemed to blend into his thin neck. 'I'd know if there was anything wrong. We're very happy together. She hasn't run away from me.' He raised his head and seemed to reach a decision. 'I don't know where she is, but I think she's run away because she's frightened of someone.'

Geraldine gazed around the gleaming kitchen. A stray plate stood on the white drainer beside the sink, together with an untidy assortment of cutlery, looking out of place in the otherwise pristine environment. It looked like one evening's worth of washing-up. Carol hadn't been missing for long enough for the dirty dishes to accumulate. Under normal circumstances a woman staying away from home for one night would be no cause for alarm, but with two people associated with Nigel's family murdered, Geraldine wanted to look into Carol's disappearance urgently.

Having made up his mind to share his fear, Nigel spoke forcefully. 'You have to find her. With a murderer on the loose, Carol's life could be in danger. What if she's come across something you've failed to discover? She's too trusting. She won't see the consequences of going off on her own until it's too late.' His cold eyes grew bright with apprehension. 'Do you understand what I'm saying? I have to find her and speak to her. She's on her own without me, and that makes her vulnerable. She could say all kinds of things she doesn't really mean. She won't be able to protect herself.'

'Who do you think she needs protection from?'

'Isn't it obvious?' he retorted, anxiety making him brusque. 'I'm worried she may be the killer's next target.'

Geraldine wondered what hidden knowledge lay behind Nigel's suspicion. 'Is there someone in particular you think might pose a threat to your wife?' she asked.

Nigel hesitated before shaking his head. 'No. It's just that after my father was murdered, and then his girlfriend, don't you think it's possible Carol could be next?'

'Surely you're an equally likely target?'

'I can take care of myself,' he replied.

Convinced he was concealing something, Geraldine asked him directly whether he knew who had killed Serena.

'I've no idea.'

'You must have your suspicions or you wouldn't be so concerned about your wife's safety. What is this about, Nigel? If you want me to protect your wife, you have to tell me what you know.'

He shook his head. His assertiveness had evaporated and he stared around the kitchen helplessly, as though it might hold the key to his wife's whereabouts. Geraldine said nothing, although she was convinced Carol's disappearance must be connected to Serena's murder. But Nigel wasn't prepared to share what he knew with the police.

'We're going to need a list of your wife's friends and associates,' Geraldine said at last. 'My colleague will be here in an hour to collect it, or you might prefer to email me.' She handed him her card.

Once again, Nigel shook his head. 'My wife doesn't have friends,' he mumbled. On his lips, the word 'friends' sounded improper. 'That is to say, she's not sociable. Neither of us are. We're serious people. We keep to ourselves. We don't need anyone else.' A faint smile crossed his lips.

'What about her family? Who is she in regular contact with—'

Nigel interrupted her. 'My wife has no family. She has no siblings and her parents died years ago, before I met her. She has no one but me.' It sounded oddly like a boast.

After urging Nigel to let her know if he thought of anyone Carol might have been in contact with, Geraldine left. On returning to the police station, she found Ariadne and discussed what Nigel had told her.

'And he says she has no family or friends of her own,' Geraldine finished. 'No one but him.'

'It sounds as though there's more than a whiff of coercive control in that household,' Ariadne muttered.

'Yes, but who is driving their isolation, I wonder?' Geraldine replied. 'Nigel or Carol?'

'If Carol witnessed Serena's murder, she could have felt threatened by the killer and run off before we had a chance to interview her.'

'He seemed frightened that Carol might betray someone,' Geraldine said.

'Is Nigel really telling us everything? And if not, why is he reluctant to talk, if he really believes his wife's safety is at stake?'

'I think he's protecting someone,' Geraldine replied. 'And that can only be his sister.'

Ariadne agreed. 'His sister, who would have wanted Serena

out of the way. And if Carol knows Daisy killed Serena, then it makes sense that her life could be at risk if Daisy finds out.'

'Assuming Daisy hasn't already silenced her,' Geraldine added grimly. 'We have to find Carol urgently and in the meantime we need to bring Daisy in and find out what she knows about Serena's death and Carol's disappearance. She must know more than she's admitted.'

It struck Geraldine that in refusing to accuse his sister, Nigel had done just that. He wasn't stupid. She wondered whether he had deliberately led the police to suspect Daisy. A full-scale search for Carol was set up and while her picture was being circulated around patrols, stations and airports, Daisy was brought in for questioning.

'What is it now?' she demanded irritably.

'How well did you get on with your sister-in-law?' Geraldine asked.

Daisy scowled. 'Carol? She was all right. Not that we were best friends or anything. We didn't hang out together or see each other more than we had to.'

'So you didn't like her?'

'Not particularly. I mean, she was all right, I suppose, but I wouldn't have chosen to live with her. Still, there you go. Nigel had other ideas. It was nothing to do with me. I know when to mind my own business and keep my trap shut.'

As though to illustrate her point, she crossed her arms over her chest and pressed her lips tightly together in an almost childlike expression.

'Did you ever see your sister-in-law without Nigel?'

'What do you mean? Without Nigel?'

'I wonder if you ever went out together, just the two of you.'

Daisy let out a raucous laugh. 'You can wonder all you like.' She leaned forward in her chair. 'Look, I told you we weren't what you might call friends. We wouldn't have spent more time in each other's company than we had to. And the feeling was mutual.'

'So you were enemies?'

'Your words not mine.'

'You need to tell me what you know without wasting any more time, if you don't want to be prosecuted for obstructing a murder enquiry,' Geraldine said, trusting her threat would have an effect.

Instead of looking cowed, as Geraldine had hoped, Daisy glared at her. 'I don't know what you mean,' she muttered sullenly. 'And if you're going to start threatening me, I won't say another word. I've not been charged with breaking the law and I've had enough of you trying to browbeat me. It's time I was off.' She clambered to her feet.

'Sit down. We haven't finished,' Geraldine snapped.

Grumbling about police intimidation, Daisy subsided on to the chair again. Hoping to catch her off guard, Geraldine asked her directly where Carol was.

'Oh Jesus, not you as well,' Daisy grumbled.

'What do you mean? Who else has asked you that question?'

'First Nigel was on at me and now you. Can't you leave me alone? I don't know where Carol is. Why would I? And what's more, I don't care.'

'What was Nigel on at you about?'

'He wanted me to tell him where Carol was. As if I would know.'

'Why did he ask you?'

Daisy shrugged.

'He thought I might know. Don't ask me why.'

'Why would he think that?'

Daisy glared at her. 'I just told you, there's no point in asking me about what my brother thinks because I've no idea. He gets these stupid ideas in his head. You've met him. He's an idiot.

You don't want to listen to what he says. He was desperate and clutching at straws, that's all. I'm going home now.'

Geraldine could see she wasn't going to get anything more out of Daisy, but she was interested to learn that Nigel suspected his sister knew more than she was admitting. Without any evidence, they couldn't charge Daisy with any crime and would have to let her go.

'We'll have to keep up the pressure,' Geraldine said to Ariadne after Daisy had stomped out of the police station, complaining vociferously about her time being wasted. 'We'll keep questioning her until she cracks.'

But she had the impression Daisy was likely to become more recalcitrant the more they questioned her.

54

THE SEARCH FOR CAROL continued all through the night without success. There was no record of her at any railway station or bus depot, no cab driver had driven her away from York, and no police car patrolling the streets had caught so much as a glimpse of her walking anywhere in the city. As far as they could tell, she hadn't left York, but she seemed to have vanished without trace. Geraldine checked on the reports regularly, even though she would be alerted as soon as there was any sighting of the missing woman. Naomi had a team checking on social media, but Carol appeared to have no presence there. None of her former classmates had seen her since they had left school, and she hadn't gone to university. Geraldine went to speak to Nigel again to see if he could shed any light on what had happened. Geraldine learned that, before her marriage, Carol had worked for several years at an accountancy firm, which was where she and Nigel had met. He had taken her on as a bookkeeper and within six months they were married. Nigel's mother had still been alive at the time and according to him she had welcomed Carol into the family, while his father had been more circumspect.

'So your father was against the marriage?'

'No,' Nigel said. 'He wasn't against it. He just wasn't as excited about it as my mother was. I think she had always been hoping for a big wedding and she was disappointed when we didn't want that. A quiet ceremony and then Carol and I went home for tea by ourselves.'

'Did you have a honeymoon?'

'No. We both thought it would be a waste of money.'

Geraldine wondered if that had been Nigel's idea, and whether Carol had really agreed with him, or if there had been another reason for the low-key wedding. But she was keen to pursue the idea that Martin had disapproved of Carol. If there had been any antagonism between them, there might even be a chance that Carol had plotted with Dorothy to kill him. It seemed unlikely, but anything was possible. Returning to her desk, she looked up details of the wedding. It was an understatement to say Martin and Ann had not been excited about Nigel and Carol's wedding; they hadn't attended. The certificate had been witnessed in the registry office by two of Nigel's colleagues. Geraldine wondered whether Martin and Ann had fallen out with their future daughter-in-law, or whether there had been a good reason for them to object to the marriage. Perhaps they had known something about Carol that the investigating team had not yet come across. She shared her suspicions with Ariadne and Naomi.

'If there was something going on,' she concluded, 'we ought to look into Carol as a possible driving force behind these murders. We shouldn't overlook the fact that she stood to gain if Nigel inherited a fortune.'

They all agreed it would be worth looking into Carol's history. When, after an hour of searching, they had found nothing, they wondered if their suspicions were justified. Carol had no presence on social media, and they could find no record of where she had worked before her arrival at Nigel's firm. This could well have been due to careless record keeping by previous employers but, whether deliberately or not, Carol's past had been effectively concealed. The only information they uncovered was that she had a repeat prescription for a common sleeping pill. This probably had no relevance to the case but, all the same, Geraldine made a note of it. Sleeping pills had uses other than to help a patient struggling with insomnia.

Discussing their frustrating findings, they agreed to tell Dorothy that if it had been Carol's idea to have Martin killed, this would mitigate Dorothy's own sentence. Dorothy had not yet been moved from the police station, so Geraldine made her way to the cell where she was being held.

'Long time since we've seen you down here,' the custody sergeant greeted Geraldine. A burly man with an even temper, he was well suited to his post. Whatever abuse or complaint was thrown at him, he treated every exchange with unwavering good temper. All of Geraldine's colleagues were trained to cope with violent members of the public, but she knew few officers who could handle relentless verbal assaults with such equanimity.

'I'm here to have a word with Dorothy McIntosh,' she said.

'Ah yes, Dorothy,' the sergeant replied. 'Full of the joys of spring, that one. If I had a packet of chips for every time she's grizzled and griped, I'd be one happy man.'

'And overweight, I dare say,' Geraldine smiled.

'Oh bless you, that ship sailed a long time ago,' he said, patting his ample belly with a grin. 'I blame the wife. Her pies would turn an anorexic into a glutton. Still, I'd rather be guzzling than grizzling, eh?' He laughed.

The sergeant accompanied her to the cell where Dorothy was being housed temporarily. Dorothy glanced up dully as the door swung open, but she didn't move when Geraldine walked in. No longer neat, her hair fluttered around her full-cheeked face in a messy mop, and she looked unwashed. Having registered who had joined her in her cell, she lowered her head and remained seated on her bunk, staring down at the floor as though she was still alone.

Geraldine went straight to the point. 'What can you tell me about Martin's daughter-in-law?'

'Who?'

Dorothy looked so dazed, Geraldine wondered whether she

had understood the question, or remembered anything about Martin's daughter-in-law.

'Martin's daughter-in-law, Carol,' she added.

'Carol?'

'Yes, Carol Reed, Martin's daughter-in-law.'

'What about her?'

'What can you tell me about her?'

Dorothy looked at her with a sly expression. 'What do you want to know?'

'I want to know what you can tell me about her.'

'Get me out of here and I'll tell you whatever you want to know.'

'Answer my question and then we'll see.' Observing Dorothy's expression grow distant again, Geraldine added, 'Tell me what you know about her and I'll get you a cup of tea.'

Dorothy nodded and licked her dry lips with the tip of a moist pink tongue in anticipation.

'Go on then,' she muttered. 'What do you want me to say?'

'Tell me about Carol. Everything you know.'

'She's married to Nigel, Martin's son,' she recited as if by rote. 'They've been married for about three years, maybe longer. I don't know exactly. That is, I might have known, but I can't remember.' She looked around with a flash of resentment. 'It's hard to remember anything when you're stuck in here and time stops and starts but mainly it stops.'

Geraldine frowned. 'We're talking about Carol Reed. What else do you know about her?'

'I only met her a couple of times when she came into the office with Nigel. They looked well suited, both equally gloomy. Martin told me his son had always been miserable, right from the day he was born. He was a fractious baby and I guess his wife was the same. They were a dismal couple all right. I don't suppose anyone ever laughed in their home.'

'How well did you know her?'

'Are you still on about Carol?'

'Yes.'

'I wouldn't say I knew her at all, really. I met her in the office a couple of times and that was it. I wasn't invited to the wedding. Martin said it was a wretched affair, just a quick trip to the registry office with no other guests. I suppose Martin and his wife went along, and I suppose their daughter was there, and afterwards nothing. No party, no celebration, not even a sociable cup of tea for the immediate family. They just went home. It sounded like a real damp squib. I did wonder if Martin made it out to be a smaller affair than it really was to make me feel better about not being invited. That would have been typical of him.' She sighed and her eyes glimmered with tears. 'He was always kind to me. But I wasn't put out about not being invited to the wedding. It wasn't like I was family or anything. And I had no time for Nigel.' She stifled a sob. 'I miss Martin.'

Geraldine found it hard to sympathise with her.

'You need to tell me the truth. Were you working with Carol when you killed Martin?'

'What? No! I told you I didn't even know her. What is all this? I've confessed to my crime. Now leave me alone.'

'Where is Carol now?' Geraldine pressed her.

'How should I know? How would you expect me to know anything about what's going on out there, while I'm stuck in here? Now, I've told you everything I know and you promised me a cup of tea. They're starving me in here. It's not even civilised the way they treat me. Wait, wait! What about my tea?'

With Dorothy's cries following her, Geraldine left the custody suite and returned to her desk to write up her notes. Even though Dorothy was a convicted killer, she believed her when she said she knew nothing of Carol's whereabouts. As for her tea, she could expect no special treatment from the police. She would have to wait for her provisions just like everyone else – and none of the others currently being held in the custody suite had been accused of murder.

55

EARLY ON MONDAY MORNING, Daisy was disturbed by the lights coming on outside. She got up to make a cup of tea and was gazing gloomily out of her kitchen window, waiting for the kettle to boil. The drizzle that had been falling overnight had cleared up and a winter sun was barely visible, rising behind a thick bank of cloud. Cursing her neighbour who insisted on installing security devices everywhere, she fetched her coat from the hall and pulled on her wellington boots before stepping outside to chase the foxes out of the back garden.

'Who do you think is going to want to break in here?' she had asked Bella who lived downstairs.

'It's all right for you,' her neighbour had replied. 'You're upstairs and you can hear if someone's coming. You'd have time to call the police if there was an intruder, but if they break in through a downstairs window, I won't know anything about it until I see them right inside my apartment. I wouldn't even hear them coming. I don't sleep in my hearing aids. I wouldn't feel safe without taking at least some precautions, and the police recommend Ring cameras and motion-activated security lights, so that's what we've got. Of course, if you know better than the police about burglar deterrents, do tell me.'

'It's not intruders, it's foxes,' Daisy grumbled. 'They set those lights off all the bloody time and it never scares them away.'

Out in the shared back garden, there was a small patch of lawn in need of attention, bordered by a few spindly trees and some scrubby bushes. Drawing in a deep breath, Daisy stood still, looking around for a moment. There was something deeply depressing about the darkness and the damp cold air. She shivered and was on the point of returning indoors when she noticed the door of the dilapidated shed was ajar.

Grumbling under her breath, she made a mental note to complain to her downstairs neighbour for leaving the shed door open. The tools kept in there were hardly worth anything, being antiquated and rusty, but her neighbour occasionally brought out the discoloured old lawnmower and pushed it up and down. It was probably time to buy a new one, but it still worked and just about kept the grass under control, so there was no point in throwing money away on a replacement. And as long as the mower was in working order, someone might consider it worth nicking. Plus, forgetting for a moment the low risk of theft, foxes or other creatures might decide to take shelter in the shed if the door wasn't secure. Daisy had once found a dead robin that had been accidentally shut in there, so she insisted Bella keep the door locked, but the stupid cow never listened to her.

Daisy tucked her trouser bottoms into her boots and tramped across the wet grass to close the door properly. Reaching the shed, she noticed the flimsy padlock on the door was broken. Something else she would have to harangue her neighbour about. Glancing warily inside, she was startled to see the outline of a figure crouching on the muddy floor.

'Hey!' Daisy yelled in surprise. 'What the hell are you doing in there?'

The figure shifted and in the shadows Daisy made out the shape of a woman. Taking a step closer, she was even more astonished when the figure turned its face towards her and, in the early morning light, she saw that the woman huddled on the filthy floor of the shed was her sister-in-law, Carol.

Daisy repeated her challenge, more stridently this time. 'What the hell do you think you're doing? Come out of there at once!'

'I need somewhere to hide,' Carol replied in a tremulous voice. 'Somewhere the police won't look for me. I came here last night, hoping you might help me but you didn't answer the door. I don't think they'll look for me here.'

Unable to contain her astonishment, Daisy muttered that she must have been asleep when Carol rang the bell, or watching television. 'I don't understand what you're doing here. And I don't know why you think the police would be interested in you anyway,' she added crossly. She was tempted to add that she couldn't imagine why anyone would be interested in her sister-in-law. 'You can't stay there. You need to leave. Now. I can't help you. Even if I could, why would I?' she added under her breath.

Using the handle of the lawnmower for support, Carol pulled herself to her feet with an effort and shook her head. 'Listen, you don't understand. You have to help me. I have to stay hidden. It's not safe for me out there.' She clutched at the handle of the rusty mower and stood quivering in the shed. 'You have to help me.' She sounded frantic.

Daisy grunted. She had always thought her sister-in-law was deranged. It made no sense that a young woman would agree to marry her brother, of all people.

'Why can't Nigel help you?' Daisy replied coldly.

'If I went anywhere near Nigel, the police would pick me up straightaway.'

'Why are the police looking for you?' Daisy asked, curiosity overcoming her irritation.

Carol shook her head again. 'I don't know. I can't say. They think – they seem to think I've done something dreadful.'

'And have you?' Daisy asked. Watching Carol's discomfort, she was beginning to enjoy herself. 'Oh, Carol, what have you done?'

'Nothing! I swear I haven't done anything.'

'Then you have nothing to be afraid of.' Daisy grinned, registering Carol's desperation with intense satisfaction.

Carol whimpered. 'No, no, you don't understand. It's all a mistake. I've done nothing wrong.'

'Well, if you've done nothing wrong, no one will be able to prove anything against you, will they?' Daisy leaned against the doorframe of the shed, watching Carol. 'What do they think you've done?'

'They think I killed Serena,' Carol said in a low voice. 'Even Nigel thinks I did it. So, you see, I can't go to him. You have to help me hide, just until I can make arrangements to get away. Will you help me?'

Daisy contemplated her sister-in-law thoughtfully. 'I suppose you'd better come inside,' she said at last. 'You can't stay out here. You'll freeze to death. Besides, my neighbour might come out here and spot you and then all hell will break loose.'

With a groan of relief, Carol shuffled stiffly out of the shed. Shivering, she followed Daisy across the grass, which was still damp from the earlier rain, and into the house. Once indoors, they hurriedly removed their outer clothes and wet shoes and Daisy offered to make tea. Carol seized on the suggestion with the eagerness of one who had been waiting for a cup of tea for hours, as perhaps she had. While Daisy was busily occupied making the tea, Carol went to the toilet. As soon as she left the room, Daisy took out her phone. Hitting the emergency button, she hung on impatiently for an answer, watching the kitchen door as she waited. Before she had time to give her location or even ask for help, she heard footsteps approach and barely had time to pull the fridge open before Carol walked into the kitchen.

'I need to pop to the shop,' Daisy said. 'We're out of milk. I won't be long. Do you need anything?'

Carol shook her head energetically.

'Well, if you're sure. You wait here. You'll be perfectly safe.' Daisy paused, all smiles. 'In fact, why don't you stay here until you get yourself sorted? It's – it's lonely living here by myself and I'd appreciate some company, at least for a day or two.' She paused, wondering if she was sounding too eager. 'Now, I'll just pop out for that milk.'

'I don't think so,' Carol said, moving to stand in front of the kitchen door.

Daisy frowned. 'What are you doing? I need to get some milk. For the tea.'

'No, you don't. I can see you've got nearly a whole bottle of milk in there.'

Daisy glanced over her shoulder and cursed herself for not shutting the door properly and leaving it to swing open silently behind her.

'Oh yes, but I wanted to get some biscuits,' she faltered.

'Why did you say milk then?'

To Daisy's shock, Carol pulled out a knife. Brandishing it in front of her, she glared at Daisy who stumbled backwards. Carol snapped at her to go in the living room and sit down.

'I don't understand,' Daisy stammered. 'What's got into you?'

Muttering that she needed time to think, Carol repeated her command that Daisy go in the other room and sit down. Not only was Carol manifestly deranged, she was also potentially violent – not a safe combination. Daisy considered her options. Her most pressing need was to get away from there as quickly as possible. She wondered fleetingly whether Nigel knew his wife was insane, but this was no time for speculation. She was being threatened at knife point in her own home and she had to act quickly. Anger seemed to course through her at this outrageous invasion of her privacy. Howling with rage, she rushed at her crazy sister-in-law. Taken by surprise, Carol fell back a step, allowing Daisy to barge past her into the hall. If her front door hadn't been bolted, Daisy might have stood a chance. As her fingers clutched frenziedly at the bolt, she heard, rather than felt, a rending. For a second, she was too stunned to react. Then a jolt of pain struck her and she staggered and nearly fell.

Stunned, she watched a trickle of blood flow from a wound in her upper arm. With a snort of irritation, Carol propelled her into the sitting room and on to a chair. Daisy sat there, feeling dazed from shock or loss of blood. Possibly both. Clutching her injured arm, she fell back on the chair in a state of near collapse. Mesmerised, she watched bright blood ooze between her fingers and drip on to her trousers where a wet patch glistened darkly. The pain was intolerable.

'I'm bleeding,' she blurted out, struggling to believe what was happening. But there could be no doubt about the pain which was so sharp she found it difficult to breathe. 'You stabbed me.'

'Stop fussing. It's only a scratch. Now shut up. I need to think.' Carol stood over her, scowling and waving the knife in Daisy's face. 'Give me your passport.'

'What?'

'Your passport. I need your passport and your money.'

The room began to spin and Daisy thought she might pass out. 'I need help,' she murmured. 'You have to get me to a doctor.'

'Not everything is about you,' Carol snapped. 'Where's your passport?'

'It's in my bedroom, in one of the drawers.'

Carol hesitated. 'Go and get it. Now!'

Daisy clambered to her feet and staggered from the room with Carol following her.

'I'll be right behind you,' Carol said, pointing the knife at Daisy. 'Don't try to slip away, or you know what will happen.' She waved her weapon in front of Daisy's face. 'Come on, I haven't got all day.'

Praying that she would somehow survive this, Daisy began to haul herself along the corridor to her bedroom. If she could only reach her phone and touch the emergency key, she might be saved, but Carol was right at her heels.

56

By EARLY MONDAY MORNING, it was beginning to look as though someone must be hiding Carol. Many man hours had been dedicated to studying CCTV on buses and trains in and around the city, searching for a sighting, and taxi companies had been questioned, but without any result. The monitoring continued, but there was no sign of her. Frustrated by the failure of the search, Geraldine went to question Nigel again, hoping he might have at least an inkling about where his wife might be. He wasn't at home, so she drove to the head office of Reed Construction, which Martin had founded and developed into a thriving company. It would now belong to Nigel and Daisy, following Serena's brief term of ownership. The head office was located in a modern block of brick and glass, situated on the outskirts of York, just north of Huntington. A large car park served Reed Construction and several other office buildings which surrounded it on three sides, and Geraldine had no trouble finding a space.

The interior of the building looked well maintained and a smartly turned-out receptionist greeted Geraldine as she stepped through the shiny glass and chrome doors. As soon as she learned who Geraldine was, the young woman ushered her into an inner office, where Nigel was slumped behind a desk. Staring dully at a computer screen, he barely glanced up when she entered the room. Not until Geraldine addressed him did he raise bloodshot eyes. Smiling thinly, he invited her to take a seat. At first sight his office was a curious mixture of order and clutter. A bank of filing cabinets stood along one side of the room, each drawer neatly labelled, while box files were lined up in a perfectly even row on shelves on another wall. Yet in front of a large window, the desk was littered with papers and files, an oasis of chaos in an otherwise tidy environment.

Fleetingly animated by her arrival, Nigel asked whether Carol had been found. On hearing Geraldine's reply, his shoulders drooped and he lowered his head with a sigh.

'Nigel, where do you think Carol might be?'

'I told you,' he muttered, 'I don't know. You can ask me as many times as you like, for as long as you like, but I've no idea where she is. Believe me, I'm more eager to find her than you are.'

'Think carefully, Nigel. Are you absolutely certain you don't know where she might be?'

Once again, he insisted in a flat voice that he had no idea where his wife could be. His pale face was even more ashen than usual, and he was studiously giving nothing away, but he avoided meeting her eye and once again Geraldine was convinced he knew more than he was admitting.

'She's an adult,' he said, staring at his computer screen. 'She'll turn up. If she hadn't forgotten to take her phone with her, she would have been in touch before now. I'm sure there's nothing to worry about. She just went away for the weekend, that's all. She'll come back when she's ready. I just have to wait.' He seemed to be talking to himself.

Geraldine didn't suggest that Carol might have left her phone at home to ensure she couldn't be traced.

'You're saying you think there's nothing to worry about, but you reported her missing,' Geraldine reminded him.

Nigel fidgeted uncomfortably in his chair but he persisted in saying that he had no idea where Carol was and repeated that he was sure she would return soon.

'It's in your wife's interests that we find her,' Geraldine said. 'Before anyone else can,' she added pointedly.

Nigel flinched and shook his head, but he refused to speak again. There was nothing Geraldine could say to persuade him to admit what he knew, or suspected, so she questioned him again about his movements on the night Serena was murdered.

'I told you, I was at home with my wife,' he said, but this time he didn't sound sure.

'Is it absolutely impossible she could have left the house?'

Nigel cleared his throat nervously before admitting that he had been sleeping so soundly, he wouldn't have known if she had gone out.

'So you're saying your wife could have gone out that night?'

He shrugged and was silent, his face a mask of indecision.

'Nigel, if there's anything you're not telling me, now's the time to come clean. Your wife's life might depend on you admitting whatever you know.'

But Nigel merely shook his head and repeated that, as far as he knew, his wife had been at home with him all night when Serena was killed, and he had no idea where she could be. Frustrated, Geraldine left, more convinced than ever he was keeping something from her.

Back at the police station, she discussed what he had said with Ariadne.

'Carol's running-off suggests she's guilty of something,' Geraldine concluded thoughtfully. 'And now there's a question mark over her alibi on the nights both murders were committed. Nigel said he's been sleeping well, and we know Carol was prescribed sleeping pills by her doctor. Possibly she drugged Nigel without his knowledge.'

'What for? Surely you don't think she killed Serena?'

'Why else would she go into hiding?'

'She could be scared the killer might attack her next?'

Geraldine shrugged. 'Whatever the reason for her disappearance, we need to find her. Don't forget that with

Serena's death Martin's fortune reverts to Nigel and Daisy, so Carol had a strong motive for getting rid of her.'

'True. We were busy looking into Nigel and Daisy, but Carol's going to benefit from Serena's death as well.'

A young constable interrupted their discussion. 'We received an emergency call without any message.'

'Probably a mistake,' Ariadne said, dismissing the constable.

'We're busy right now,' Geraldine added, frowning. 'Can't the switchboard trace the caller and deal with it?'

'They couldn't trace it, the caller rang off too quickly. But not before she muttered a name, Daisy Reed.'

Geraldine was instantly alert. 'Where is she? What did she want?'

'She just phoned but left no message, apart from the name.'

'Where was the call made?'

'We couldn't track it. The caller rang off almost immediately.'

'Rang off or was interrupted?' Geraldine said.

Taking Ariadne and the young constable Sam Cullen with her, Geraldine drove straight to Daisy's home off the Holgate Road and rang both bells. No one came to the door. Remembering that the woman living downstairs was deaf, before trying the bell again, Geraldine hurried around the house to set up a watch on the back door. The wooden side gate was locked, but with Sam's help she kicked it, hard. After a few attempts, the wood splintered around the lock and the gate swung open. If Daisy had thought better of telling the police what she knew, they would make sure she didn't leave the house without speaking to them. There was no response from inside the house when they banged on the back door. Leaving Sam guarding the door, Geraldine returned to the front of the property. As she made her way quietly along the side of the house, she noticed one of the upstairs windows wasn't properly shut and decided to mention it to Ariadne. Perhaps between the two of them, with Sam's help, they could enter the house unseen and confront Daisy.

But when she reached the front entrance, there was no sign of Ariadne.

Geraldine tried her colleague's phone, but Ariadne didn't respond. Struggling to control her alarm, Geraldine rang the bell again and this time a voice shouted at her from the other side of the door.

'Go away! You need to go away, now! Go!'

Geraldine didn't recognise the voice. There was the sound of scuffling and then Ariadne called out. 'Do what she says. She's got a—' Her words were cut off abruptly.

'Ariadne! Are you all right?' There was no answer. 'Ariadne?'

A second voice shrieked out suddenly. It could have been Daisy. 'Go away! Do what she says! She's used—' Once again, the speaker was abruptly silenced.

'She's got a knife!' Ariadne shouted and was again cut off.

Geraldine drew in a breath and sprinted to the street, already on the phone summoning urgent back-up, with an armed response team. Whatever else happened, she had to focus all her energy on rescuing Ariadne, if it wasn't already too late. She tried not to think that she had brought Ariadne to the house and was responsible for whatever happened to her.

57

WAITING FOR THE ARMED response team, Geraldine ran silently round to the back door to inform Sam of the latest developments. Despite his training, his face fell when he heard that Ariadne was trapped in the house with a woman who was armed with a knife.

'What can we do?' he asked, poised to run.

'We wait.'

'We can't just stand here and do nothing,' he protested, raising his voice in dismay.

'There's nothing we *can* do until back-up arrives,' she replied in a whisper. 'I've put in an urgent request for an armed response team and a negotiator. Don't worry, we'll get Ariadne out of there.' She wished she was feeling as confident as she sounded. 'You wait here, and no heroics if Carol tries to escape this way. Remember, she has a weapon and may have killed before.'

Sam nodded uncertainly.

'That's an order, Sam,' she said sharply, trying to ignore the accusation in his eyes. 'Don't even think of disobeying.'

With that, she ran back to the front of the house. Inside, all was silent. Knowing Ariadne was in there, the waiting was unbearable. Suddenly, she could bear it no longer and hurried to the window she had noticed earlier. It was quite high off the ground but she thought it was large enough for her to wriggle through. She asked Sam to help her and he nodded, eager to assist.

'I can reach it,' he said.

'No,' she replied. 'I sent Ariadne in there, it's on me to help her. You wait for the armed response team. They'll be here soon. I just want to check out who's in there,' she added, not quite truthfully. 'And you might not fit through it,' she added, truthfully this time. 'Give me a leg up. That's an order.'

Sam hesitated before making a stirrup of his hands, so she could climb up to the window.

'I should be going in there,' he muttered. 'I could overpower her easily.'

'No one's going to try and overpower a knife-wielding killer,' Geraldine said. 'I intend to see what's happening in there so I can report the details back to the armed response team.' She stared up at the window, judging its height. 'You stay here so you can help me down again.'

'Wouldn't it be better to wait for the armed response team?' Sam asked.

Geraldine frowned at him. 'When I need your advice, I'll ask for it,' she replied, more abruptly than she had intended, partly because she suspected he was right and she was being foolhardy. 'I'm only going to sneak inside, take a quick look at who's there and where they're positioned, and then leave before anyone spots me. It may sound like a rash strategy, but I'm not going to take any risks. I'll make sure no one sees me.'

Before Sam could challenge her about taking risks, she stepped carefully on to his interlaced hands and hoisted herself swiftly up to the bottom of the window frame until she could peer over the edge. She couldn't see anyone inside. With a huge effort, she heaved herself silently up and over the sill. Clutching both sides of the frame, she manoeuvred one leg over the window sill and dropped gently into the room. It was nearly dark inside, but she could see enough to know that the room was empty. So far she was safe. She was in what looked like a small dining room. Silently she moved towards the door. As she stood perfectly still, scarcely daring to breathe, she thought she heard voices. Quickly she stole across the room towards the door. Reaching it, she peered out into a narrow hallway. There were three doors leading off it and she heard a woman talking. The sound seemed to be coming from the door that was nearest to her. Holding her breath, she crept into the hall and made her way closer to the door.

'You know you'll never get away with killing a police officer,' Ariadne was saying.

Geraldine nearly cried out on hearing that her friend was still alive.

'Shut up,' Carol barked. 'One more word out of you and she dies.'

It must have been Daisy who let out a cry of fear. There was a retort that sounded like a slap. Geraldine started and pressed her hand to her lips. Having discovered where Carol was keeping Ariadne captive, it was time for her to withdraw but as she turned away, someone screamed. Geraldine ran to the door and flung it open.

'Ariadne!' she yelled and froze at the sight of the tableau in front of her.

Carol was standing with her back to the door, waving a large knife. Ariadne was seated on the other side of the room, with Daisy on the floor beside her, apparently unconscious. Startled, Carol spun round. The instant she turned towards the door, Ariadne leapt at her and grabbed her arm just as she lunged forwards to thrust the knife at Geraldine. The blade missed her by a few centimetres. Before Carol had time to recover her balance, Geraldine punched her in the face, knocking her to the floor, and sending the knife skittering across the carpet. It came to rest beside Daisy's inert figure.

'Get the knife,' Geraldine panted as she snapped handcuffs on Carol.

'If it was a gun, you'd be dead,' Carol hissed.

Ariadne seized the knife, and Geraldine darted over to Daisy to check whether she was still alive.

'Geraldine, what are you doing here?' Ariadne asked, her voice shaking so much she could scarcely force the words out.

Before Geraldine could respond, a loud voice reached them from the street.

'We have the house surrounded,' it announced calmly. 'Come out with your hands in the air.'

'She's still alive,' Geraldine said and pulled out her phone. Having identified herself, she reported that the situation was under control. 'We have a civilian here who requires urgent medical attention. I repeat, a civilian has been stabbed and needs urgent attention.'

She ran to open the front door and within a minute paramedics and armed officers charged into the house. They had arrived more quickly than Geraldine would have thought possible. She moved aside as Daisy was carried out on a stretcher, seriously injured but alive.

'When can we question her?' she asked one of the medical team as they passed her.

'Not now,' the paramedic replied and turned away.

58

CAROL'S EYES GLITTERED COLDLY at Geraldine across the table in the interview room.

Geraldine met her gaze steadily. 'You stabbed Daisy,' she began.

'What are you talking about? You can't say that. Is this being recorded?' Carol spluttered, gazing around the room. 'That's a lie. It's an outright lie.' She tapped her fingers nervously on the table as she spoke, the convulsive movements at odds with her decisive words. 'Did you see me stab anyone?' Her usually neat hair was a mess and without make-up her features looked stronger.

Geraldine spoke softly. 'You know perfectly well I'm telling the truth. You can't pretend otherwise.'

'You can accuse me all you like, but you won't get me to confess to something I didn't do.'

Geraldine raised her eyebrows sceptically. 'There's no point in denying it. My colleague was in the room with you when you assaulted Daisy. I'm referring to my colleague who you took hostage and threatened with that same knife, the one you tried to stab me with.' She gestured towards Ariadne. 'There's no point in pretending none of it happened.'

'I saw you stab Daisy,' Ariadne agreed evenly. 'And I witnessed your attempt to stab my colleague.'

'That's a lie,' Carol blurted out frantically. 'You're both lying. You've got your story neatly together but just because you're both lying doesn't make it true. You think you can use me to wrap up your murder enquiry. Do you really think I'll be that easy to frame? Do you take me for an idiot? I can see what you're trying to do, and it's not going to work.'

'It's pointless to deny you stabbed Daisy and tried to stab me,' Geraldine repeated. 'That's not even a discussion. And when Daisy recovers, she'll remember what happened. Now, we need you to confess you shot Martin.'

Carol looked startled and then she laughed mirthlessly. 'So you think you can pin that one on me as well, even though you know it wasn't me? I know Dorothy confessed she shot him when he sacked her. After all her years working for him, she ended up with nothing. We all know that's why she shot him. It had nothing to do with me. As for what happened this morning, I was acting in self-defence.' She leaned back in her chair and crossed her arms in an attempt to look confident. 'I thought Daisy was going to attack me. And then I mistook both of you for intruders. You broke in. A woman is allowed to defend herself.'

'Let's talk about Martin,' Geraldine replied. 'You just told us Dorothy killed him.'

'She confessed to it, didn't she? You can't argue with that.'

'Where did Dorothy get hold of a gun?'

Geraldine placed the gun on the table, inside its evidence bag. Carol's eyes widened in alarm, before she fiercely denied having seen the gun before. Geraldine was convinced she was lying. Dorothy had confessed to killing Martin, but Geraldine was sure Carol had been involved. She took a break to allow Carol to call her husband who agreed to arrange for Mr Higgs to come and represent her. While they were waiting for the lawyer to arrive, Geraldine went to talk to Dorothy to find out whether she could shed any further light on the circumstances surrounding Martin's death. This time, Geraldine was determined to persuade Dorothy to tell her everything that had happened.

'Dorothy,' she said urgently, 'if you lied to the police, I'm offering you a chance to put the record straight. Do you want to make any changes to your statement?'

Dorothy's eyebrows rose in astonishment. 'Lie? What are you talking about? I haven't lied to you about anything. You arrested me and I confessed, didn't I? So that's that. Everything I told you was true. Every word. It was a terrible thing I did. If I could turn the clock back—'

She spoke so fervently, it was hard to doubt her. Geraldine tried asking her directly why she had confessed to a crime she hadn't committed, but Dorothy shook her head. She looked genuinely surprised.

'I don't understand,' she wailed. 'First you tried to pin Serena's murder on me, and now you're saying I didn't kill Martin after all. I don't understand what you're playing at and now I'd like you to leave me alone, please. I can't take this any more.'

'Tell me again what happened on the night Martin died,' Geraldine persisted calmly. 'And this time, start right at the beginning. How did you come to be on the river bank that night?'

Dorothy frowned. 'I was so angry about the way he had treated me after everything I'd done for him.' She began to mutter about the twenty years she had devoted to Martin, but Geraldine steered her back to the night of his death. 'I followed them to the river,' Dorothy said.

'Them?' Geraldine repeated, picking up on how Dorothy worded her response. 'Who was "them"?'

'Martin and a woman. I saw them leave his house and get into his car.'

Dorothy had given her statement earlier, only until now she had never mentioned seeing another woman with Martin on the night he was killed.

Geraldine hesitated, uncertain whether to believe this new claim. 'Why didn't you tell us this before?' she asked.

Dorothy hung her head. 'I didn't want anyone to know I'd been watching his house,' she mumbled.

Even though she had confessed to killing Martin, Dorothy was embarrassed to admit she had been spying on him.

'I'd been sitting outside his house, watching, and saw her go inside.'

'Tell me about the woman you saw with Martin that night. Who was she?'

Dorothy shook her head. 'I couldn't see much. It was too dark. But it must have been Serena. Who else could it have been? They drove off together in his car. I could see it was him. I'd have known him anywhere.' She sighed softly.

'The woman, the one you saw leaving his house with him. What can you remember about her?'

Dorothy shrugged. 'What more can I tell you? I assumed it was Serena. But there was something odd about it, actually. I thought so at the time.'

'What was odd?'

'The woman was sitting in the back of the car when they drove off. I wondered about that when I saw them getting in the car, but I never saw who she was. Her hood was up and her face and hair were hidden. I'm sorry, but I can't tell you who she was. I shouldn't have mentioned it. What does it matter? He's dead and nothing can bring him back now.' She began to cry.

'Tell me again how he died. Was the other woman there?'

'No, no, she'd gone. It was just me and Martin beside the river, and I killed him.'

Geraldine urged her to think carefully and try to remember more about what she had seen but Dorothy shook her head and refused to say another word. Frustrated, Geraldine sent her back to her cell. Something about Dorothy's account didn't add up, but Geraldine couldn't work out what it was. If she could spot the missing piece of the puzzle, she would solve the case, but the answer remained tantalisingly out of reach. Serena was the key; Serena, who could no longer tell them what had happened that night.

59

A GAUNT MR HIGGS looked glumly at Geraldine, but his expression gave nothing away. She wondered what he had discussed with his client.

'My client is accused of murder,' he said severely. 'Can you name the victim?'

'We have witnesses to the stabbing of Daisy Reed—' Geraldine began, but the lawyer raised his hand for silence and interrupted her.

'You have witnesses that my client brandished a knife at Daisy. Her intention was to intimidate her in the course of an argument during which my client felt threatened. Unfortunately my client caught Daisy, although she has made it clear the injury was inflicted by accident. My client never intended to cause any injury. But whatever injury was sustained, there was no murder. Daisy is alive and recovering in hospital. Carol was frightened and lost control of the weapon, and that was her only crime.'

'So her defence for stabbing Daisy is that it was an accident?' Geraldine repeated, shaking her head at the audacity of the claim. 'That doesn't explain what Carol was doing with a dangerous weapon.'

'According to my client, she found the knife in Daisy's residence. No one can be convicted for keeping a knife in their kitchen, to be used when cooking.' He raised one eyebrow and looked shrewdly at Geraldine. 'You seem to forget that this was a kitchen knife that was found in Daisy's house. Surely that is reasonably conclusive?'

Carol nodded her head vehemently, appearing to suppress a grin.

'It was Carol's knife,' Geraldine said firmly, 'and she's the only person who has used it.'

'It was never her knife.' The lawyer leaned forward. 'There was a scuffle during which Carol took the knife from Daisy. As I explained, my client was acting in self-defence. I think we can dismiss any case against her over what was clearly an accident. You can question Daisy about keeping a knife in her kitchen, but that is hardly going to get you anywhere. And now, I suggest you allow my client to go home.'

'Let's leave the attack on Daisy for now,' Geraldine said. 'Forensics confirmed that this gun was used to kill Martin Reed.' She turned to Carol and spoke softly. 'It would be understandable if you were responsible for shooting your father-in-law. You suspected he was going to cut his children out of his will, which meant you stood to lose all of the fortune you had been led to expect Nigel would inherit. That must have made you very angry.'

'So now I'm accused of killing Martin?' Carol asked, her eyes alight with fury. 'If you can't convict me of murdering someone who's still alive, you'll find another trumped-up murder charge to pin on me.' She let out a bitter laugh and turned to her lawyer. 'This is all nonsense. They can't just invent a crime to accuse me of and make the charge stick, can they? Not when they know I've got an alibi for the time my father-in-law was murdered.'

The lawyer gazed evenly at Geraldine and insisted they release Carol. Given that someone else had already confessed to shooting Martin, the lawyer pointed out it was unacceptable to keep Carol in custody on suspicion of committing that same crime, regardless of whether or not she had an alibi. When Geraldine said the police needed more time to investigate what had happened, Carol muttered an expletive and demanded to be released. Her eyes glowed darkly and she scowled, grumbling crossly at her lawyer.

'I'm afraid that's out of my control,' Mr Higgs replied, 'but don't fret. We'll have you out of here in no time. In a day or so, all this will just be an unpleasant memory.'

Carol was taken back to her cell. 'This is blatant injustice,' she called out over her shoulder as she was led away. 'I'll get you for this.'

Geraldine shrugged and went to find Ariadne. 'I know Carol was shocked that we found the gun. Either Dorothy and Carol used the same gun, or Carol shot Martin,' she said.

'But if Carol shot him, then why did Dorothy claim she killed Martin?' Ariadne asked.

'Who could she have been protecting? Unless she was mistaken,' Geraldine murmured.

'What do you mean? Who was mistaken, and about what?'

Geraldine jumped to her feet. 'Dorothy said she saw Martin down by the river with another woman. What if it wasn't Dorothy who shot him after all?'

'But she confessed to the murder.'

'She confessed to killing him, yes, but not to shooting him.'

'It comes to the same thing, doesn't it, because we know he was shot.'

'Maybe Dorothy only *thought* she had killed him. What if he had already been shot when she found him?' Geraldine explained her theory. 'Carol shot Martin, heard Dorothy approach and fled, leaving Martin lying dead on the river bank. Not knowing what had happened, Dorothy found him lying there, perhaps drunk, pushed his body into the river and then ran off. Then she came to the conclusion that she had killed him, not realising he was already dead when she found him.'

Geraldine shared her theory with Binita who agreed that it might be correct. They just had to prove it. While Geraldine interviewed Dorothy again, Ariadne arranged a search of Nigel's house. He was reluctant to let her in, but changed his mind when she threatened to return with a search warrant. Meanwhile,

Dorothy was describing how she had been watching Martin and his unidentified companion drive down to the river. She left her own car near Martin's and followed them on foot. In her anger, she had called out to him, but neither he nor his companion seemed to have heard her. By the time Dorothy reached them, the woman had disappeared and Martin was lying on the bank in what she thought was a drunken stupor. In a fit of rage, she had shoved him and he had slid, unresisting, into the water.

'I couldn't believe what I'd done but I was too scared to stay. I was afraid the other woman would see me. The next morning I went back. I thought he might still be alive and in need of help, but by the time I arrived, the police were there and I didn't dare go too close. Then I learned it was too late to save him. He was dead and I killed him.' She broke down in tears. 'I killed him.'

Geraldine leaned forward and spoke very gently. 'You may be charged with attempted murder, but you didn't kill anyone. Are you listening to me? You didn't kill Martin.'

Dorothy looked up, her face wet with tears. 'What do you mean?' she stammered.

'You didn't kill Martin because he was already dead when you found him lying beside the river. Martin didn't drown. He was shot.'

'Shot?' Dorothy repeated wonderingly. 'Shot? What do you mean?'

With a sigh, Geraldine told Dorothy what had happened. Geraldine watched her closely. Dorothy couldn't have looked more taken aback if Geraldine had told her Martin had been carried away in an alien spaceship.

'Shot?' she repeated again. 'You mean with a gun?'

Geraldine waited to hear what Dorothy would say next. Recovering from her astonishment, Dorothy shook her head. 'Why would you think I shot him?'

'Because we know Martin was shot and you confessed to killing him,' Geraldine replied.

'But I didn't shoot him,' Dorothy said. 'I found him lying on the river bank and in a moment of madness I pushed him in. I heard the splash of him hitting the water and ran away leaving him to sink or swim, just as he had abandoned me.' She shuddered. 'In that moment, I thought it served him right. I'm not proud of what I did, or of running away and leaving him to drown, but I was scared. And the next day, I heard that he was dead. Murdered. And it was my fault.' She burst into tears. 'If I had rescued him when he was lying there drunk, if I had helped him home or gone for help, called for an ambulance, anything, he would be alive now.'

Geraldine nodded, realising how the confusion had arisen. 'You thought he was unconscious when you pushed him in the river, but he was already dead.'

Dorothy raised her tear-stained face and stared at Geraldine. 'Who shot him?'

60

HAVING ESTABLISHED THAT DOROTHY had not shot Martin, the question of who had shot him remained unanswered. Geraldine scanned through her notes and her eye was caught by a comment Nigel had made, almost in passing.

'Actually, since my father died,' he had said, 'I've been sleeping better than ever.'

She called him to check whether he was on any medication, mentioning that it was common for the bereaved to be prescribed drugs to help them through a difficult time. It had occurred to her that if Nigel was taking sleeping pills, he might have given some to Carol to ensure she wouldn't wake up when he slipped out to kill Serena. Nigel was adamant that he had felt no need to request anything from his doctor since his father's tragic death, adding with a touch of arrogance that he was on no medication at all. He was so insistent that Geraldine decided to pay a visit to his doctor to find out whether he was actually telling her the truth.

The doctor's surgery was not far from the police station but she decided to drive there as she was impatient to find out whether her theory might be possible. She parked right outside, wondering how members of the public ever managed to park in the town, where every street had yellow lines and the car parks were often full. There were not many perks to being a police officer. She worked long hours and was permanently stressed and under pressure, but at least she had no trouble from parking wardens.

It took ten minutes for her to gain access to Dr Cotton, and even then the receptionist was reluctant to let her go in ahead of patients who were waiting to see him. A small round-shouldered man, the GP peered at her anxiously through rimless glasses and was reticent about divulging any details about his patients. More time elapsed while she persuaded him it was not a good idea to withhold evidence pertinent to a murder investigation. Only by threatening to have him summoned to court as a witness, was she able to persuade him that discreet cooperation at this stage of the process was the most prudent course of action.

After Geraldine had wasted twenty minutes following her hunch, the doctor confirmed that Nigel Reed had not been prescribed any medication following his father's death. However, police enquiries had already established that Carol was prescribed sleeping pills. Nigel hadn't taken steps to make sure Carol would sleep well, but the reverse might be true. Nigel had told her he had been sleeping better than ever since his father's death. With a shock, she wondered how she could have missed the implication of his admission.

'But we know you prescribed sleeping pills to Carol Reed,' she said, struggling to conceal her sudden excitement.

With a slight incline of his head, the doctor responded without speaking. 'Now, would you please leave? I have patients waiting,' he added.

Geraldine was already on her feet. She had learned what she needed to know. Driving straight back to the police station, she went to speak to Binita to request an urgent search warrant for Nigel and Carol's flat. Binita wasn't in her office and Geraldine learned that she was away at a meeting. Requesting a search warrant where no one's life was in danger would not be considered a sufficiently urgent reason to disturb the detective chief inspector.

'Well, that's it for now,' Ariadne said, when Geraldine shared her theory with her friend and told her the detective chief inspector was unavailable. 'We'll have to wait for Binita to come back and request a search warrant. She probably won't be around until tomorrow. So in the meantime what do you want me to do?'

'In the meantime, nothing. We need to get on with searching Nigel's flat before we do anything else,' Geraldine responded firmly.

'We can't enter the property without a warrant,' Ariadne objected, sounding shocked. 'Even if we manage to gain access, you know perfectly well that evidence collected illegally is of no use whatsoever. We can't break in, Geraldine, and even if we could, there's no point.'

'Who said anything about breaking in? Trust me. I know what I'm doing,' Geraldine replied.

'Geraldine, if we enter the flat we'll be trespassing.'

Geraldine smiled. 'Not if we're invited. Now, we need to bring an experienced search team with us. As long as they know what they're doing, it shouldn't take long. We're looking for something very specific. Come on. Let's get started.'

Ariadne organised a search team and on the way Geraldine briefed them about what they were looking for. She went into the block of flats with Ariadne first, and spoke to the concierge who told them Nigel was out.

'Please call him and ask him to come home at once,' Geraldine said. 'We need him to get here as soon as he can.'

The concierge raised his eyebrows, but he reached for his phone without demur. Listening to his half of the conversation, it became apparent that Nigel was remonstrating about having to come home. After a moment, the concierge turned to Geraldine.

'He says can't it wait?' he reported with an apologetic shrug.

'Tell him it can't wait and if he isn't here within fifteen minutes, we'll enter his apartment with a search warrant,' Geraldine replied. She didn't add that it might take a few days to obtain such a warrant. Instead, she asked the concierge to inform Nigel that she had a search team waiting outside who would join her the moment she summoned them.

With an anxious glance at the door to the street, as though afraid a bevy of police officers would come charging in, the concierge spoke rapidly on the phone. After listening for a moment, he looked up with a nod. 'He's says he's on his way now. He should be here in ten minutes.'

Geraldine breathed a silent sigh of relief. Nigel's presence was vital if her plan was to work. Now all she had to do was convince him to let them into the flat. And if she suspected Carol might be guilty of murder, she was fairly sure Nigel would already be thinking along the same lines. On the other hand, if he remained convinced his wife was innocent he would have no good reason to deny the search team access to the flat. Either way, he should be willing to cooperate, if only to clear his wife of the new accusation Geraldine was about to level at her. A large clock in the entry hall ticked loudly as she waited impatiently for Nigel to appear.

61

AFTER SEEING NIGEL, GERALDINE and Ariadne faced Carol across an interview table. The lawyer, Higgs, was beginning to seem all too familiar.

'I want to protest in the strongest terms,' Carol began in a strident tone.

Mr Higgs scowled at her with a vague wave of his hand in a tentative attempt to silence her. 'Let's hear what the inspector has to say, shall we?' he murmured. 'We can answer any further questions they have, I'm sure, and then we'll be on our way.'

'You shot your father-in-law,' Geraldine said.

'That's not true,' Carol protested. 'We told you, we were together all night, Nigel and me.'

'He has slightly changed his account of what happened the night Martin was shot,' Ariadne told her. 'He says he was fast asleep all night.'

'We both were, so how could I have gone out and shot Martin? It's ridiculous. Don't you think he would have woken up if I'd gone out? He's always been a very light sleeper.'

Geraldine nodded. 'It was Nigel who gave me the idea that it must be you, when he admitted he's been sleeping more soundly than ever since his father died.'

'We searched your house,' Ariadne took up the account.

'You did what?' Carol blurted out. 'You had no right to do that.' She turned to Mr Higgs. 'They can't do that, can they? It's illegal. They had no permission. If they came across anything, it can't be used against me, can it?'

'We had permission,' Ariadne said. 'Your husband let us in. We would have got a search warrant if he hadn't.'

Carol listened in silence as Ariadne told her what the search party had found. Then she placed an evidence bag on the table. It contained a bottle labelled Mirtazapine.

'What's that?' Carol asked, but she sounded belligerent and Geraldine suspected that was a cover for her fear.

'I think you recognise the sleeping pills your doctor prescribed for you.'

Carol shrugged. 'Oh yes,' she said. 'Now I see what that is. So what?'

Geraldine leaned forward. 'Carol, we don't need you to confess, because we know exactly what you did. You drugged your husband so he would sleep through the night and not wake up when you left the house. While he was asleep, you visited your father-in-law and somehow managed to lure him down to the river bank where you shot him using a pillow from his own bed to muffle the noise. You left him lying on the bank when you were disturbed by someone else turning up, because just after you shot Martin, Dorothy arrived and scared you off. She saw him and thought he was drunk so she pushed him in the river in a fit of anger. That's why she confessed to killing Martin. She thought she had. What a miraculous escape that must have seemed to you, because it wasn't Dorothy who killed Martin, it was you. There's no point in trying to deny it any longer. You're going to be convicted whatever you say, because we have enough evidence to prove you planned and carried out the fatal attack, enough evidence to convince the most lenient jury that you murdered your father-in-law.'

The lawyer interrupted her crossly. 'Inspector, you know perfectly well that's not a given. Are you judge and jury now as well as detective?' He raised his eyebrows sceptically. 'Or are you just trying to browbeat my client into saying something she'll regret?'

'If you confess,' Geraldine pressed on, ignoring the interruption, 'it will help your case. A jury could be persuaded that this was an act of passion, not deliberate aggression, if you show remorse for what you did. But that's not going to happen if you persist in refusing to admit the truth. We know what you did, Carol.'

The suspect's face flushed and her eyes gleamed with sudden desperation. She clenched her fists, and her red cheeks paled as she glanced at the tape before lowering her gaze. Geraldine waited. When Carol looked up again, her eyes were bright. She turned to Higgs.

'Is that true?' she hissed at him. 'Why didn't you tell me to say it was a crime of passion?'

He stared at her in surprise. 'I need to talk to my client,' he said. 'Alone.'

Carol seemed to reach a decision. 'I don't know what came over me,' she said loudly, directing her words to the tape and letting out a loud sob. 'I'm not a violent person. I believe in the sanctity of life. It wasn't like me at all, but I was driven to it. Normally I wouldn't – I would never – but—' She hesitated and drew in a shuddering breath. 'Martin deserved it. He kept pestering me. I couldn't tell anyone because it would have really upset my husband. You can't understand how difficult it was for me. What was I supposed to do? I couldn't tell Nigel that his father was molesting me. He kept – trying to get me on my own, so he could touch me. And in the end, I just flipped. I couldn't take the abuse any longer. I had to stop him.'

Carol sounded almost hysterical, but Geraldine didn't believe a word of her story. The trouble was that Martin was dead and unable to defend himself. Before she could challenge what Carol had told them, Mr Higgs rose to his feet and demanded time to discuss his client's defence with her. In view of all the new information that had come to light, he insisted it was essential he speak to her in confidence. But Geraldine had not finished.

Now she knew Carol was capable of murder, she was almost certain she had killed Serena as well.

'You killed both of them, Martin and Serena,' she said. 'It was all about the money for you, wasn't it? We know it was you and we have the proof, so you might as well confess. Carol, I'm offering you the opportunity to confess and it might just get the jury on your side. Confess, before it's too late.'

Carol glared at Geraldine. 'I told you, Martin was a dirty old man.'

Geraldine hesitated but unless she could gently persuade Carol to confess, there was a chance the jury would not convict her of Serena's murder. With the story she had concocted about Martin, she might even escape a custodial sentence.

'Martin had a girlfriend,' Geraldine said softly. 'Serena was young and beautiful.' She paused, leaving the conclusion unspoken.

Carol was silent.

Geraldine tried once more. 'Do you seriously believe you can convince a jury that Martin was pursuing you while he was living with Serena?'

'I thought Martin's death would be the end of it,' Carol said. 'The end of the abuse,' she added quickly.

'You thought Martin's death would make you and your husband rich,' Geraldine prompted her.

'But then we heard his will and discovered he hadn't left it all to Nigel, as he had promised. Instead he left everything to *her*.'

'So she had to go,' Geraldine said quietly. 'You killed two people, just to get your hands on some money.'

'Some money?' Carol cried out with a manic shriek of laughter. 'Have you any idea how many millions the old man had stashed away?'

'And that was worth killing him for?' Geraldine asked.

'It would have been, if she hadn't come along to ruin everything.'

'So you killed Serena too?'

'Oh, very well,' Carol burst out suddenly, her face flushed once more. 'You're right. I killed her. Of course I did. He'd left everything to her in his will, everything, just because he was besotted with her. And what was I left with? What right did she have to steal his inheritance from us? Nigel had been expecting that money all his life.'

'That's why you married him,' Geraldine murmured.

'Martin's fortune belongs to Nigel, not some girl who pushed her way into his life at the last minute. Nigel was Martin's son. Are you listening to me? His son! I couldn't sit back and let her take it all, not after everything we've put up with from his family.'

'You mean, after you shot Martin?'

Carol's cheeks paled and she looked down.

'I need to speak to my client,' Mr Higgs said.

62

IT WAS THE WEEKEND. With Ian available to take over when Geraldine had to attend meetings, she was working from home on the bulk of the seemingly endless paperwork needed to support the charge. Celia had departed, promising to see them again soon, next time with her whole family. Geraldine would have loved to invite them to stay in York over Christmas, but her flat was too small to accommodate everyone comfortably, so Celia had invited Geraldine, Ian and Tom to stay with her. Ian would have preferred to celebrate Tom's first Christmas at home but, after Celia had helped them, they felt they couldn't refuse her invitation. In any case, as Geraldine pointed out, Christmas was a time to spend with family.

'As long as members of your family aren't trying to kill you,' she added sombrely.

Tom seemed to settle down without any problem with his new childminder, Andrea, a motherly woman whose credentials were impeccable. After their experience with Zoe, Geraldine had looked into Andrea's background in meticulous detail and had found no whisper of suspicion against her. What was equally important was that none of Andrea's relatives had a criminal record. So it seemed all was well, at least for the time being.

'I can't believe both of our cases have resolved themselves in time for us to be completely finished before Christmas,' Ian smiled. 'I couldn't have wished for a better Christmas present.'

'Let's hope nothing turns up to scupper our plans,' Geraldine replied.

After everything that had happened recently, she found it hard to believe nothing else could go wrong, even though they both knew that was unlikely. It would have to be something fairly drastic for either of them to have to cancel their leave over the Christmas period when they had both booked two weeks off work. While spending four days with Celia, Ian hadn't once complained, but he was clearly pleased to have Geraldine and Tom to himself again. Although he had been very welcoming to their guest, Geraldine could see he was more relaxed when she returned home from dropping Celia at the station.

'At last I can walk around naked in my own home again,' he said with a grin.

'You never walk around naked,' she replied, laughing.

'Are you complaining?' he teased her, pulling her into an embrace which was interrupted by Tom bellowing from the nursery.

'Leave him for a bit,' Ian said. 'He won't come to any harm in there. It's not going to be long before he's able to climb out of his cot all by himself. We should make the most of the time we've got to ourselves.'

There was a thump and they ran into the nursery to see Tom sitting on the floor, looking as surprised as they both felt. Once they had reassured themselves that he was unhurt, Geraldine scooped him up and carried him into the living room.

'Looks like you spoke too soon,' she said.

Geraldine fed and changed Tom while Ian made a start on preparing the dinner. Once Ian had bathed Tom, Geraldine put him to bed while Ian finished cooking. At last they were able to sit down and have their supper in peace.

'This is perfect,' Geraldine said later that evening as they sat in the living room listening to music and finishing a bottle of wine together after a steak dinner.

'Couldn't be better,' Ian agreed, and Geraldine was shaken by a wave of happiness so powerful it was almost sharp.

'We've come a long way,' she said. 'You know, I never used to believe I would ever find a partner in my life. Someone like you, I mean. I never thought one person could mean so much to me. More, even, than my career. More than anything.'

Before Ian could reply, they heard Tom yell.

'But not more important than Tom,' she added, laughing. 'So much for the romantic mood. He has an uncanny sense of timing. Poor little thing, it must be his teeth.'

'He'd just started sleeping through the night as well,' Ian sighed.

As he spoke, Geraldine disentangled herself from his embrace and clambered to her feet. Tom stopped crying as soon as she leaned over the side of his cot and he reached out to her with his chubby little arms, his tiny fingers wriggling with excitement. She picked him up and carried him into the living room. Ian smiled and Tom gurgled with pleasure on seeing him.

'I wasn't the only one who missed you,' Geraldine said contentedly as she settled back down beside Ian on the sofa with Tom propped up between them. 'You never did tell me about your undercover job.'

Ian grinned and tickled Tom who chuckled.

'Actually,' he said, 'there's not much to tell. It was all pretty dull, really. You think undercover work is going to be dangerous and exciting, but I can tell you it was nothing like a James Bond movie. We got the job done all right. That was never in question. But there was no drama to speak of and I didn't even get the glamorous girl at the end of it all, so I decided I might as well come home to you instead.'

Geraldine slapped his leg and Tom squealed with delight.

'So we're definitely going to your sister's for Christmas?' Ian asked.

Geraldine nodded. 'If you're sure that's okay with you.'

Ian shrugged. 'If that's what you want.'

'What would you like to do?'

Ian hesitated before replying that it would be Tom's first Christmas and he had been looking forward to spending it at home.

'Don't you think it would be nice for Tom to get to know his cousins?'

'Celia's it is then,' Ian agreed.

'As long as you're sure you're happy to spend Christmas there.'

'I don't really care where we are as long as we're together,' Ian said, leaning across to kiss her gently on the lips.

63

NIGEL STARED UNEASILY AT Carol across the table and hesitated before speaking. Her face was more lined than he remembered, her eyes looked bloodshot and her skin had a greyish tinge. Besides her evident exhaustion, the environment was hardly conducive to having a cosy chat. He shuddered and kept his eyes lowered. In the periphery of his vision he could see a guard standing impassively by the door. In spite of his bored expression, Nigel felt sure the guard was watching them. Doing his best to ignore their surroundings, he forced himself to focus his attention on Carol. It was almost impossible to believe she could be guilty of two murders, but there it was. Not only did the police have evidence of her guilt, but according to what they had told him, she had confessed. He wasn't sure he believed she had caved in under questioning, but if it was true, she would be facing a custodial sentence.

If a jury found her guilty, he wondered how long she would have to spend behind bars, leaving him at home on his own. Not that he would want to live with her again after she was released from prison. He tried to suppress his feelings, but he was terrified. According to the police, his wife had killed two people, one of them his own father, and she had attacked his sister with a knife. Possibly there had been other victims they didn't know about. He had no idea what to say to her. He only knew this couldn't be happening. He must have misunderstood. Her arrest would turn out to be a blunder by the police. He shook his head, as though that could shake some sense into his confused thoughts.

Higgs had proved useless. It was his job to get Carol off, but he had achieved nothing, his defence of her a complete fiasco. All he had done was collect an exorbitant fee. When Nigel remonstrated, Higgs had protested that no lawyer could have done more to defend the indefensible. Once Carol had confessed, against his advice, his hands were tied, he had said.

'What am I paying you for then?' Nigel had fumed. 'If you can't get her released?'

With exaggerated patience, Higgs had explained that it was no longer a question of trying to prove Carol was innocent. All he could do now was try to make sure her sentence was as light as possible, given the circumstances.

'What the hell am I paying you for?' Nigel repeated crossly.

Higgs insisted Carol had disregarded his counsel. 'She's a headstrong woman,' he added ruefully.

'It was your job to guide her,' Nigel snapped. 'This is all your fault. I should complain to the Law Society.'

'Good luck with that,' Higgs replied.

The lawyer was right to be complacent. Carol had confessed to two murders. Only Nigel knew she had been planning a third – and perhaps even a fourth. He shuddered to think that she had quite possibly been intending to do away with him once she had despatched his sister, but he tried not to dwell on that. She was still his wife and he loved her. That was to say, he loved the woman he had married, the woman he had believed her to be. But the Carol he had married had been replaced by an evil doppelgänger, a creature of nightmares. Something must have happened to cause such a change in her. He refused to believe she had always been a psychopath, hiding her true nature from him. Facing her now in the drab visiting room, he studied her face, searching for the woman he had married, while Carol stared back at him coldly, as though they were strangers.

'How are you?' he enquired awkwardly. The question sounded inappropriate and formal.

Carol let out a bark of laughter. 'Oh, I'm just great,' she replied. 'Couldn't be better.' Without warning she leaned forward and hissed at him. 'Get me out of here, Nigel. You have no idea what it's like. The place stinks. You have to do something. You can't leave me here to rot.'

Again he had the sensation that he was listening to a stranger. Tempted to retort that it was her own fault she was in prison, and she ought to have thought of the repercussions before she killed his father, he shook his head, muttering that he would speak to Higgs.

'I'm sure he's doing everything he can,' he added helplessly. 'He's the best—'

Carol's face twisted in an ugly snarl. 'The best? The best?' Her voice grew shrill. In the corner by the door the guard stirred and she lowered her voice. 'He's useless. I don't know what you think he's doing but whatever it is, it's not good enough, is it? Because I'm still here. Get rid of that useless idiot and find me a proper lawyer. If you'd done that in the first place, none of this would be happening.'

Nigel didn't even try to hide his surprise at her belligerent tone. 'I don't know what you're talking about. Bertram Higgs is the most prestigious law firm in York, and William Higgs is a senior partner. He's been—'

'Senior is right,' Carol interrupted him. 'He's practically senile. He must be at least eighty.'

Nigel ran out of patience with her griping. He stood up abruptly, telling her there was no point in him visiting her if she was going to spend all her time complaining.

'It's all right for you,' she snapped. 'You can go home to a nice flat and sleep in a comfortable bed and eat whatever you want whenever you want while I'm stuck here in this hellhole with no prospect of ever getting out, being slowly starved to death. Your precious Mr Higgs hasn't even managed to get them to fix a date for my trial. Although why I should be put on trial when you stand to benefit even more than I do is beyond me. Why is this all my fault?'

'Because you killed two people,' he replied quietly. 'That's why you're here.'

'But I did it for you,' she went on, growing tearful. 'You have to get me out of here.'

Once he would have been desperate to alleviate her distress. Now he just thought how ugly she looked with her face contorted in misery. He tried to explain that it was impossible for him to grant her request, and Higgs was equally helpless to influence the justice system. Her case would have to follow its due course and there was nothing anyone could do about it. The more she protested, the more unhinged she seemed. He supposed the experience of being arrested and locked up might have tipped her over the edge, but he had a horrible suspicion that she had always been deranged. After all, she had admitted to killing two innocent people without showing a shred of remorse. That was hardly sane. He had to accept that his wife was a psychopath, possessed of enough cunning to fool her own husband.

Until recently, he had been an easy target, wilfully blind to her wickedness. Admitting she was insane placed a serious question mark over his discernment in choosing a wife, and he had never before had cause to doubt his own judgement. Now he was forced to acknowledge what might have been in store for him if she hadn't been stopped. He shivered and gazed apprehensively at her, wondering what he would do if, by some fluke, she escaped a prison sentence. The prospect of her returning to his house made him tremble with fear. Looking at her now, with her greasy hair and smouldering eyes, he wondered how he had failed to see the terrible psychosis that must have always been present, lurking beneath her mask of sanity.

He hesitated to ask, but he had to know. 'Were you planning to kill me too? After a reasonable interval, of course,' he added bitterly.

Carol eyed him speculatively before answering, but her vacillation was all the confirmation he needed. Far from being shocked by the suggestion, she was calculating how to respond.

'Don't be ridiculous,' she said, shifting uneasily in her chair. 'Are you suggesting I don't love you?' She stared into his eyes, seeming to grow in confidence as she slipped into her familiar wheedling. 'I wouldn't have married you if I didn't love you, would I?'

He tried to recall exactly when she had learned about Martin's financial position, and whether that was before or after he had proposed. Strictly speaking, he had never actually asked her to marry him. The idea had just evolved and he wasn't sure which of them had suggested making their relationship permanent. He had a sinking feeling she had probably known about his expectations right from the start. He remembered her job interview and the impression he had of her when he first saw her inviting smile. In a way, he had been at her mercy ever since. But not any longer.

'Now focus on getting me out of here,' she said plaintively. 'I hate having to meet you like this, unable to touch you. Get me out of here so we can be together again. Nothing else matters right now. Only us.'

'Does my father's death not matter?' he asked sadly, feeling a shutter closing between him and the wife he had loved.

'How can it matter when he's dead?' she asked, but he was no longer listening to her. 'Now, what are you going to do to get me released? There must be a way.'

Nigel rose to his feet. 'I'm sorry,' he mumbled. 'This is over. I won't visit you again.'

At the door he turned his head to glance back; her jaw had dropped open in astonishment while her eyes blazed with fury. He walked away, blinking his watering eyes.

64

DAISY WAS BACK AT home, claiming to be over her ordeal, but Nigel wasn't convinced she had made a full recovery. She was bound to experience some after effects from being held captive, not to mention being stabbed. Apart from the terror she had suffered, her injury must have been agonising. The wound was not yet fully healed after three weeks, and the dressing was still being changed regularly, which involved regular trips to the hospital. Nigel was on hand to drive her there and back each time. He did so not just because she was his sister, but also because he couldn't help feeling at least partly responsible for what had happened to her. After all, he was the one who had introduced a violent maniac into their family. Of course, at the time he had married Carol, he had not entertained the faintest suspicion she would turn out to be mentally ill. Daisy refused to concede that Carol was unhinged, preferring to believe she had plotted quite deliberately and coldly to get her hands on Martin's money.

'If she was prepared to go to any lengths to get hold of his fortune, including murdering innocent people, then you have to agree she's ill,' Nigel argued. 'Killing people isn't exactly normal. She's a psychopath.'

Daisy was recalcitrant. 'You of all people would have known if she's a psycho. You married her. Dear God, Nigel, you *lived* with her. How could you not have seen what she was like? She was your *wife*. Surely even you can't be that blind.'

Nigel merely shrugged and was silent. He had no defence against her accusation. It was true he had been utterly oblivious to his wife's true nature, the side of her she had concealed from him for years. He actually sympathised with his sister's scepticism, because he too found his own poor judgement hard to believe. Seeing the doubt in Daisy's eyes, he shivered as she reflected his own misgivings back at him. He felt he was living on quicksand; everything he had once trusted was collapsing around him and there was nothing he could do to escape the ensuing chaos. If he could live with a killer and not have the faintest inkling about her true nature, what else might he have failed to understand about the world and about himself? He trembled to think that he might have been drawn to Carol because he was unconsciously attracted to her violent nature.

'Well, obviously, had I known about her sickness, I would have had her committed,' he muttered sullenly. 'I would have done something about it. You seem to think I'm happy to discover my wife suffers from some devastating mental illness,' he ended lamely, because he wasn't quite sure what was wrong with his wife. He cursed his fate. 'If I'd known, I'd have got her help,' he bleated. 'I never wanted any of this. But you can't blame Carol. She needs professional help. Surely you can see that?' He was pleading with Daisy now. 'She needs help.'

'What she needs is to be locked up,' Daisy answered promptly.

Perhaps her refusal to compromise was understandable, given that Carol had tried to kill her, but it was typical of Daisy to be difficult. He wanted to support her, driving her wherever she needed to go and taking her shopping, but he couldn't carry on like this indefinitely. She was taking advantage of his good nature... or his guilt.

'None of this was really my fault, you know,' he pointed out. 'I'm the one who's lost a wife.'

'Oh well, poor you. I only nearly lost my *life*,' Daisy retorted promptly. 'You can divorce her and get yourself another wife. But make sure you make a sensible choice this time, instead of going for someone years younger than you. Didn't you ever wonder why she wanted to marry *you*?'

He couldn't bring himself to reply that he had believed Carol loved him. He listened in silence as Daisy continued to harangue him about his wife. Nigel had always found his visits to his sister thoroughly depressing, but she was the only close family he had. Besides, she needed ferrying around and there didn't seem to be anyone else in her life able to help her.

'You need to think about how you're going to manage when you're older,' he said, in an attempt to steer the conversation away from the painful subject of his marriage.

'I'll manage how I always manage,' she replied. 'I've got you, haven't I? We've got each other.'

He wanted to shout out that she couldn't keep relying on him for support, and it was unfair of her to even think of doing so, but instead he merely pointed out that he wouldn't be around forever. He spoke mildly, but she bridled visibly.

'What's that supposed to mean?' she snapped. 'Who said I want you to be around forever?'

Carefully avoiding mentioning Carol, he told her that he was missing their father, and she began to cry.

'Don't worry,' he heard himself say, almost automatically. 'I'm still here.'

Daisy nodded and mumbled incoherently. They both knew he would be back at her door ready to ferry her to her next hospital appointment. They were trapped together in a relationship built up over decades of loneliness and mutual dependency. While Nigel had Carol for company, he hadn't spent much time with Daisy. Now that he was on his own again, he and his sister would be thrown together more than ever. Even spending time with his sister was better than spending every evening alone nursing his bitter disappointment.

'At least we're both still alive,' he said. 'We had a narrow escape. You do realise that sooner or later we'd both have been killed if Carol had managed to get her way. As for Serena, she did nothing to deserve what happened to her. All she did was give our father some happiness to help him through his grief. She didn't deserve to be murdered any more than we did.'

He had been trying not to dwell on his last conversation with Carol, but it was difficult to forget how she had glared at him when he left, her eyes filled with hatred.

Daisy sniffed. 'I'll never understand why you didn't see through that wife of yours,' she said. 'You always were an idiot.'

Miserably, he left. As he turned into Leeman Road, there was a flash of lightning and it began to rain. He swore as his wipers smeared water across the windscreen. Once he would have been pleased that he was nearly home, but he could never go back to those days. The sense of loss hit him like a punch in the chest and he realised he was crying.

65

GERALDINE SMILED AS ARIADNE put a couple of pints on the table and sat down. They had agreed to join their colleagues at the pub nearest to the police station to celebrate the successful conclusion to the case, and were waiting for the others to arrive.

'I can't stay long,' Geraldine said, glancing at her watch. 'One pint and I'm off.' She sighed. 'It's difficult, but hopefully, we've made the right decision.'

She was glad Ariadne hadn't responded glibly that she was sure Geraldine would have found the right person this time.

Ariadne grunted. 'Parental duties,' she said, a trifle wistfully.

Geraldine had never wondered whether her friend might want a family. Until Tom had come along, quite unplanned, such questions had never occurred to her.

'You've got to feel a bit sorry for Nigel,' Ariadne said, picking up her glass and studying the head on her pint. 'I mean, imagine discovering you've been living with a psychopath. Do you really believe he didn't know what she was capable of?'

Geraldine shrugged. 'It's difficult to say. People can be wilfully blind to faults in the people they love.'

Ariadne laughed. 'Being a killer is some fault!'

'And what about his sister? She's a real piece of work,' Geraldine said.

'I guess any woman would seem appealing compared to her.'

'But I agree, I do feel a bit sorry for Nigel,' Geraldine said. 'Even though he's hardly someone you can warm to.'

As she was speaking, a group of their colleagues arrived.

Sam came over trying not to spill his pint and sat down next to Ariadne. There was a buzz of excited conversation for a few minutes, with some of their colleagues standing at the bar waiting to be served while others found seats or stood around chatting. Naomi dragged over a chair and joined Geraldine, Ariadne and Sam.

'I know this is a gathering to congratulate everyone on a successful outcome,' Ariadne said, 'but before Binita starts holding forth telling us what a wonderful team we are, I want to add my thanks to Geraldine for saving my life.'

A few colleagues standing nearby cheered.

'Sam helped,' Geraldine said quickly.

'All I did was shove you through a window,' he protested, laughing.

'Sam wanted to go inside instead of me but I felt it was my duty seeing as I'd brought you there in the first place,' Geraldine said. 'But what I still don't understand is how you ended up in there with Carol? I left you on the doorstep. What were you thinking of, going inside?'

Ariadne nodded and put down her pint. 'I know it looks as though I was taking a stupid risk, but we didn't know Carol had a knife when I went in. In fact, we didn't even know she was there. As far as we knew, Daisy was at home on her own, so there was no reason not to go in. Daisy had never said Carol was at her house. So as far as I knew, we were going there to help Daisy. At first no one answered when we rang the bell, but after you went round the back, Daisy opened the door. It was only after I'd gone inside and she'd shut the door that I saw Carol behind her, holding a knife at her neck. At that point, there wasn't much I could do without endangering Daisy. I could see she'd already been stabbed at least once, and was bleeding quite badly. Then we heard you calling from outside, and it was as much as I could do to warn you that Carol was armed.' She shuddered.

'Well, she didn't kill anyone on that particular occasion, and it's all over now,' Geraldine said.

'Thanks to you,' Ariadne replied.

'And Sam, and everyone else here,' Geraldine smiled. 'Like Binita is about to tell us, we're a team.'

Binita tapped a glass with a teaspoon and cleared her throat.

'If there's one thing I want to say to you all, it's that we are a team,' she began.

Geraldine and Ariadne looked at one another and raised their glasses in unison. 'We're a team within a team,' Ariadne whispered, and they both smiled.

Acknowledgements

I never imagined we would progress beyond twenty books featuring my detective, Geraldine Steel, but readers keep wanting more and so here we are, launching *Deadly Will*, the twenty-second title in the series. I couldn't be prouder of all that Geraldine has achieved, but none of this would have been possible without the wonderful team at No Exit Press, Bedford Square Publishers. I would like to thank Polly Halsey for her invaluable help in production, Jem Butcher for his brilliant covers, Anastasia Boama-Aboagye for her enthusiastic marketing, Jayne Lewis for her highly skilled copy editing and Rachel Sargeant for her eagle-eyed proofreading.

Ion Mills has championed Geraldine Steel right from the start, and his support has been key to the success of my books. I am also indebted to Jamie Hodder-Williams and Laura Fletcher at No Exit Press, Bedford Square Publishers, for their continuing faith in Geraldine Steel. It is a privilege to work with such a professional and good-natured team.

I am very fortunate in my editor, Keshini Naidoo, who has been with us from the beginning, and I look forward to continuing to work with her on more books in the series.

My thanks go to all the bloggers and interviewers who have supported Geraldine Steel, and to everyone who has been kind enough to review my books. Your support is sincerely appreciated.

I am grateful to readers around the world for showing interest in Geraldine's career. I really hope you continue to enjoy reading about my detective.

Last but by no means least, my thanks go to Michael, who is always with me.

A LETTER FROM LEIGH

Dear Reader,

I hope you enjoyed reading this book in my Geraldine Steel series. Readers are the key to the writing process, so I'm thrilled that you've joined me on my writing journey.

You might not want to meet some of my characters on a dark night – I know I wouldn't! – but hopefully you want to read about Geraldine's other investigations. Her work is always her priority because she cares deeply about justice, but she also has her own life. Many readers care about what happens to her. I hope you join them, and become a fan of Geraldine Steel, and her colleague Ian Peterson.

If you follow me on Facebook or Twitter, you'll know that I love to hear from readers. I always respond to comments from fans, and hope you will follow me on **@LeighRussell** and **fb.me/leigh.russell.50** or drop me an email via my website **leighrussell.co.uk**.

To get exclusive news, competitions, offers, early sneak-peaks for upcoming titles and more, sign-up to my free monthly newsletter: **leighrussell.co.uk/news**. You can also find out more about me and the Geraldine Steel series on the No Exit Press website: **noexit.co.uk/ leighrussellbooks**.

Finally, if you enjoyed this story, I'd be really grateful if you would post a brief review on Amazon or Goodreads. A few sentences to say you enjoyed the book would be wonderful. And of course it would be brilliant if you would consider recommending my books to anyone who is a fan of crime fiction.

I hope to meet you at a literary festival or a book signing soon!

Thank you again for choosing to read my book.

With very best wishes,

Leigh Russell

noexit.co.uk/leighrussell

About the Author

Leigh Russell is the author of the internationally bestselling Geraldine Steel series, which has sold over a million copies worldwide. Her books have been #1 on Amazon Kindle and iTunes with *Stop Dead* and *Murder Ring* selected as finalists for The People's Book Prize.

www.leighrussell.co.uk

@LeighRussell